ALSO BY J.MERCER:

DARK & STORMY

WHAT READERS ARE SAYING:

"Complex characters give way to a brilliantly written story."

"J. Mercer combines her gift for poignantly haunting characters with a plot that is intriguingly complicated."

"Great small town setting with an awesome cast of characters. J. Mercer masterfully takes you on a journey full of twists and reveals that are woven so skillfully into the story you'll want to read it again and again."

"There is an underlying darkness throughout the narrative which keeps the reader on edge, and the threat, which starts as a reasonably low level one, gradually ramps up to the shocking conclusion. A gripping read."

"I can't wait to read this book again! I was captivated from the very beginning. This story is romantic, then it's thrilling. It has so many twists and turns and layers that I guarantee when I read it again, I will find something new I missed before."

After They Go

J. Mercer

Published 2018 / Bare Ink
Printed in the United States of America
Print ISBN: 978-1-7321332-1-1
E-ISBN: 978-1-7321332-0-4
Library of Congress Control Number: 2089674
After They Go / written by J Mercer

Cover design © Chris Slabber
Edited by Gina Ardito

For my girls, who taught me of sisters—
That you will always be each other's joy and solace.

CONTENTS

"One of the secrets of life is to be honestly who you are. Who others want you to be, who you used to be, or who you may someday become . . . these are fantasies. To be honestly who you are is to give up your illusions and face today with courage."

– Bill Purdin

SEPTEMBER

The store was still, silent, and stifling tonight, in this farce of a town.

No busy rush of traffic outside, no excitement of what might come next, no scent of promise—that's what Gwen wanted, instead of the face they put on for the tourists.

She belonged in the city, and she'd known it since the day she'd first heard of one. She promised Gage it would happen as soon as her grandpa died, but now her father was telling her it was her responsibility to take over the store.

Gwen swallowed her shock, a lump in her throat stopping up her words. He had to know how much she wanted the opposite, to not be tied to this small town and their store, both at the mercy of the tourist season, their lives taken over by strangers for five months, then a desolate emptiness sweeping in for the other seven. And she wanted out of a life of *shoulds*.

"It's how we do it, Gwennie." They stood on either side of the front counter, the register open next to her as she collected the day's deposit. The front door was already locked, and most of the lights were off.

Gwen dug her nails into her palm. She should have gone after high school graduation four years ago, but her mom piled on a load of 'shoulds' then, too. A load she slowly struggled out from under until there was this last one left—*stay until Pops is gone; help your father with the store so your sister can focus on taking care of him.* The other shoulds, the saving money, she'd saved—for three years she'd saved. And the concern she wouldn't make it because she was a small town girl? Well, now she had Gage.

Shaking her mother's guilt off her shoulders, Gwen stood taller. "Give it to Betta."

"Betta has been under such strain taking care of Pops. She can't come in right now and handle all this."

"All what? The tourists are almost gone. It's the best time."

"It's the hardest." Her dad glanced at the bundle of cash and credit card receipts in her fist. She let out a steady breath and smoothed the pile on the counter. "Give it a month, Gwen, maybe two. Let your sister recover. Who knows when she last had a full night's sleep."

Gwen took in his doughy face, the line of his nose that was both hers and her grandpa's. The years there which spoke of the many Aaldenbergs before him, all who worked this store in the same way. When the oldest generation passed, the property was left to the next, who then retired to live off the rent their children paid them, while their children managed the store and took a salary.

So far, so good. They were a fixture in town and held their

heads high. Aaldenberg Hardware, though it was more than that—a general store, really, providing everything for everyone—reached back to a time before the big developers claimed the suburbs, back to a time when no one else provided much of anything.

It was what her father stood on. And her mother, after she failed at the city. It was what Betta lived for. Her dad was right, though. Betta was exhausted. As miserable as Gwen had been, waiting to get out, Betta had done the hardest work. She did deserve a break.

It had already been three years, what was another month or two? And with her mom's words of caution in her ear— her doubt that Gwen had the fortitude to last in Boston— she'd been hoping Gage would propose. It would be a little more insurance that she'd make it, that she wouldn't be back.

Because once she was gone, coming back would be failure. She refused to come back. She refused to fail, especially at this, and so she must do it right the first time.

She must set them up to succeed so she could be free.

* * *

Betta didn't want to be grateful her grandpa was dead, but the sense of relief was overwhelming. She tried to tell herself that anyone, had they been there in the night hearing his moans and pleas, knowing they were coming up from a consciousness supposedly flattened by pain meds, would feel the same as she.

Still, the guilt circled her.

She wondered if her tears were more from that than from missing him. Pops, she was sure, had been gone for at least three months before he actually passed.

It had been a long two years, not that she would've traded the first year and a half for anything. Most of it reminded her of when she was little, when he'd bring her home after she followed him around Aaldenberg Hardware all day and fry her up a grilled cheese sandwich with tomatoes. When she'd moved into his small rented duplex, he told her that as long as he was able, he'd keep making her those sandwiches.

Then she had to start making them for him. Until he wanted nothing to do with food. Until she took to betting him on their cribbage games—if she won, he would eat.

That was another thing—if she never saw a cribbage board again, it would be too soon. The very thought of it made her more tired than she already was.

She and Van sat on wooden folding chairs in the living room, dinner plates on their laps, while Gwen and Esmerelda helped their mom in the kitchen, serving casserole to those who stopped by to express their condolences. Generally this meant dropping off yet another pan of something-with-noodles and telling Wanda how very sorry they were for her loss. They'd grab a plate to try someone else's concoction, while cooing over Gwen, the brightest and most golden of the family. Then they'd chat with Ez as she poured them lemonade, ask her about starting high school, *how exciting*, and last, they'd wander into the living room and pat Van on his shoulder.

No condolences for Betta.

Then again, next to the recently graduated high school football star, anyone might be invisible. Did invisible mean she could fall asleep against him and no one would notice? But it was loud, and Betta's head hurt going on about three months.

Grabbing Van's empty plate, Betta forced her way through the crowd to the kitchen. She tossed the trash into the large round can someone brought in from the garage, and plodded through more people until she could squeeze her way outside.

The back door swung shut behind her, sealing off the chatter of hushed voices, and the pale fall sun opened up the sky above.

"Too many people in there," her dad said from an old Adirondack chair. He patted the one next to him. "You doin' okay?"

Betta slumped down and threw one leg over the other. "Yeah." She'd be doing even better if she could take a nap out here. It was a good day for it: cool enough to be comfortable plus a light blanket of sunshine. "I know I look like death, but I'll be ready to run the store come Monday."

She could sleep all day tomorrow. She *would* sleep all day tomorrow. Then she'd be ready for her new life. The one she'd been waiting for since she dropped out of school.

Boston had been too cold for Betta—cold in its anonymity. Not that people weren't kind and welcoming, but they were hard to get a read on, the endless parade of strangers. Streets full of people you'd never seen before and every day new faces. So even if the last few years had been exhausting, she was glad she'd done it. Someone had to. It's not like they could afford in-home care, and they certainly wouldn't have shipped him off to a nursing home.

Plus, the city was too much. Noise and traffic and onslaught to the senses. Fuel and stink and waste. The town—the store, her family—was more important, plucking at her insides like fingers on a harp. The *pluck, pluck, pluck* sending reverberations of belonging through her, straight down to her toes. She didn't need college to run the family business anyway; she'd grown up there. She could do it in her sleep.

"Your sister's got it under control. You take some time to recover, okay?"

Betta's lids closed; she couldn't keep them open any longer. "When's she moving?"

"Hopefully never. Maybe she'll realize this is a better place to raise a family."

Forehead creased, Betta forced herself to wake up enough to look at him. He was joking, right? Nothing would keep Gwen here.

He patted her hand. It was what he did to tell them the conversation was over. "You deserve some time off."

That wasn't how she'd been bred, to take time off. They never took time off. What would she even do with it? Her very few friends went to college, and when she chose the town over an education, they mocked her. Because they mocked her—gotten on her case, really, and never bothered to understand—she stopped talking to them. Not all at once,

6

of course, but little by little until she nearly forgot she had friends in the first place. Which was okay, because she had her grandpa.

Now it was time to rebuild, to show them what she'd been aiming for, to show them it could be worth it. But rebuilding took a lot of effort. And it would have to wait until after a nap.

* * *

Once the lemonade was tapped, Esmerelda escaped the pruning faces. Nearly all of town had been at the funeral, so how come there was no one her age at the after party? Slipping up the stairs, she dragged her hand along the wall, setting her feet directly in front of each other, heel to toe. Rounding the corner, she checked behind her before sneaking into Gwen's room, a lilac-scented cloud of yellow and white.

It was safe while everyone was here. Gwen wouldn't leave their mom to do the hosting alone. Besides, death or not, everyone knew it was Gwen and Van the guests wanted to see.

Someday it would be her, too.

Ez sunk down onto Gwen's white, fluffy rug and leaned against her quilted yellow bedspread. This was the spot with the best view of Gwen's boyfriend. It wasn't the long chiseled nose, the definition of his chin, or even his perfect ears. It wasn't that she wanted him even, but that she wanted what he was to Gwen. She wanted that for herself.

Ez found it hard not to want things.

She wanted so many things, in fact, that sometimes she thought she might burst. The only release was scribbling it out on paper, a collection of lists that could be found folded into perfect, tiny squares and shoved in the back of her underwear drawer.

She started the first one when Pops was diagnosed. *I want cancer to disappear. I want Pops to live. I want heaven to be real.* Now, with the whole page filled up, the things she wanted weren't so serious. She'd lowered her expectations when the first two proved a bust.

What she didn't want was what she had: a flat chest, pimples on her cheeks that seemed to move around instead of going away, dirty dishwater blond hair that curled instead of settling, and the anonymity of being the fourth Aaldenberg.

With a sigh, Ez stood and made her way to the dresser. Staring at Gage's face, she pulled out Gwen's brush and ran it through her fuzzy hair. Setting it down in exactly the same spot, she picked up Gwen's eyeliner and traced it almost completely around her eyes. Not thick and winged like Betta's, though; unlike Betta, Ez wasn't trying to distract people from a scar. Last, she chose Gwen's favorite lipstick, pulled off the cap to set it on the worn wood, and placed the color to her mouth.

The buoyant Aaldenberg lips was one thing she did have, and smiling proudly at them, she clicked the cap back on the tube and set it back in its place.

Grabbing the marbled hair pin Gwen had found at an

antique store, Ez brought it back to her room and hid it in the corner of her closet.

* * *

After everyone left and the house was cleaned up, Wanda sat on the front porch swing in her dressiest coat. It comforted her when she needed to be soothed, the elegance and dignity of the rich fabric reinforcing the weak supports she'd erected over a lifetime of ups and downs.

Right now, she didn't feel so much down, but lost, and it wasn't because of her father-in-law's death. Rather, Labor Day had come and gone, marking the moment each year that her children scattered back into their own lives, no longer reined in by the needs of the store. It meant winter was coming, and winter was a cold, barren season.

She imagined, in the city, that there was no such season. Though Boston broke her heart many times over, she figured that was her own fault. If you were the type of person who could take a beating and get right back up, the city would surely offer limitless possibilities.

Unlike the limited ones here.

The screen door creaked open and shut, and Wanda felt her husband's thick hand on her shoulder. "Want to go for a walk?" he asked.

She didn't, but she would. Glancing down, she wondered when she'd stopped wearing her heels and jewelry around the house. At least she didn't need to change shoes. Standing, she slid her hand through his, and they stepped off the porch.

Wanda was comforted by the sound of their soles slapping on the street at regular intervals as they walked the few blocks from home—an old Victorian only slightly bent with age—past Aaldenberg Hardware, and on to the town square.

There, three streets met around a central fountain, the most important of which ran along the ocean's shore. This was commonly known as the port road, but officially as Beach Street. North Beach Street, after sandy public stretches, restaurants and tourist shops, trailed off into nothing, a dead end field that seemed to hold no life or reality on the other side of it, while South Beach Street, set upon a stretch of rockier shoreline and holding more restaurants and shops, ended at the marina.

The other two roads converged diagonally on the opposite corners of the square. Main Street—otherwise known as "the way in"—was where the locals lived and worked. It was home to art galleries and handcrafted shops, along with some of the best restaurants and candy stores. Town Hall Avenue—or "the way out"—housed the government properties and businesses that tourists didn't need: dentists, accountants, lawyers, etcetera. The locals joked that unless you lived there, you would never need the way out.

The rest of town was mostly residential. A few homes had been gobbled up for seasonal residences, but overall the real estate agents and local developer did their best to keep things close and small, which was the very charm. The large hotel chains formed suburbs around them, but at least inside town limits, the locals could hold tight to their roots and character.

They respected the visitors who searched out the little bed and breakfasts amidst their streets, the ones who rented the seasonal homes when the owners couldn't be there, the ones who took them seriously and didn't view them as a commodity.

Sometimes Wanda felt like a commodity. A servant, or support system, for each member of her family. Dishes, laundry, dinner, work. Dishes, laundry, vacuum, work. Dishes, laundry, dusting, work.

Yet, at the same time, she couldn't bear the thought of them getting older and leaving her. She shouldn't be glad housing was so expensive it forced them to stay home as long as possible, but she was.

"It's so pleasant without the tourists," Harvey noted as they headed toward the port.

Wanda, however, thrived on the energy they brought. "I hate it without the tourists."

Harvey squeezed her hand. "Calm and peaceful." He drew in a deep breath, like everything in front of him was clear and made sense.

"Boring and stagnant," Wanda snapped back. Nothing in front of her felt clear or sensible, and she hated how he always tried to turn her mood. A little acknowledgement or a dose of commiseration would make the difference, not blatant disagreement.

He nudged her. "Are you upset about Dad?"

They were next in line to greet death, so that was a bit disconcerting. But she'd stopped crying over Pops' cancer a year ago. She shook her head. What she was, was sick of this same old argument they'd had, going on twenty-four years. No matter how many times Harvey tried to convince her that the slow pace of winter was worth relishing, Wanda knew she'd never feel differently.

It was fact, that with fewer bodies on the streets, there was a subtle stillness in the air. Just like it was fact, that with fewer people needing her, there was a subtle emptiness in her soul.

* * *

The cobblestone path of the port walk was lit up with fairy lights—strings of them looped from store awnings on one side to waterfront canopies on the other. The ocean lapping at the boats set the background noise during the off-season, when the restaurants weren't blasting music from open doors, a lure to the tourists looking for a good time.

Sitting down, Gwen inhaled the cool, briny air coming off the sea. She picked a table sticking out from under the canopy so she could see the stars, which were much clearer here than they were in Boston. But if she and Gage were in the city, she wouldn't have to work the next day, and they wouldn't have to settle for ice cream. They could go to the chocolate shop on the corner by his apartment, where they served real hot cocoa, melted from actual chocolate.

Handing her a cone of butter pecan, he sat down next to

her. "It's our four month anniversary."

"On the day of my grandfather's funeral," she said.

"Well, say it wasn't, what would you want?" This was a game they often played. What do you want—now or later, big or small?

She appreciated he was trying to take her mind off what kind of day it had been and considered his question while taking a few lazy licks of her ice cream. She wanted Boston and him and a life that wasn't anchored to this place and her family. Not that she didn't love her family, but nothing was new here, ever. It was the same, mind-numbing, over-and-over she couldn't stand. All the same people with all the same problems, doing all the same things. She could tell you what everyone spent their free time doing, what their secrets were—*secrets*, she snorted. The very thought of actually keeping a secret here was ludicrous.

What would she want, if she hadn't buried her grandfather that day? "Fancy shoes," she replied. "And a place to wear them."

Gage bent sideways to see what she was wearing, and she kicked a foot up to table height. "Those are pretty fancy," he said.

She shook her head. "Espadrille wedges are beachy."

"Espa-what?"

"Espadrille." Gwen settled her foot back on the ground and leaned toward him with a sultry whisper. "Canvas-bottomed."

"When you say it like that, they sound fancy."

"What do you want?" she asked.

"To buy you fancy shoes and take you somewhere to wear them." It was delivered casually, but the look in his eyes was far from flippant.

Gwen sighed. "I have to run the store for a bit."

"Okay."

"I mean, I have to stay here longer. I can't move to Boston yet."

"Okay." A higher tone and more clearly two syllables, like she hadn't understood he meant it the first time.

"That's it?"

"Well, sure." He let out a small smile. "You want me to *not* be okay with it?"

"*I'm* not okay with it."

Gage licked his mint chip while keeping an eye on her. "Then don't do it."

"I'm supposed to. I should." These words were chains, even if they were comfortable ones. "Really, though, he could do it himself."

"Do what himself?" Gage asked.

"He could not retire yet, so I don't have to stay."

Leaning forward, Gage whispered, "You don't have to stay."

"I do, though." *I should*—it echoed again in her mind.

"If you left, he'd take care of it."

"I don't think so. I think he'd throw it on Betta, same as he did Pops."

"Betta wanted to come back, Gwen. She wanted to help out."

"Are you saying I didn't?" she snapped. Because she didn't,

14

it was true. One afternoon was all Gwen could handle, taking care of an old man. She couldn't stand it, and for that she owed her sister whatever Betta wanted—whatever her father asked of her for Betta's sake.

Gage raised an eyebrow. Infuriating how he did that, knowing she'd bite off whatever he returned with. Safe. He played it safe. Gwen was so sick of playing it safe. This town was safe. *Waiting* was safe.

"So stay a little longer. Enjoy it." Looking out at the black expanse of ocean before them, Gage added, "Stay forever."

Now it was her turn to raise an eyebrow. "Really?"

He grinned and scooted closer to her. "I'd move here for you."

"No." She put a hand up.

"I would. I could be an accountant anywhere."

"Not here. There wouldn't be enough work for you here."

"I wonder, though."

"No," she said, but he was finished with his cone now and sliding a hand up her leg. Her stomach caved first, then her irritation, then her face.

"That's more like it," he whispered, dropping kisses along her chin. "Because, see, you don't know what tax season is like."

"What's it like?" she murmured, melting into him the way her ice cream was melting into her hand.

"Busy. So busy, you'll never see me. It'll be like I don't exist."

"No," she whispered, but it was confusing how she meant it—her tone breathy and high. No, he shouldn't move here,

15

everyone knew that. And no, don't cease to exist. And no, don't stop.

She was a good girl, though, and Gage nearly a saint. They were in public, and she lived at home, and he was staying in Van's room, and she was waiting. Waiting because four months wasn't that long, and her mother always insisted Gage stay at the house instead of the inn.

So she closed her eyes and remembered the one weekend she'd been able to sneak away from the store to visit him in Boston, when they drank hot cocoa and nearly undressed each other. When they got to know each other on another level, just not *that* level. That's what started her itch.

Too soon, he'd said. *Next time.* But he didn't know what the store was like… what the town was like… what her family was like. He didn't know it wasn't so easy to get away.

* * *

Esmerelda hurried to the dirty white cavity that was the high school lunchroom, dumped her brown bag in the nearest trashcan, and blew into line behind Georgia. Georgia dyed her hair the shade of blonde Esmerelda wished she'd been born with, which was the second reason Ez liked her best of all the girls in their class. The first was that she was Celia's best friend.

Crossing her fingers, Ez threw out a "Hey, Georgia."

Georgia turned with a friendly, confident smile Ez tried to

copy. "Hey, Ez."

"What's up?" Esmerelda placed all the same things on her tray Georgia did, only she organized them better, squaring off the containers and leaving equal space between each item: one piece of sausage pizza (though Ez preferred pepperoni), one bottle of water, one apple, one fork, one knife, and two napkins.

"Not much. You?"

The third reason Ez liked Georgia more than the other most-popular-girls was that she was polite. Like Gwen, she was nice to everyone and had an air of maturity about her most high-schoolers couldn't pull off. She was many of the things Ez wanted to be: classy, liked by the masses, and inside Celia's inner circle.

"I'm good," Ez answered. "Mind if I sit with you?"

"Sure, if there's room."

Ez followed with fingers crossed. Esmerelda zoned in on Celia as they zigzagged through the space. High school had bigger tables than middle school, which meant Celia's circle had room to grow, and one of those seats was on Esmerelda's newest list, folded up on pink paper and hidden in her underwear drawer—Gwen was her happiest sister, and Ez attributed this to who she'd been in high school. It was what she wanted for herself.

Ez sat down, almost too quickly, sliding into a spot before anyone else could claim it. Celia raised one perfect eyebrow at her—*what are you doing here?*

"Hey." Ez delivered this with the same nonchalance Celia was putting off and fanned her hair out across her shoulders.

The conversation drifted around Esmerelda, noise she couldn't quite catch. She tried to jump in, but it never seemed like the right time. That, or Celia made sure to never give her an opening.

She'd need to work her way up out of invisibility, she knew. Besides, she couldn't talk and eat at the same time anyway. It took a lot of focus to pick the sausage off her pizza and not lose any cheese in the process.

"Gavin asked Christine to the party," Celia said, directing her attention toward Georgia more than the rest of them.

"What party?" Ez tried.

"Didn't she already tell him she wouldn't take him back?" Georgia asked.

"Yes." Celia snapped off a bite of carrot with her teeth. "But he's moping instead of getting on with his life."

"That's stupid. So he's not going at all?"

"Why can't he go without Christine?" Ez asked.

"It is stupid," Celia agreed with Georgia. "He can't not be at our first high school party."

"Plus, Ben's his best friend," Georgia added. "He'll go."

"He swore to me this morning that he won't without Christine. And she already asked someone else."

"Ben's having a party?" Ez tried again, this time catching Celia's attention.

Throwing her board-straight hair over her shoulder and squinting her exotically-shaped Brazilian (or so she said) eyes, Celia looked in her direction. "You weren't invited or you would know."

"Everyone has to have a date," Georgia explained. "So

there are an equal number of girls and boys."

Ez set her fork down. "So he just needs a date."

"Duh. Have you not been listening?"

"I mean, what if someone asked him? He won't ask anyone but Christine, but if someone asked him…" Ez wondered if they would follow where she was going, and if not, how hard she should push it. This could be her in.

Celia squinted at Ez, but did not berate or dismiss her.

Esmerelda let out a steady breath. Problem was, Gavin hadn't spoken to her since third grade. "Or just *tell* Ben I'm going with Gavin, and then the numbers will be even."

"I'm not sure Ben cares enough that Gavin shows up, if it means you're there." Celia followed this with an *oomph*, and Ez figured Georgia had kicked her under the table.

"Do you want Gavin to go or not?" Georgia asked Celia.

Celia scanned the rest of the girls at the table. "You all have dates?"

They nodded in turn as her gaze landed on them.

"And you both do, I'm sure." Because if they wanted him there so bad, why didn't they just ask him themselves?

"Girl, I was the first to have a date." Balling her lunch bag in her fist, Celia caught Georgia looking at her with a raised eyebrow. "Fine, you were. But you didn't have to be asked. You and Ben planned it. Doesn't count."

"If she asked Gavin," Georgia leaned forward, "he'd probably say yes."

"Yeah, he's a softy for people like her." Another oomph from Celia and then one from Georgia. Whatever, Ez would win them over. Ez would become so much like them that they couldn't group her in any other category ever again. All she needed was an angle. And maybe a little time.

Georgia turned to Ez. "You'll ask him, then?"

Ez nodded.

Celia rolled her eyes. "She can't ask him. Look at her. She's about to pee her pants at the very thought."

Clutching her shaking hands together, Esmerelda thought of snow and icebergs and Popsicles to cool her heated, surely blushing face. "I can. I will." But her words betrayed her, scratchy and dry.

"Who has a pen?" Celia asked, and a redhead at the end of the table supplied one. Grabbing for the cleanest napkin, she put both in front of Esmerelda. "Write him a note, and we'll deliver it. We'll say how cute and pathetic you were, and how he has to throw you a bone."

Georgia nodded, smiling at Ez. "Great idea, by the way."

Celia snorted. "I don't know about that, but it's worth a shot."

The conversation continued on, taking another path, and Ez worked at steadying her hand. The fewer words the better, especially if she couldn't smooth out her handwriting. *Please come to the party with me.*

She signed it with an E. Short and sweet. Quick and simple. Celia and Georgia could do the rest of the work, and Ez would save her energy for when she'd need it.

* * *

Betta, tucked in her favorite nook at the store, looked up when she heard the steady rhythm of Van's shoes in the hallway. Stepping past the bathroom and office, he entered the back room and stopped in front of her with a shake of his wide head.

Reaching over her, he pulled down a box of napkins. "You're supposed to be sleeping."

"This is my favorite place." She set her book on the floor and grabbed the steel shelving to help her up, then followed her brother out of the charcoal-shadowed back room to the wide center hall that led up to the front door.

Crossing her arms, Betta watched her dad heave himself through the aisles and around the corners, huffing with the exertion it caused.

She picked up the candy bar wrapper someone had tossed on the floor and walked it to the nearest garbage, straightening things as she went. There was something peaceful about working this place where she'd grown up. Lines of stacked toiletries next to Tupperware and baking dishes, a world where one could buy anything they might need for their home away from home—or even just for their home. They sold hardware of course, and garden plants, clothing even, sewing supplies, greeting cards, basic non-perishables, small appliances, vacuums, the list went on.

Her father spotted her and waved her over. Giving her a one-armed hug, he said the same thing. "You're supposed to be sleeping."

"I know, Dad." As if it was a family edict.

"So go sleep." He wandered off, inventory list in hand. As

if it was that easy to do nothing.

Van marched down the aisle and prodded her toward the front door. "James should be done with work. Go sleep with him if you're not going to sleep by yourself."

"Ew," she drew it out with a face that said likewise. Van was eighteen and probably beyond hormonal, but really? He had to go there? Continuing to step toward her, he forced her backward until she stumbled into the vestibule. Their most regular customer, the woman who owned the gourmet sandwich shop next door, squeezed past them with a bright smile.

"Look. There he is right now." Van squinted out into the rain-soaked afternoon at her boyfriend's yellow Volvo.

Betta sighed. "Fine." She supposed she could do him. Except she wouldn't, not literally, because of the whole he'd-been-with-Gwen-first thing, and she hadn't quite gotten over what they might have done together and how she might match up.

She didn't match up anywhere else in life, except maybe in the schoolwork department, and schoolwork no longer mattered.

Van opened the door for her, and she stepped out. A thin veil of dreariness blanketed the sky, and the trees swayed in the wind. Betta stood straighter, loving the weather for its honesty.

James leaned over the passenger seat and rolled down the window. "Are you working? I thought you were supposed to be sleeping."

With a huff, she got in and rolled up window. James

leaned over to kiss her neck, his favorite spot of anyone's ever, or so he said. His loose brown waves—just long enough to be in a constant state of disarray—tickled her earlobe, and she shivered into a smile. "I was reading in back," she explained. "Van kicked me out."

"You missed it that much, huh?"

"It's why I came back."

"Mmm. I thought I was why you came back."

"Well, I didn't know that at the time."

Gwen had sat in this seat too, more times than Betta. How many days were in a school year, the one they'd been together? It wasn't until years later—*years*, Betta wanted to scream at the locals who raised their eyebrows—when she was back home with her grandpa, after having already grown tired of her friends' judgments, that James showed up with a model car kit for Pops and stayed to do it with him. Betta stood in the kitchen, resting against the counter while they worked, listening to her grandpa's Johnny Cash and Willie Nelson CDs, and six months later, James pulled her onto the back porch and kissed her without a word.

It was a small town. She'd been lonely. He felt like home.

She hadn't realized she was stepping into the looming shadow of her sister. Not that James put that on her. She knew it was her problem, her issue.

Betta tried to get a handle on it, tried to squeeze the intolerable until it settled back inside, before she blurted out something stupid. She didn't want to start a fight today, not when there was such a lovely drizzle settling over everything outside.

"Are you okay?" he asked. She had stiffened; he was perceptive. "Are you upset I wasn't there yesterday?"

Betta had told him not to come to the house after the funeral, and she meant it. One, his best friend Eddie was in town for the day, and two, everyone still thought of him as Gwen's boyfriend. Having both Gage and James there would only be confusing to all of Pops' acquaintances.

Betta shook her head. "No. I'm sorry, I don't know what's wrong with me."

"Nothing's wrong with you."

She sighed, because there were a whole many things wrong. Her grandpa just died. He'd been her life for the past two years. She wanted the store, wanted to do something, yet she was supposed to recover, like she'd been the one with cancer. Her frown pulled tighter. "I don't know what to do with myself," she admitted, turning the radio off as James pulled away from the curb.

"I have the perfect thing," he said.

"What?"

Strumming his fingers on the wheel, he glanced at her. "Marry me."

She shook her head. "You don't want to marry me."

"Yes, I do. I've told you a million times I do."

"No, you've told me a million times you want to whisk me away to California to start over. I don't want to start over." And she definitely didn't want to move in with Eddie, which is what they'd have to do if they moved to California.

James grabbed her fingers. "You need more sun, babe. You're always happier in the summer."

She was happier in the summer because it was when the store needed her. But the store wasn't in California.

He pulled into the parking lot of their favorite diner and grabbed his cigarettes, unable to part with them the way some were unable to part with their cell phones. It was his only flaw, in Gwen's eyes, but Betta didn't mind it much. She kind of liked the smell of fresh cigarette smoke.

They hurried through the rain to the front door, which he opened for her, and slid into the same side of their regular booth.

"I get that taking care of someone else is all you've done for the last two years, but how about taking care of yourself for a bit?"

"You think I should be sleeping too?"

He collected her hair over her shoulder and kissed her earlobe, then the scar on her jaw—she tried not to cringe—all while his knee bounced a steady beat under the table. "I think, if you need to take care of somebody, you should take care of me."

"Yeah?" She thought about this—moving in with him, taking care of him in a totally different way than she'd taken care of Pops—and that was when she realized she did, indeed, need a break. Because the thought of taking care of another person pulled her down into a kind of exhaustion she never thought she'd feel again. "No," she said, shrugging him off. "No, they're right. I need a break."

"Too bad." His voice held its regular teasing lilt, and he relaxed back into the booth. "Because if you took care of me, I could trick you into taking care of yourself."

She laughed. "Not now that I know your plans."

"That's better."

"What's better?"

"Your smile. I've missed it."

Betta fingered the menu, not that she needed it, but it gave her something to do. It had been hard to smile. It had been hard to do a lot of things while Pops wasted away in front of her. Perhaps she'd make a list of all the things she stopped doing while waiting for him to die.

She could then climb them, one by one, out of the hole she'd descended into with him. Back to life.

OCTOBER

Esmerelda sat in front of her large vanity mirror, and Gwen stood behind her.

They both studied Esmerelda with a smile—she was ready for the party—and Ez took stock of the differences between their reflections.

"Can I borrow your necklace for good luck?" she asked, it being the most obvious and easily fixable of the disparities. Ez wanted the locket since she first saw it—on Gage and Gwen's one month anniversary—and liked to imagine their faces matched up inside, forced to kiss until released by a fingertip.

"You're already wearing my earrings."

And your socks, but Ez didn't say it, because she'd taken them earlier, and they were tucked deep inside her boots. "For luck." To bring it home, Ez added, "It's my first date."

A lie? A little. Though it technically was her first date, Celia made it very clear Gavin was only being polite.

Pursing her lips, Gwen unlocked the clasp and placed the necklace around Esmerelda's neck. Ez's fingers, all ten of them, crawled up to touch the chain and make sure it was real.

"One night and one night only," Gwen said. "I want it returned as soon as you get home."

Ez pumped her head up and down before returning her focus to the mirror. Her hair, flat-ironed, looked almost as natural as Gwen's, and her makeup was an exact copy. The top she wore was Gwen's, the jeans used to be Gwen's, the jewelry Gwen's, and the socks. Head to toe.

Feeling complete, Ez stood with a squeal and threw her arms around her older sister.

Gwen laughed. "Have fun tonight."

It was the first real party she'd been invited to—or gotten herself invited to—and Gavin was picking her up (on foot) like a real first date, though Celia kept reminding her they were only going as friends.

The doorbell rang, and Ez raced for it. Flinging it open, she pretended she hadn't charged for the door the way she had. Gavin wore a lightweight jacket and stood with hands stuffed into his jean pockets.

His brown hair was thick and long, angled forward almost as if it was being pulled invisibly toward his nose, and his lips were short, narrow but round, a slight downturned pout in their natural state. His grin, however, brightened his otherwise very serious face.

Ez couldn't seem to get her tongue or mouth or words working, and it took three minutes of their feet on the sidewalk (Ez counted in seconds) before Gavin blurted out, "You have pretty hair."

Only, she didn't. Not usually. Esmerelda could hardly

believe her luck, this magic that was Gwen on her face and in her hair and on her feet. Ez tucked her bottom lip into her mouth and felt the dimple in the center with her tongue. A compliment for a compliment, that's what her mom had taught her, but "I like your jacket" felt about as stupid as she could get.

It came to her as he opened the front door of Ben's house, something Van would do, something Van would say. "You have pretty hair, too." With the kind of smile that made it obvious she was teasing (not an idiot who was serious and trying to be cool), she ducked her head and stepped past him into the house.

With an amused quarter-smile, Gavin led her through the first floor and down to the basement, where they landed under the head of a buck and surveyed the room. The music was loud, and the crowd chaotic—showing off for each other in the most obvious of ways.

Gavin was probably drawn to it, to the energy and the vibe. Ez was sure this was the moment they'd split up, and she'd become Cinderella tripping on her broken shoe, so she scanned the heads for Georgia and Celia, the only two she cared about. That's where she'd go.

Except he grabbed her fingers and led her to a cobwebby corner.

She looked down at their hands, loose in each other's grip as if this was a thing they did now.

Gavin's grin slid up sideways. "I have a problem with wasting time. If I want to do something, I do it."

"Okay. What do you want to do?"

"I want to kiss you."

Esmerelda blinked.

It couldn't be that easy. She glanced around again for Celia—what if she'd put him up to this, what if it were a joke?

"Ez? That okay?"

"Of course that's okay," she replied. It was a first date if she were kissed, no matter what Celia had to say about it.

His mouth pressed on hers, and her eyelids fluttered in response—*keep them closed,* she instructed herself. Ez didn't have much practice, but she was good at following, and Gavin had no trouble directing traffic.

When he released her, Ez blushed and looked down to her toes. Her stomach was hot. Boiling. She didn't know stomachs could catch a temperature.

But. It did not escape her that they'd barely spoken. That a few days ago, it had been reported he was still into Christine. That so far, what he liked about her was only her mouth and her hair.

Cinderella had dealt with the same thing though, and Cinderella hadn't doubted herself in front of the prince. She didn't ask him why he liked her when she was only Cinderella, and if Ez remembered correctly, they didn't speak much either, only danced.

Dancing, making out, same difference.

"Are you okay?" Gavin asked, because Ez was staring at a cobweb, deeply considering the implications of a fairytale.

Copying what she'd seen Gwen do when she and Gage said goodbye last weekend, Ez grabbed hold of Gavin's shirt and pulled him back for more.

This time, he waited for her to stop, and as she retreated, he smiled. "I'm glad CeCe set us up."

"CeCe?"

"Celia."

"You call her CeCe?"

"Sure, it's what her parents call her."

"Oh." Esmerelda worked her lip with her teeth. She'd noticed how Gavin watched it last time, and wanted to see how quickly it might catch his attention again (two seconds). "So, you guys are close?"

Before he could respond, Celia grabbed Ez's arm, yanking her away with a warning look in Gavin's direction. "What part of coming as friends do you not understand?" she seethed.

"*He* kissed *me*."

"He's trying to get over Christine," Celia snapped. "Do not take advantage of that."

Ez studied her, this very cool cucumber of a girl, currently red in the face, and it hit her. Celia liked Gavin. She wanted him for herself. So if Gavin wanted Esmerelda, if Ez could keep him, then Celia wouldn't let her out of her sight.

Celia was totally the type to keep her enemies close.

Well, that worked for Ez; she'd win her over eventually. Plus, it was too late to *not* kiss him. It wasn't like she'd say no now. If being Celia's frenemy was her in, then it was her in.

Blinking over wide eyes, as if she didn't know any better, Ez defended, "I don't understand. If he likes me, and I like him…"

They stared at each other a beat, searching out the truth of one another and not finding it, until Celia broke the moment by rolling her eyes and playing it off. Ez tucked that victory in her pocket for later.

"Be careful," Celia said, like she was doing Ez a favor. "Rebounds always get hurt."

That was the hole in her plan, Ez realized. Once she no longer had Gavin, she was no longer Celia's enemy, and she'd be dropped like a hot potato. It was further than she'd been that morning, though.

She'd have to be on her best behavior and look for something else Celia might want as backup. So she spent the night observing, being careful not to step on toes or be too much of anything, lest she be too much of the wrong thing. Kids made out, they snuck cigarettes out the bathroom window, and Ez sipped the tiniest sips out of the beer Celia handed her, dumping it in the bathroom whenever she got the chance.

Hell if she was going to lose control of the situation.

Celia kept her eye on Gavin, and Gavin kept his eye on Ez. Ez got to practice coy, and interested, and amused, and a look that intimated the softest *hi*.

It was beyond exhausting, honestly, and when Gavin slipped his hand into hers a few hours later, as he tugged her into an oversized armchair, she breathed easier.

Kissing wasn't a game, like pretending. It just was.

She landed on his lap, and he shifted her a bit sideways. The making out went on longer than Esmerelda could have ever imagined, and when she started to wonder if lips could bruise, Gavin's hands began to wander her chest. It was curious and felt strange.

Until it felt a little less strange.

Until she sort of liked it.

Until she wondered when they could do it again, and it wasn't even over yet.

Gavin stopped only when his friends started making fun of him—and her, Celia at their side. Stupid boy jeers—*Where's Christine, Gavin? Weren't you just crying about Christine?*—while Ez's head spun. She didn't care what they were saying. She didn't care that Celia was orchestrating it. She didn't care because she was here, at a legit high school party, part of the action, with the maybe fifth coolest guy in their class.

Their words swirled around her, almost as if she were drunk, only she knew she wasn't, she'd dumped three beers down the drain that night. She could act it, though, seem like she didn't know what was happening: innocent Esmerelda, sorry Celia, oops, bad call to pair us together, the kissing *not my fault*.

Gavin defended them both, declaring he was over his ex— what was her name?—because, I mean, come on, look at those lips. No, he said then, don't look. She's mine.

She's mine. That's when the world came back into sharp focus.

Could it be so easy?

Ez repeated it numerous times in her head as Gavin walked her home, which almost made her stumble and land on a crack in the sidewalk. Ez did not step on sidewalk cracks. Or blacktop cracks. Or dirt that had dried and separated into a crack.

Especially not now; she was not about to tempt her luck.

All of this because of the locket, Ez was sure, and as they turned onto her block, she reached up for it.

Panic slammed her chest as her fingers rested on a blank expanse of collarbone. She clawed for it, but no necklace, no chain, no nothing was there. Ez stopped walking.

"What's up?" Gavin asked.

"My locket!" Tears sprang to her eyes. "It's gone!"

"Was it special?"

"Of course it was special!" she cried. "When is a locket not special?"

He put his hands up. "Do I look like I wear lockets?"

Fisting her hands at her sides, she calmed herself with a forced sigh. The last thing she wanted was to alarm him, even though she was so terribly alarmed herself. "I'm sorry, it's just... I can't lose this locket. Do you think we could go back?" She checked her phone. But they'd been one of the last to leave, and her curfew was looming. "*Crap.*"

"Hey." He squeezed her hand. "I'll be there tomorrow. I'll check it out. It's bound to be in that chair."

Ez cringed with the realization that she was being punished for believing in luck, or for letting Gavin grope her, or maybe for stealing all the things she'd stolen from her sister over the years. Yet here was a boy who was promising to find it for her, to fix the problem. It was something she'd never known before.

"You'd do that for me?"

"Of course."

Ez breathed. And nodded. And decided to stay upbeat. Because that was what Gwen did. So far, acting like Gwen had not only gotten her a boyfriend, but also had her making out for the first time, not to mention felt up like she'd never expected.

She'd march inside and tell her. Tell Gwen she lost it and her boyfriend was going to find it the next day. And he would. He'd bring it to her house, she'd introduce him to the family, she'd give Gwen her locket back, and Gavin would kiss her like Gage kissed Gwen.

* * *

Maybe Gwen's mood was about the missing locket, or maybe it was just the time of month discontent rode in on. Then again, it could be that it was Sunday, and she was shut up in a drab office with the teeniest of windows and no direct sunlight.

Gwen put her pen down and surveyed the clutter that was running the family business. Her father had given up his big desk and worked at the smaller one, doughy face pinched as he finalized the inventory he planned to order at one o'clock.

"Daddy, we aren't even covering expenses right now. Why are you spending money?"

"I always do one last inventory to stock up for the winter."

"Maybe you shouldn't."

His pencil kept moving, head down.

Gwen tapped her screen. "Maybe you should come look at this."

"I know what it looks like, Gwen."

She rolled her neck, trying to release her tense muscles. "I don't think you do." He couldn't. How could he, and then spend money anyway? She'd seen the numbers dwindling all month, while hoping she could leave the store in a better state for Betta. The last thing her sister needed was more stress after the year she'd had.

Her dad ripped into the candy bar he'd set on his desk first thing that morning. "It's always like this in the winter," he admitted.

"What's it always like, exactly?" Because the way it looked to her, she wasn't going to have money to pay their parents rent next month. The rent that paid for the family's groceries.

Chewing on the nougaty caramel, he came around to stand behind her. "Yep, like that."

"It can't be," she muttered. "Do you have backup?"

"What do you mean, backup?"

"I mean, a stash?'

"A stash of what?"

"A stash of money."

"Naw, summer always makes up for it. Things are worse than normal because of Pops' funeral expenses, and, well, he had some debt. Hadn't been paying rent, either, but they let that slide until he passed." He patted her shoulder. "Like I said, summer always makes up for it. I'm sure it will this time, too."

"Betta wasn't paying his rent?"

He shrugged. "His meds were very expensive, it was rent or food."

Gwen blinked into her computer screen. "What you're saying then," Gwen wanted to be clear before she made yet another *should* decision she knew already she was going to regret, "is that you're retiring, no matter what. You are no longer in charge."

"That's how we do it, Gwennie." He sat back down in his chair and finished off his candy bar.

She stared at him.

"I'll be here to help," he added. "But it's time for the next generation to step up and make something to be proud of."

Gwen swallowed hard. She was hot. Sweaty. Still, she had to say it. "Dad. You have to fix this."

He picked up his pencil and dipped his head back down to his work. "I figured it out when I took over, and you'll figure it out now."

"I thought I'd be in Boston by Christmas," she muttered.

"Your mom would really love you to stay through Christmas."

She felt a scream building, teapot steam and the subsequent squeal. Pressure. So much pressure. *She needed out.*

"If you want to go now, Betta can handle it."

"You just told me she wasn't paying rent and ran up credit card bills."

Still, with his head down and only half there, her dad replied, "She didn't have much of a choice."

Clutching the edge of her desk she sat, stunned, as the facts tumbled about inside her head.

She could leave and watch from Boston. Maybe they'd pull through, or maybe they'd lose everything.

Losing everything was not uncommon. It happened all the time. The money didn't live in town, it only visited, and only for a short time each year. It was not an easy life.

She could watch them flounder from afar, or she could stay and help.

Helping is what she *should* do. And failure wasn't an option.

* * *

"What do you mean, the locket's not there?"

As Wanda brought the lasagna to the table, she pretended they could salvage a lovely family dinner, and that Gwen's reaction to Esmerelda's news would not instead start a fight.

Due to tourist season store hours, tonight was the first meal they'd all shared since April, and Wanda had painstakingly whisked fresh salad dressing and labored over lasagna to make an event of it.

All that work to bring her family together, and now two of her children were whining and distraught. Something was up with Gwen anyway, and now Esmerelda lost her locket. It went to show, you could set up everything perfectly, and still someone would ruin it.

"He looked everywhere," Ez whimpered.

"How do you even know you can trust this guy?" Gwen

asked. "Maybe he found it and gave it to his girlfriend."

Esmerelda jutted her chin up. "*I'm* his girlfriend."

"Really?" Gwen laughed. "One night and you're his girlfriend?"

"It isn't my fault!"

"Then whose fault is it?"

"It must have a bad clasp. Or you didn't latch it right! I never took it off!"

"Calm down," Betta said, standing and taking the spatula out of Wanda's hand. "It's just a locket."

Gwen bit her lips shut.

Wanda looked to Harvey as she set the napkins on the table. "Let's pray?"

He nodded and bowed his head, clasping his hands in front of him. "Lord, we give thanks today that you have blessed us with another good season, and we pray you meet our needs in the slow months of winter to come. We thank you for the shelter over our head, the love of our family, and the delicious food you have provided. Amen."

"Amen," the table chorused, a medley of tones from cheerful to not, and they dug in.

"I'm thankful we're all together for dinner again," Wanda said, trying out a tentative grin. "The up side to the season being over, right?" There was no pointed look there; she didn't mean to glance at Gwen, but this was Wanda's night, all of them together. She wanted a nice dinner. It shouldn't be too much to ask.

Esmerelda cut her lasagna in the most perfect of squares, her bony elbows vicious with the movement, while Gwen shuffled the chunks of beef around on Wanda's old china.

See? She even got out the china. That should've been a hint to be on their best behavior.

Gwen's fork clattered to the table. "This is why I don't lend you things."

Esmerelda slid her phone across the table to Gwen. "Look! I'm not lying! I'm freaking out, too, okay? It was an accident, completely, one hundred percent!"

Wanda sighed, about to give up on the illusion of a happy family meal, as Gwen snatched the phone and skimmed through. Whatever she saw brought her back from furious to distraught.

"I'm sure Gage'll buy you something else," Betta said, and Wanda couldn't tell if she was trying to help or being a brat.

"It's not the worst thing that's happened," Van added. "I mean, my friends all left me for college, and Kate won't be home again until Thanksgiving."

"Pops died," Betta reminded.

"And had cancer for three years. That sucked."

"Perspective." The two of them nodded together.

"Perspective?" Gwen echoed with a raised eyebrow. "You want perspective, let's talk about how much debt you racked up while taking care of him."

"What do you mean?" Betta furrowed her brow. "I saved us money."

"What debt?" Wanda asked her husband, who straightened from where he'd been hunched over his plate.

"Don't worry, honey. It's nothing."

"*Nothing?*" Gwen cried, spearing a look at Harvey.

Gwen was already worked up, Wanda told herself; surely she was exaggerating. Harvey was calm, not a ripple. He would know if they were in trouble. In fact, he was so unconcerned, he picked up his phone from next to his plate.

Gwen's cell pinged and she snatched it. After reading, she narrowed her eyes at Harvey, who set his phone down with a smile.

"Good news, Wanda!" he said. "Gwen's planning to stay through Christmas. Probably through summer."

Betta sat back in her chair. "What are you going to do here for that long?"

"Run the store," Gwen clipped.

"You don't want to run the store."

Gwen ignored that. "Honestly Betta, with sales down and winter staffing, I won't really need you."

"*You don't want to run the store*," Betta repeated.

It made sense to Wanda. Harvey usually worked winters with only weekend help from the kids and a little morning help from herself. Now it was Gwen, with Harvey in the morning taking the deposits to the bank.

"I'll likely be working seven days a week," Gwen added. "I have plans for a store transformation before next season."

"What kind of transformation?"

Gwen shrugged. "Mostly cleanup."

"I can do that, Gwen. I can help."

"I won't pay you for what I can do myself."

"You'll work yourself silly, seven days a week."

"If it makes you feel any better, I'm letting Van go altogether." Her gaze darted over to Van, who swallowed hard.

"Uh, thanks for letting me know?"

"This doesn't make sense, Gwen. You quit, Van works part-time, and Mom and Dad help out when they need to. I'm good. I got it."

"No, *I've* got it."

Betta squinted. "Did you and Gage break up or something?"

Gwen shoved her plate away from her. "No, this is just what I want."

"But you don't!" Betta cried.

"Maybe I do."

"I'm not the one who lost your locket," Betta said. "Why are you taking it out on me?"

"I'm not taking it out on you," Gwen snapped. "Not everything's about you."

"No. I guess it's not." Betta gathered herself tall. "I guess it's about you."

Gwen huffed, gaze darting to Harvey. Her words were a plea. "Help me out here."

"Store goes to the oldest," he affirmed, then lowered his head back to his plate.

Betta put her hands to her head, elbows out. She blinked at her sister, and Wanda skirted her gaze as it came for her next. Wanda was missing something, she was sure. Yet Gwen staying in town was good news—her family, all together. So why weren't they celebrating?

It was like they wanted to be unhappy, when truly they couldn't yet fathom what desperate unhappiness was.

Throwing her napkin down, she began collecting plates.

So much for her family dinner.

* * *

Betta checked every one of their faces—her dad's, mom's and sister's—and each said the same thing. Gwen was taking the store. For now and for who knew how long. Long enough she couldn't count on it happening for her anytime soon.

Shoving her chair back, she walked out of the kitchen and to the front door, outside where she might be able to breathe a little better, where the air was cold enough it might hold her up. She leaned into it, hoping to numb the bits of her that currently ached and spun.

She'd known Gwen was pissed Betta was Pops' favorite, and maybe she'd actually been a little pissed about James too, but Betta hadn't believed any of that mattered, because Gwen got everything she wanted. She was the world's favorite, and Betta only theirs.

She'd presumed all this living in her sister's shadow bullshit was her own insecurity, but as she stood, feet half off the curb on their very quiet street, she wondered if Gwen had actually been trying, all these years, to keep her there on purpose.

The door opened and shut, and her brother's heavy feet made their way to her side. He slung an arm around her shoulder, and she rested against him while blinking the tears back inside.

"What the hell just happened in there?" she muttered.

"I don't know," he replied. "But since my hopes and dreams of working part-time at the store for my sister the rest of my life are crushed, I guess I better start looking for a job."

She looked up at him. "I'm sorry."

He smirked. "Don't worry. I know this is about you."

Betta pinched him, but he didn't flinch, only held tighter to her at his side. It wasn't his dream, and he'd already been making other plans, had spent the summer lifeguarding and working the store per usual, then Pops...

Everything had been twisted and off since, and Betta took in a great gasp of air to help flush out the tears crawling up her throat.

"Is that your way of saying I should look for a job?" she asked.

"No." He dropped his arm, and the cold swept back in around her. "It's my way of telling you I'm going to look for a job."

Betta hugged herself. "Mom and Dad knew I was charging his meds. They could have brought groceries over; I wasn't going to take them."

"You did good, Bets."

"Yeah?" She glanced at him for confirmation, and he nodded. "Because suddenly it doesn't feel like it."

"Mom and Dad charge stuff all the time, stuff a lot less important than food and meds."

"Exactly!" She threw her arm back. "You can't tell me that we have cash for that in the winter. No one here has money for stuff in the winter."

"Seriously, don't worry about it, okay?"

She nodded.

"Come back inside and finish dinner."

She shook her head.

"Lasagna's your favorite."

"I can't eat another bite right now."

"Then what are you going to do?"

"I'm going to find a job." With a pat on her brother's arm, Betta took to the sidewalk and hurried down the street. Good thing she had her black turtleneck on, and her thickest knit sweater.

She would start at Mae's sandwich shop right next door to Aaldenberg Hardware. Convenient and close, in case Gwen ever needed anything. Not that she was sure she wanted to help Gwen at this point, let her do it on her own, but she doubted she'd be able to turn her back on the store so easily. If it needed her...

At the halfway mark, where a broken brown house sat nearly in the intersection, Betta had to compose herself one more time. It used to be her favorite saltbox in town, back when she was a kid and her mom pointed out the styles of homes on their walks to the hardware store, and now it was in such a state of disrepair it might need to be torn down.

It reminded her too much of herself. An empty, tired shell after the passing of her grandfather, in such a state of disrepair that her sister could so easily demolish her to crumbled pieces.

She'd made her list of the things she'd stopped doing

during Pops' care, and the first was the store. *Work.* She liked to work. She'd been sitting happy on the thought that when she was ready and rested, she'd be welcomed back and it would be hers to take over. If not, well, then she was still going to work. A contributing member of society did things; they produced. And she needed a job to do that.

Swinging the door open to Mae's, which sounded identical to the entrance next door—same weight and feel too—Betta was glad to see it was quiet. Mae sat behind the register with a cup of tea and a book.

"Hi, dear," she said, looking up and standing to attention.

"Hi, Mae." Betta rested her fingers on the counter and straightened her shoulders. "I was hoping you might be hiring."

"Oh." The woman gave her a small smile—a sad one? "Oh, honey."

Betta cleared her throat. Why did pain and sorrow and disappointment always come up from the throat? Was that the nearest exit from the heart? "Do you have any positions available?"

"Surely you realize no one is hiring right now."

"I want a job." Betta averted her eyes from the woman's pitying look and rubbed her thumb along a divot on the edge of the counter. "I need a job."

"I don't have anything, I'm sorry. Come back in the spring, okay?"

Swallowing her disappointment and all the other things that were threatening her, Betta nodded and spun on her heel. She walked straight out with purpose, so Mae wouldn't feel too sorry for her, and stood once again on the sidewalk, staring at the bookstore across the street.

The bookstore.

She loved bookstores, and she loved the owner. She loved books. Reading was the third thing on her list of living. It was perfect.

Without looking, because that was how dead the town was on a Sunday night during the off-season, Betta marched across the street.

She yanked open the worn wooden door, aching for familiarity the moment her fingers touched down on the handle. Aching for comfort and the reminder of old plans, even if they'd just crashed around her.

Shelby was on a stool at the register, watching something on her phone, but she glanced up with a smile. Betta passed in front of the bookshelves on her left and the seating area in front of the windows on her right. Standing with fingers tentative on the counter once again, she asked, "Are you hiring?"

Removing a pair of purple reading glasses from her nose, Shelby disentangled the rope they hung on from amidst her thick red hair. "Coffee?" she asked, standing to pour her a cup from the station behind the desk.

"Is that a no?"

"Girl, I live here to get through the winter. That's the only reason I'm even open right now." The woman turned back and handed the mug over, then guided Betta to the soft green couch with a hand to her back. "Sit."

Betta took the mug from her, folding it into her palms,

and Shelby sat at the edge of a green-shaded paisley armchair, setting her phone on the coffee table. It was cluttered with books and sat in the center of a well-worn rug.

Betta blinked into the bulbous glass lamps on the end tables which lit the space with a cozy glow. It lent a feel of interminable time—endlessness stretching out in front of you with infinite possibilities.

Or, normally it did. Today, it felt dreary and depressing, highlighting how the world could let you down. Without the sunlight that normally shined in the window, it was dark enough Betta almost felt like she couldn't see—couldn't discern what was real and what was not. Same as she felt about her sister's words.

"You live here?"

"There's an office space upstairs that makes a lovely bedroom, and I use the storage room in back for my office."

"Do you own the building?" She asked because they owned theirs, but most of the street rented from Mas Properties.

"Business rent is cheaper than housing rent around here. Brennan's really great about it." Brennan Masowicz. He took over his father's real estate business the minute he was able. No waiting for him.

Her dad told her not to worry, but now she wondered where all the money came from, if no one else had any. And Gwen was definitely worried about something, maybe about more than the locket.

"Have a sip of that coffee, Betta. Looks like you need it."

She did, and a warmth rushed through her, soothing the nips she'd taken from the cold outside, and also the nips she'd taken from her sister.

"This is fantastic."

"Thanks, it's the Baileys."

Betta sputtered a little.

"Aren't you twenty-one now?"

"No. Well, almost."

"The Aaldenbergs are a good little Christian family, I know." Shelby smiled warmly. "I won't tell. You look like you could use it."

This was definitive. If ever, in her short years, she needed something to take the edge off and blur her confused mind until it might resemble something that made sense, now was that time. She took a larger drink and heaved a shaky sigh.

"Rough day?" Shelby asked.

"Most of them are," Betta admitted.

Shelby waved this off. "Most of them are adventures."

Betta didn't remember when she had her last adventure. What she remembered was the funeral and watching someone die. Leaving school, too, had been as difficult as living in a city she could never love. And before that, coming up in a place that worshipped Gwen, beautiful and untarnished, having to hide your face and your scar—the literal representation of your *less than*—those had been some rough days, too. Even if Betta never wanted what Gwen had, she'd wanted her happiness, her ease.

Now, Betta realized, she actually wanted what Gwen had. What Gwen was taking. Maybe therein lay the problem. Gwen always took what she wanted when she wanted it, and Betta had learned to wait her turn.

"Why do you stay?" Betta asked, but to the window and the world outside. If you had to live where you worked, why would you stay?

"For the ocean. Anyway, I don't need much."

"Mae doesn't live at her store," Betta pointed out. Her house sat behind the Aaldenberg's; they were backyard neighbors.

"She gets her husband's social security and retirement, and they paid off the house before he died. Plus, she doesn't make soup in the winter only because it's warm."

Betta glanced at her with a furrowed brow.

"Soup is cheap and goes a long way. Anyway, people eat more than they read."

Betta chugged the rest of her coffee, then held onto the mug for its lingering warmth as the Bailey's burned through her, heating with false hope.

She felt stupid, like she should have realized. She knew the house they lived in went back to the first Aaldenberg's, same as the store did. She knew Pops moved out when her parents had Van, so the new family had more room. She should have connected the dots and not charged anything—she should have scraped by. Maybe, even, she shouldn't have trusted her father.

"Does she think I can't do it?" Betta wondered aloud.

"Do what?"

"Run the store."

"Your mom?"

"No, my sister."

"It's up to your sister?"

"Tradition," they echoed at once.

"Ah, yes." Shelby offered her a sad smile. "I forget about that sometimes. How this town is stuck in its ruts." Shelby had blown in from nowhere about ten years ago.

The woman stood to rummage along the shelves, searching out the kind of medicine that had always worked for Betta in the past.

"Maybe fantasy," Betta suggested.

If there was anything that could counteract the utter, heart-aching reality, Betta thought, it would be a heavy serving of fantasy.

NOVEMBER

About a month after Esmerelda lost Gwen's locket, Celia started wearing one.

Esmerelda didn't notice right away, but it didn't take long. Then she didn't say anything right away, because though she was sure, she couldn't be absolutely sure. There were a million gold heart lockets in the world with soft scrolling at the edges.

At first, Ez figured Celia had found it, and not knowing who it belonged to, took a liking to it and kept it for her own. Then she realized if you found a locket, you'd open it up and look at the pictures. Ez was pretty sure there was no mistaking the photo inside for anyone but her sister, and everyone knew her sister.

Esmerelda puzzled over this for days before deciding none of it mattered. She needed to say something. Plus, Gavin thought it'd be easy. They'd been spending afternoons making out at his house—empty until 5pm on the dot—and Saturdays wandering town, holding hands and talking.

When she mentioned it to him, he shrugged. "So tell her

it's yours, and you want it back."

Of course, she could have guessed that's what he'd say. Everything was simple to Gavin. Black or white, obvious or more obvious. Ez sighed.

Squeezing her hand this first Monday after she'd told him, Gavin left her at her new lunch table, and she took a seat next to Georgia. Gavin sat with his friends one table over, and as soon as Celia joined them, Ez busted out with it. "That's my necklace."

Celia smirked at her with a haphazard sort of confidence. "Really? How do you know it's yours?"

"I lost it at Ben's party."

"Does it have your picture in it?"

"No, it's my sister's. It has her picture in it."

"Hmm. Well, let's see." Celia opened the heart to reveal a picture of herself on one side and the indistinguishable face of a boy on the other. She leaned over the table so far Ez had a hard time seeing anything but Celia's well-developed cleavage.

After a moment, Celia slapped the sides closed again and sat back. She offered a sympathetic smile. "Guess you must be mistaken."

Esmerelda's jaw dropped, but the world continued on like normal. She didn't say another word, and eventually went to eating her lunch. Thoughts tumbled around in her brain, disorganized and on top of each other, but she could at least control her movements. She could cut her cheeseburger into the same sized pieces, but for the edges which she left discarded to the side uneaten. She could pull her fork to her mouth on the same trajectory with each bite, chew fifteen times before swallowing, and repeat.

In focusing on these motions, her brain sorted itself out.

It had to be her locket. It just had to.

"Where'd you get it, then?" Ez blurted out, interrupting a story Georgia was telling.

The corners of Celia's lips snaked up. "Are you calling me a liar?"

Ez blinked. "Of course not." No one would call Celia a liar. No one would call her anything but the things she wanted to be called. Not if they wanted to stay at the table, which Ez wanted almost as much as she now wanted Gavin. Actually, she wasn't sure which she wanted more, so she dropped it.

Even so, Ez thought of nothing else as she walked back to her locker and then on to gym. There, she sighed deeply and doubly, because at the same time she admitted to herself that she'd have to wait out getting the locket back, the teacher paired her up with Christine for their weightlifting unit.

"Hey," Christine said, breaking into her thoughts.

Ez stood. "Hey."

"This doesn't have to be awkward. I know you're with Gavin now, and that's totally no problem for me."

But Ez couldn't have totally no problem with Christine, because Celia had a problem with her, which meant—Ez had at least figured this out—that to stay on Celia's good side, she also had to have a problem with her.

Really, Ez decided, Christine looked like a softer, nicer version of Celia. Maybe that's what Celia had a problem with.

Christine tried to make it less awkward with a whole lot of

talking, but it wasn't until the end of the hour when she mentioned the locket that she made any sort of breakthrough at all.

"Did you give that locket to CeCe?"

Esmerelda dropped her weighted legs with a thud. "I don't know. I mean, no. I mean, she said it's not mine."

"Of course she said that."

"You call her CeCe, too?"

"We've been friends on and off for a very long time. Probably won't be again though."

"Why not?"

Christine shrugged. "I don't like her very much anymore."

"Oh." Ez figured, however, that Christine was covering for not being liked by Celia anymore. "I asked her about it today. The locket."

"Yeah?"

"She said it wasn't mine."

"Well, she lies."

"Yeah?"

"Yeah, she's probably not going to give it back, but it is yours. I saw her pick it up off the floor when you and Gavin were making out at the party. About that, by the way, you don't have to worry that because he felt you up right away he's expecting anything else. All of eighth grade, we never even got to second base, *technically*, since he was always on top of my shirt."

Esmerelda didn't know what to think about this. She hadn't really been worrying about it. She hadn't even known she should be worrying about it. "Did you *want* to get to second base?" she asked.

"Sort of."

"Oh."

"Anyway, I'll help you get it back if you want."

"I can't believe she lied to me." Actually, that wasn't true. She could believe it. She just couldn't believe how good she'd been at it—so certain and straight-faced, one hundred percent committed.

Esmerelda wanted to be that sure about something, or about herself. It was admirable, honestly.

* * *

"You don't have a million dollars hiding under your mattress, do you?"

Gwen was on the phone with Gage, alone in the store office, now completely intimate with the state of her family's finances. She'd asked her dad straight out last week, and he mumbled something about January loans she couldn't decipher. She'd pushed him further, and suddenly he remembered he needed to run something over to Mae's. So that was a lot of help.

The next chance she got, she rummaged through his desk and logged onto his computer, feeling like a snitch and a liar and a cheat. But if he wasn't going to be honest with her, then she knew there was more to it, and if she wanted out, she needed to find the whole of it.

"Your parents do not live like they're a hundreds of thousands of dollars in debt," he replied. "Your mom just redid her kitchen. And didn't they buy new bedroom furniture?"

"Exactly. They spent it when they had it, instead of saving it for Pops' funeral expenses, which duh, were obviously coming. Not to mention hospital bills from his last round of chemo—his insurance was nearly useless—plus Dad was on his credit card, and Betta maxed that out. The house is paid off, unless there's some second mortgage hiding somewhere. Crap, there probably is. I don't know how long it's going to take to right this, Gage."

"It's okay, Gwen. Take all the time you need."

She tightened her fist around the chunk of hair in her hand until it hurt, until it was painful. Time was not what she needed; she needed a release. Like a boiling kettle, she'd reached a suspended state of anxiety. If someone would only pull her off the heat and stop the damn whistle in her head.

She'd taken to drinking coffee, not that caffeine helped. Instead, it amped up her skittish thoughts even more. What she needed was a noose for them, the pack of mad dogs barking from chains inside her head.

How, how, how, how, how?

Gwen couldn't see around having to stay through next summer, getting her parents' fingers off the pulse of the financials, and holding tight to all that tourist season income before her mom could get any big ideas on how to spend it. If sales were anything like last summer, they should be able to pay off all debt and save enough to get them through the next winter, barely.

Meanwhile, Betta was walking around like Gwen had stabbed her in the back, when really she was saving her from more doom and gloom.

Sometimes, when Gwen sat up at night, she reminded herself of this. Two plus years of wiping an old man's ass equaled at least the same of digging a store out from certain ruin, if that's what it took.

"Why don't you send me an accountant's copy," Gage said, startling her from her thoughts, from her feeling of certain suffocation. "I'm sure I could shave a couple hundred a month, if not more."

"I've *shaved*," she replied. "I've shaved everything I could."

"Maybe there's something you're not seeing."

Seeing it was worse than being told, and she didn't want him to see it. The door chime rang out, and her father was once again next door at the sandwich shop, eating his way through semi-retirement. "I've got to go. I'll see you this weekend?"

"Yes, for sure."

Gwen slid her phone into her back pocket and hurried out into the hall, only to run into her dad. "Someone here?"

"Your mother."

"For what?" Because the schedule was pretty clear: Gwen, Monday through Sunday 9am to 5pm; Dad, Monday through Friday 9am to Noon; Betta, Saturday 10am to 4pm.

"She's picking up a few things."

Gwen blanched. "Picking up a few things" meant taking inventory off the shelves, and generally, her parents didn't *buy* anything, they took it.

That would not help her shaving.

Stalking down the hallway and through the aisles, Gwen found her mom roaming with a cart.

A cart! As if she planned to be at this for awhile.

A recipe box, which she didn't need. A stuffed animal, for who? A romance novel with a hunk of meat on the cover, holding a heroine in a ripped bodice, both of them sweaty in the desert...

"What are you doing?" Gwen wished she were in some desert and a half ripped bodice. Honestly, anywhere but here. "You don't need any of this stuff."

Her mom gave her a funny look. "I want it."

"Too bad. We need inventory on the shelves."

"Oh, honey, no one will miss what I'm shopping for." She tried to push past, but Gwen jumped in front of the cart.

"You don't know what people will be looking for in the next five months, Mom. Someone might come in for something, and if we don't have it they might go online, and if they go online and realize how easy it is, they might never come back."

"That's silly."

"No, it's not."

"Yes, it is. There's no immediate satisfaction of clicking a button. Not like bringing your purchases home and putting them away."

"Mom." Gwen pursed her lips. "You are not shopping here."

She grabbed a candle from the shelf. "Says who?"

"Says me." Gwen yanked it from her hand and slammed it back in its spot.

Her mother huffed. "Your father always lets me shop here."

"Then pay for it."

"The whole point," she cried, "is that I don't have to pay for it. If I was going to pay for it, I'd shop for clothes. I'd shop somewhere else!"

"If you don't pay for it, it's not shopping. It's shop*lifting*."

Wanda put a hand on her heart. "I would never."

"Then pay for it. I can't handle losing any more money."

"You aren't losing money, it's just stuff."

"It *is* money, Mother. Don't you get it?"

She grabbed a butane lighter fashioned like a double barrel shotgun. "Apparently not."

"No, no, *no!*" Gwen yanked the cart from her mother's fists, emptied it haphazardly onto the nearest shelf, and marched it up to the front of the store.

She heard her mother's footsteps behind her. "Maybe we should demote you, if you can't handle the stress."

"Good. Please. But then don't come crying to me when you don't make it through the winter."

Her mother's eyes widened with alarm. "Why wouldn't we make it through the winter?"

"Dad says we hardly ever make it through the winter!"

As her mom absorbed this information, Gwen put a hand to her stomach and breathed slowly to calm herself. She shouldn't have said that. She shouldn't have said any of that. But they shouldn't have left her with this, either. And they did.

"Listen." Gwen took a deep breath in. "The store is mine now. You can't demote me, and I'm doing things my way."

Her mother blinked. She blinked and blinked again. Was the tenuous financial position news to her?

Whatever, she wasn't going to worry about how it felt going down. She knew how it felt and was still struggling with it herself.

Gwen stalked behind the register to keep an eye on things. It was what she did now. It was her job.

Her mother stood blinking for a few more moments, then without a glance in Gwen's direction, walked out the door and down the sidewalk in the direction of their neighborhood.

Good, Gwen thought. She couldn't get into any trouble there.

* * *

Wanda paced their bedroom, going on three hours. She'd years ago worn a path in the carpet: from the door, past the TV, between the window and the foot of the bed, past the closet, to the small bathroom.

And back.

Back.

Then back again.

They should have replaced the carpet when they got the new bedroom furniture. Wanda hadn't noticed it was so worn. Next summer. Carpet would be next summer.

She trusted Harvey, she did. He'd always managed their finances—the way they'd always been managed, he said. Then what was Gwen talking about, last month yelling at Betta about Pops' credit cards at dinner, and today yelling at her about not making it through the winter? It made her heart race, and her heart racing picked up the pace of her feet.

It wasn't that she thought winter was easy, she knew it was hard; this was the primary reason she despised it. Every winter she wore her way through this carpet, every winter when Harvey froze the credit cards and especially in January when he went to the bank for the loan. They'd never denied him—they'd never denied an Aaldenberg—but every time, she worried her way along this path.

Gwen must know something Wanda didn't, if she felt this winter to be even worse than the others. Perhaps she knew the lender at the bank. Perhaps their previous loan had been their last.

Wanda twisted her hands together to keep them from shaking and took the length of the room again.

She knew she shouldn't spend money this time of year, that's why she shopped at the store. What else was she supposed to do with her time? An idle body; an idle brain.

As she heard Harvey's feet come up the stairs, Wanda forced herself to sit on the edge of the bed, looking out the window at the home behind them. Mae's house, Mae of the sandwich shop. But what took billing above that, in Wanda's mind, was Mae, widower and empty nester.

She couldn't imagine anything worse. Again, she was up

and pacing.

Harvey entered the room, stopping inside the doorway as she flew by. "Wanda?"

"I feel like you've been keeping some things from me."

Harvey glanced out the window. "What do you mean?"

"Gwen is freaking out about the store, about winter. Didn't you tell her we get loans every January, and that by June, they're always paid back?"

"I did." He stood in front of her. "She's overreacting."

Wanda set her palms on his blue oxford shirt, above his protruding belly. "Maybe we shouldn't retire yet. Maybe you should send Gwen to Boston and work our way through the funeral expenses, until things are back to normal."

"She chose to stay, Wanda. And this is normal. A bit bigger of a loan, that's it."

"How much bigger?"

"You might have to hold off on whatever you wanted to do next. Wait till you actually have the money in hand." He delivered it politely, but it still went down like a punch in the throat.

Wanda frowned.

"Gwen's too old to live at home and be our child. She needs something of her own, even if it's a struggle. She needs to accomplish something and be proud of her work. At the end of this, that's how she'll feel."

"She's really staying?"

Harvey put his hands on her arms. "Would Betta be so upset if she weren't?"

"Shouldn't we give it to Betta?"

"It's not ours to give. It's Gwen's."

"That's tradition," they said together.

Wanda sighed and dropped her hands from her husband's chest. "I don't know what to do with myself. Esmerelda won't let me pour her cereal. She doesn't even want me to make her lunch."

Harvey grinned. "That's a good thing. That means you did your job."

Now that she wasn't needed at the store, couldn't smother her children, and couldn't spend money, all her coping mechanisms were void. "Christmas is right around the corner. Probably the last one they'll all be here for."

Harvey winced, but at least he said what she wanted to hear. "One last time, Wanda, but that's it. Then we really have to get on top of it."

* * *

Betta was to meet James at his place in three minutes, but instead of heading over, she was watching Gwen and Gage on the front porch. It was as far as Gage got before Gwen melted into him, eyes closed and face upturned.

The way he fawned over her—hands in her hair, thumbs on her cheeks—whispers of sweet nothings, Betta was sure. Half of her was sickened, and half of her wanted that kind of happiness so badly she could taste the flavor of envy on her lips.

Perhaps that envy was drowning her in waves because of the store, not Gage, but she couldn't look at Gwen any longer without it coloring things, without feeling like she had everything Betta did not.

When the revulsion won out, Betta slipped past them to the sidewalk, only to replay it in her mind a million times as she walked the ten minutes to James' house. By then, she was back to envy.

He met her at the side door that led directly down to his Mom's basement, which he called his own apartment because he paid rent. A fraction of the rent any actual apartment in town would charge, but what might be normal for most small towns that didn't jack up prices for the sake of year long leases with seasonal occupants.

"Why aren't we affectionate?" she asked, as they descended the steps to the beat-up leather couch that smelled of him—spearmint and spring-scented soap; a little oil, gasoline, and smoke.

"We're affectionate," he countered.

"I mean, like,"—she threw her arm up and pushed past him—"why aren't we all over each other, falling into each other as if it aches to be apart?"

He let out a short laugh as they sat on the couch. "You'd crawl out of your skin."

"I would not!"

He smirked, as if it were a dare, and slid his right hand along the outside of her thigh, coaching her leg onto his. Fingers on the skin of her hip, he snuck his other arm around her shoulder and rubbed his cheek against hers. "I missed you yesterday."

She tried not to squirm, tried instead to focus on the picture of them on hanging in front of her. They were wrapped around each other in the photo too, her in a red retro two piece and him in board shorts. It had been cold that day on the beach, and she'd forgotten a sweatshirt.

"Ask me what I missed about you," he whispered.

"What'd you miss about me?"

"I missed your soul."

She rolled her eyes as he peppered her with kisses. "That's the stupidest thing I've ever heard," she said.

"You're not playing along."

"Because you're not being serious!"

"Actually, I am. I did miss your soul yesterday, that deepest part of you I sometimes see in your eyes. I thought about you a lot." He leaned further into her, burying his face into her hair and holding onto her with both hands—one on the back of her neck, the other climbing her arm to pull her closer.

It was too much—the grasping, pulling, needing— different than when they were making out on purpose. This was more intimate, if it were possible, him trying to reach for her insides in a way that was more than physical. When she could take it no longer, she sprang up like a startled cat. Nearly panting, she looked down at him.

Ugh. He was right. So why did it look so good on Gwen and Gage?

He relaxed into the couch. "You aren't that person, Bets."

"What if I want to be that person?"

"Do you, though?" He grabbed her hand and rubbed his thumb along her skin. "Why can't you be happy for her and what she has, and happy for yourself and what we have, even if it's different?"

She narrowed her eyes. "Who's her? Who said anything about her?"

"I love you." He shook at her hand where it was settled in his. "I think we're perfect, and I wish you did too."

James accepted all the things about her, things she wasn't even sure she liked. Thinking of him, being with him—it was a hug from the inside—but it wasn't enough. Why wasn't it enough? "She has my life. Maybe if I were her, I'd have my life too."

"Gwen doesn't want the store. I don't know what's happening, but she does not want that store."

"Then what? She doesn't want me to have it?"

He tugged her back onto the couch. They sat turned into each other, knees touching and shoulders resting on the cracked camel leather.

"As much as I've dreamt of the west coast, she's dreamt of the city. It's what brought us together." He inched in a little closer, always a little closer, and kissed the top of her head. "She will not stay forever."

"What if Gage wants to move here? What if that's why?"

He snorted into her hair. "Then I imagine they break up."

Betta pulled away from him to look at his face.

"Yeah, I think she's that motivated. And the appropriate amount of selfish."

"Okay, but what if?"

"I'm telling you, she'll leave."

"What if it takes her five years to actually do it? Or ten. No one is hiring; I've asked every store in town. I'm supposed to be satisfied working eight hours a Saturday in the meantime?"

"You could move to a little town in the mountains with me." James turned her hand over in his, watching it carefully while he spoke. "Finish school. Get away from all this and come back refreshed when it's ready for you."

She rested her cheek against the couch and inhaled its smell of him, closing her eyes tight. "I don't like the mountains," she murmured. "I don't like anywhere but here."

* * *

"One of us could turn out the lights, and the other could rip it off her neck," Christine proposed. Gym had become a plotting session. It helped Ez feel better.

"Ripping it off her neck would break it," Esmerelda pointed out. "We can't break it."

"Couldn't you unclasp it in the dark?"

"I don't remember what kind of clasp it has. Doesn't she ever take it off?"

"Maybe at night," Christine offered. "We could sneak into her room and snatch it off her dresser."

"She'd have to invite us over." Ez might be close, thanks still to Gavin, but she wasn't that close. And for Christine, her ship had sailed. "There has to be another way."

"Have you offered her money?"

"I don't have any money." Esmerelda lifted a weighted bar with her ankles, working her quads. It was their last day of this unit. Testing day. Ez wondered how likely they were to be paired up again in the future. Celia couldn't be mad at her for talking to her gym partner. She had no choice, really; she had to talk to her gym partner.

"Have you offered her Gavin?"

Ez sat up straighter. "I knew she liked him!"

Christine leaned closer. "I cannot tell you how pissed she was when I let him kiss me. And then, when I didn't make him stop."

Ez frowned. For her, Gavin was the key to staying close to Celia, but if she'd known he was the ticket out, she would have stayed far away. So far away that she wouldn't have known how much she could like him. Because she did like him, a lot. He was almost perfect, and she had a boyfriend.

Esmerelda Hannah Louise Aaldenberg had a real, honest-to-goodness boyfriend.

"Sorry. Maybe that was a little awkward." Christine's focus skittered away to the other side of the room. She watched the football players, loud and noisy in the corner.

"Oh, that's okay," Ez said. "He'd go right at it, so why can't we?"

"Truth." Christine grinned. "He would."

Esmerelda nibbled on the inside of her lip. "So... does he know she likes him?" Because who in their right mind would pick her over Celia?

"Yes, he doesn't care. If you offered him, though—you only need the time it takes for her to give you the locket."

"Why wouldn't he care?"

Christine studied her for a minute. "Do you have a crush on Celia?"

"No. I like Gavin." Ez paused. "And boys." Except they sure did make this weight room stink.

"I mean a girl crush, like you want to *be* her. Or, like, you'd want her if you were a guy."

"No." If Esmerelda had one of those it was directed at her sister first and Georgia second. "Not at all. It's just that she's, you know, *Celia*."

"Listen, Gavin doesn't mess around. He does what he wants and doesn't think too much about it. If he likes you, he likes you. If he doesn't, he doesn't. If he's with you, you can be sure that's where he wants to be."

Ez nodded. That's how he made her feel, but again, Celia was *Celia*.

"Anyway, I'm saying if you *offered* him, maybe she'd give you the locket back."

Shifting uncomfortably on the bench, Ez lost control of her legs and let them drop, hard.

"You need to keep control on the way down," Christine said.

"I know," Esmerelda snapped. Then, "I'm never getting this locket back."

"We'll think of something."

Ez hoped she was right and went back to work on her legs—more slowly this time, thank you very much. After

71

Christine's turn, and as they were heading back to the locker rooms, Christine asked Esmerelda if she'd ever been in a play.

"No."

"Me neither. Wanna try out with me? They're casting after Christmas."

Esmerelda stared at her. Being on stage would mean all attention on her. Not on her sisters or brother or Celia. And if she tried out, she and Christine would have more time to plot about locket retrieval. She'd have another excuse to hang out with her, on accident.

"I have a huge thing for Mr. D." Christine fanned her face. "Mr. D for Delicious. And I'd feel better not doing it alone."

Esmerelda didn't answer, but thought about it as they changed clothes. None of her siblings had ever done a play, been in a musical, or pursued any other kind of art. Gwen had ruled via cheerleading and student leadership, Van sports, and Betta with her grade point average.

"Do you think I'd be any good?" she asked. This was the roadblock—if she wasn't any good, then she'd only be making a fool of herself.

Christine shrugged. "Can you act?"

"I don't know."

"Can you pretend?"

If pretending meant keeping things from people and not letting on about anything, then Esmerelda figured she could.

Christine must have noticed her interest piquing, because she leaned forward with a smile. "Haven't you ever wanted to be someone else for a little bit?"

This hit Ez like a fist to the gut. She hadn't ever wanted to

be someone else for a *little bit*, because what she wanted—
what she'd always wanted—was to be someone else for a
whole darn stinking lot.

DECEMBER

Betta needed to get out of the house. Since she couldn't find a job, she'd been spending way too much time at home—doing many of the same things she would have been doing at the store. Due to Wanda's flurry of pre-Christmas activity and her strange, hooded mood, there'd been more than enough chores to pick up.

If Betta wasn't careful, she'd soon be organizing and deep-cleaning her brother's disgusting room, and that was where she drew the line.

At home, and at Shelby's—because after "work" on her list of living came "friends" and "books," both of which she could accomplish inside the bookstore.

Today, she dragged Van along. He couldn't find a job either, and was roaming the house, aimless and whining about how far away Kate was. Betta felt the need to make him do something, even if that something was the same sort of nothing in a different location.

Shelby did not disappoint. She'd started on her Christmas baking and candy making, and there were cookies and toffee and caramels for them to gorge themselves on. Van and Betta shoveled these sweets into their mouths while Shelby sipped her coffee and studied them.

After two good handfuls of caramels disappeared from the silver tray on the table, she asked, "What's with you two?"

"We've learned to cure illness with food," Van offered, while crunching on a piece of toffee.

"Usually a doctor hears the symptoms before they prescribe the medicine."

Van finished chewing this time. "I live at home, I have no job, I'm not in school, and I miss my girlfriend."

Shelby tilted her head at him. "It seems you need to find someone to do with your time."

"Yeah, but what? No one is hiring."

"Some*one*, Van. Not some*thing*."

"Oh." He blinked into stillness, and Betta swallowed a too large chunk of toffee, causing her to sputter and cough.

"Kate and him have been dating since third grade," Betta said, after she recovered.

"I would never do that to her," he added.

Shelby leaned back in her chair. "I've been telling Betta that's what she needs, but she won't listen to me. If James is willing, it would really take her mind off this store situation."

"It doesn't matter if James is willing. I have to be willing." It's not that she wasn't, but if he and Gwen were lying, saying they hadn't had sex, if her sister really had been James' first...

The mere thought was intimidating, completely twisted, and kind of gross. If she couldn't stomach sleeping with him, she should probably break up with him, but he was her favorite person. Cutting herself off from her favorite person was a feat near impossible, especially when she had so few people to begin with.

Shelby took a sip of coffee. "Your parents sure did something right to raise such pure, law-abiding citizens."

Van snorted. "I mean, except for the scar incident."

Betta glanced at him and his loose lips.

Shelby set her mug down on the coffee table and leaned forward, Betta hoped not for the sake of beguiling her brother with cleavage. "Tell me," Shelby coaxed, her eyes dancing between them.

Van watched Betta, waiting for the go-ahead. Whatever. Gwen and her parents were the ones who hated anyone knowing, but Betta didn't care how they felt anymore, now that they were colluding against her.

"Fine," Betta said. "Tell her."

"It's the one mark on Gwen's otherwise flawless record," Van started, voice hushed like he was telling a ghost story. "The beginning of the end for two sisters, raised side by side and inseparable."

Betta rolled her eyes and stuffed a caramel in her mouth. She was long over the scar incident. Really, it was everything that happened after. Gwen took what she wanted, and Betta's hand was slapped. *Wait your turn, Betta, be patient. You're two years younger. You can't compare yourself to who she is now, what she's doing now, what she's capable of now.*

Except, every time she reached the age Gwen had been, only the scraps were left. Betta was nothing more than a shadow people trampled on to get to the shining star. That's why they'd drifted apart. Sisters were supposed to stick up for each other, protect each other. Gwen only ever stuck up for herself.

You get the inside brownies, Betta, because I like the outside. You get the blue bike, Betta, because I like the purple.

"They were playing doctor-"

"She was always the doctor," Betta interrupted. "She wouldn't have it any other way—if I wanted to play with her, I had to play by her rules." Everything was on Gwen's terms. *All kids are like that*, Gwen would say, *you were just weaker and folded faster.*

"Betta had a strawberry-shaped birthmark on her jaw," Van continued. "She asked Gwen to cut it out."

Betta put a finger up. "I asked no such thing. She was jealous because I got to be Strawberry Shortcake that year for Halloween. It was the first fight I ever won, and all because of that birthmark."

Shelby gaped between the two of them. "She didn't cut it out."

Yeah, Betta would have a hard time believing it too, if she hadn't lived it. "She definitely cut it up."

"Wait. How old were you?"

"Four. Gwen was six. According to her, she didn't mean to, of course, but I freaked, her hand slipped, all an accident, etcetera, etcetera. Apparently, I pushed myself up into the knife, so, you know, it's mostly my fault."

"And," Van chewed his way around the word, "Gwen has spent her entire life trying to make it up to the world."

Betta swatted at him. "I can't believe you're telling *her*

version of the story."

He peeled his gaze from Shelby. "I guess it's the one I know best."

Successfully brainwashed by the family, even though he was more her brother than anyone else's. "I did love that strawberry birthmark," she admitted.

"Did they ever try to fix it?" Shelby asked. "Like, with a real surgeon?"

"They couldn't afford it—it was November. By the time they had the money, I didn't want to go through the pain of it. Then, when I was old enough to start hating it…" Betta shrugged. She couldn't explain her attachment to it because she didn't understand it completely herself.

Betta traced the line, fine from the middle of her cheek down to her jaw, where it was more a mess of tissue than anything else. Like a badge of honor or an angry tattoo, it scared people away.

"At least it's attractive, as far as scars go," Shelby said. "Almost like a star. Or an asterisk."

It didn't matter; it was as much a part of her face as her nose or eyeballs were. She'd learned to embrace it. Even so, she didn't want to sit around and witness Shelby absorbing it.

Betta finished her coffee and set the cup back in its saucer. Shelby had such pretty cups and saucers. None of them matched, but all were delicate and beautiful, fitting together perfectly when grouped together, even if they weren't from the same original set.

Sort of like a family.

Standing, she announced she was going to James'. This

was not an easy decision, as his best friend Eddie from California was back again. He'd told her she was welcome to stop in, but neither of them thought this would happen. Eddie always asked Betta where Gwen was, and why didn't she bring her, and when might he be able to see her. Even so, she knew James meant it when he said it.

Betta wasn't going to sit here in the remnants of her scar and watch Shelby stroke her bare collarbone with pointed eyes on her little brother. Nope. Gross.

Van stood to leave with her.

"You're welcome to stay, Van," Shelby said, fingering the necklaces strung around her neck. The beads rubbed softly together, and the noise brought Van's eyes back to her cleavage.

Betta knew he'd keep it in his pants, but there was no doubt the offer was there if he wanted to take it. Shelby was at least ten years older than him, and they were talking about her brother. She tried to elbow the stupid out of him. "Are you just now getting a grip on your hormones?"

Van's eyes shot away from Shelby's chest, and Shelby stood with a little laugh, as if—Betta hoped—she was only having some fun. "I'll get you some career books to pore over," she told Van. "Find you something to do with your time."

* * *

Betta hurried up the street, past Aaldenberg Hardware to the end of the street where the faded chocolate saltbox—the one in a state of disrepair—nearly protruded into the street. Its corner was long and triangular, and the house sat at its narrow end at the tip of the neighborhood.

There she stopped, because a "for sale" sign stood new and bright on the front lawn.

Catching the briny, raw scent of the ocean, Betta wondered if the second floor windows might catch a view of it. A mere twinkle of the sun on the water, the smallest slice, was all she needed, more than she needed.

"Good spot for a shop," came a voice behind her—smooth and silky, yet beneath that a shy rumble. Brennan Masowicz of Mas Properties: hometown developer. She envied him that his reign came earlier than expected. As soon as he got licensed, his dad took off for the Bahamas. No college distraction, no dying grandpas, no out of reach mothers.

Betta hugged herself, arms tight to her parka, but she couldn't afford it anyway. If Brennan snatched it up, he'd at least do something good with it, rather than tear down the block and put up an eight story hotel.

Fine, she'd play along: "Perfect for a bed and breakfast."

He glanced over with surprise. "Have you been in?"

"When I was little." Betta smiled at his mustard turtleneck and wool coat. Spiffy for a guy in his late twenties. "I delivered something to Miss Lundquist before she died."

"It's been vacant since," he said, turning back to the house in front of them.

"Probably a mess." The fence was rickety—Betta imagined

she could shove it over with the slightest nudge, and the multi-paned windows, all the same size and evenly spaced across the front of the house, were beyond grimy.

"Could refurbish it and make it my new office space."

"No way." His current office was on the square, two chairs out on the sidewalk in perfect view of the water. He could not be serious about moving. "If this isn't going to be a house, it needs to be a bed and breakfast. Or a little shop."

"Then we're pushing the residences out further, and before you know it, downtown is one big conglomeration."

Betta grinned at his frown. So serious. "I think you have a ways to go before that happens."

"It's something to always be thinking about, though, or it'll happen before we know it."

"Then keep it a house."

"You make it sound like it's a done deal. Like I'm buying it."

"Well, I mean... in this state... the wrong hands... it might get torn down."

Brennan chuckled, all the severity dropping from his face. "Not the best investment, though. Only tourists pay top dollar for refurbished originals, and this isn't close enough to the water for them."

"I'd pay top dollar for it," she said wistfully, studying its cute front door. She would paint it green. Or blue. Or blue-green. Something that looked good with the chocolate wood siding.

"If you can see the ocean from even the top corner window, it could go for over five hundred thousand." He tilted his head at it. "Then again, seeing it juts out in the middle of the street—an intersection really—and is essentially in the business district..."

"Five hundred thousand is better than over a mil." Over a million was baseline for waterfront, and close to a mil was baseline for a real ocean view.

She felt him watching her. "You can't live at your parents' forever."

"I don't have a dime to my name, Brennan." She might have enough for a monthly mortgage if the store was hers, but even then she had no down payment. Also, lest she forget, the store wasn't hers.

"It's old and rundown. It'll be a steal."

"Not a dime," she repeated. "It's all yours."

They gazed at it for a while longer, side by side.

"Word is your sister's engaged to some city slick," he finally said.

Betta nodded. "He's a good guy."

Brennan crossed his arms. "If I fixed it up and couldn't find a buyer, I'd be looking for a renter."

"Yeah?" What was she thinking? She couldn't afford rent.

"Yeah." He grinned. If there was anything Brennan Mas was, it was sure. Sure of his life, of his place in town, sure of his decisions and what needed to be done. He was a doer, Betta imagined, everywhere, all the time.

Doers said yes. They didn't wait, and they didn't say no. They willed things into being. Maybe she should try it. "Once Gwen moves to the city and I have the store, I'll be first in line."

Brennan flipped up the collar of his coat. "Best I get going, seeing I've got an offer to make."

She opened her mouth to stop him, because it was stupid. She'd already tried to will the store hers. Most likely, she'd never have it. She might never have anything.

Oh, how she wanted to dream though.

Plus, he was the right person to buy it. Whatever he did with it would be better than most.

So she snapped her jaw shut and kept moving, uphill, to see her boyfriend.

* * *

"How much does a poinsettia cost, Wanda?"

"I don't know, Harvey. Can you put a price on Christmas cheer?"

They stood near the old white fridge, where one week ago, Harvey pulled the credit card out of the freezer for gift shopping. She'd been so invigorated decorating at the beginning of December, hauling boxes out of the basement and moving things around until she couldn't anymore. When she started to fade, that was when he handed over the card. Wanda snorted. Probably figured if she only had a week and a half, she wouldn't be able to go overboard.

Lesson learned.

"I'm guessing ten to fifteen dollars, Wanda, and there is one in every room of this house. Three on the dining room table."

"There's one in the garage for the store too," she grumbled, wishing he'd stop watching over her shoulder as she made dinner.

"I got a call from the credit card company today. They said you tried to increase the limit."

"No need to worry, Harvey. They needed you to sign off on such a thing." She dropped the potatoes in the boiling water with a vicious splash, the spray sizzling on the exposed burner below. "Couldn't imagine how little wifey might be able to make her own decisions."

"No." He stepped away and paced behind her, the short length of the stove and back. "They couldn't imagine how anyone could spend five thousand dollars in one week."

"You told me this was it." She turned to him with a circus smile on her face—overworked and underfed. "I wanted our last Christmas with the kids all under one roof, all waking up together Christmas morning, to be one we remembered."

Harvey ran a hand over his spiky, graying hair, and Wanda wondered when she last did that herself. "I don't need a fancy new TV," he said. "I want to take it back."

She dropped a knife on the counter with a clatter. "How do you know about the TV?"

"They thought someone stole our card and went on a shopping spree."

"That's what kids want these days, Harvey, electronics." Imagining that her tight, forced smile was spinning poisoned sugar at him, she shuffled over to the cutting board and went at the onions in a way that caused her to wonder if she might cut a nail off. She paused, took a deep breath, and explained, "A laptop for Gwen, so she can bring her work home when she wants, some fancy headphones for Ez, an e-reader for Betta, did you see Van got a TV too, Harvey? And a sound system. I didn't want the sound system in our room, but I thought he might like it for football. It's the best they had, the man said. Best for the best, I said."

"Wanda, I-"

"Don't worry, Harvey," she clipped, cutting him off. "I took care of buying myself something too, so whatever you and the kids got me wouldn't seem anticlimactic in the face of everyone else's presents." Wanda took the knife with her as she crossed the room for her purse. One-handed, she found her wallet, pulled out the credit card, and slapped it on the kitchen table.

She went back to the onion near tears, and let their scent, their acid—whatever—seep in and put her over the edge. She had control over nothing. Not the store. Not her kids. Not their money. And not her husband.

She heard the plastic slide off the counter into his hand, but he didn't have to worry.

She was done.

* * *

Lunch was proving uncomfortable.

Gavin, proud boyfriend that he was, had jumped the gun

and gotten a group together to go to the play Esmerelda and Christine hadn't even auditioned for yet. Which meant that as soon as Ez sat down in the chaotic, bustling lunchroom, Celia led with: "A. the play? And B. Christine?" She put all her weight on one elbow and raised her eyebrows like everyone should know what a stupid decision this was. "Really, Esmerelda?"

Ez cut her spaghetti with a fork and knife; she liked her pasta in pieces no longer than an inch. "You don't think that could come in handy?" she asked. "Learning how to convincingly play other people?"

"Not on stage," Celia rolled her eyes to Georgia, who shrugged. "Actresses are a bunch of drama queens, and no one appreciates a diva."

Yeah, Ez thought, because there could only be one diva, and Celia was going to make sure it was her. "I'm not a diva. I'll never be a diva."

"Why the hell are you hanging out with Christine?"

"She's only my gym partner."

"You're trying out for the play with her."

"She thought I'd be good at it."

"Well, you wouldn't. Anyway, that's totally weird, hanging out with your boyfriend's ex." Celia popped a fry in her mouth. "You talk about what his hands feel like?"

Ez nearly spit out her milk.

"Also, no, on the play. Got it? There will be no theater geeks at my birthday party."

The others murmured, as if this birthday party had already been planned and talked about. Which meant if Celia was bringing it up now, she was dangling a carrot. A birthday party was another step in, another step closer to the locket. Maybe she could somehow have both.

"When's your birthday?" Ez asked, taking a bite of spaghetti like she barely cared.

"January." Celia sat back in her chair. "Only my closest friends will be invited."

Ez swallowed hard and a chunk of meatball lodged itself in her throat. Georgia patted her back as she sputtered.

"There's still plenty of time, I suppose,"—Celia drew her words out—"for those friends to prove themselves."

Ez caught the rolling of Georgia's eyes and the kick Celia subsequently delivered her under the table, but she didn't care if she was being toyed with. She knew, if she made it all the way in, that Celia would move along to toy with someone else.

She also recognized her chance.

A birthday sleepover was her best bet to get that locket back.

* * *

Gwen could barely hold it together.

Aside from continued lack of sales and dwindling inventory, she'd noticed the poinsettias, and Van mentioned their mother had taken the car shopping last week.

She forced herself not to imagine how much money it

would take to fill a car and checked her parent's credit card statement as soon as possible, which had been that morning after her father left for the bank. With cold, naked fear, she sat at his desk, in front of his computer, pulling up the site and his saved password. As her eyes took in the recent charges, she took to sobbing.

Maybe, if he hadn't texted her during that dinner fight, warning her to back off and not alarm anyone, maybe then her mother wouldn't have spent an entire month of their rent income on Christmas.

Five thousand dollars, gone.

Gwen couldn't seem to stop her hands from shaking at the same tremble and speed that her heart was palpitating, and if she stopped moving for too long, it became hard to breathe. So she straightened shelves, she paced, and she swept, all while praying she'd be calm enough to hold a reasonable conversation with her father when he got back. Reasonable insomuch she could get clear words and concise thoughts out instead of screams and whimpers.

Things got better when the first customer of the week came in the front door.

Things got worse when said customer slid a pack of ramen noodles down his pants.

With an embarrassing primal scream, she launched herself down the aisle and dug her hand right in after them. Harvey came running from the front door, and the young man faced their red faces and heavy breaths—one of fury and the other of exertion—with hands up and eyes wide.

Gwen was screaming still, words that made sense in her

head but broke on her tongue and came out sharp and chaotic. They'd always dealt with a bit of shoplifting, but she couldn't right now. *She just could not.* The box of granola bars missing the day before, and the can of beef stew the day before that— she wound back to slap him, but her dad caught her arm.

"Gwennie, I'm sorry," the man was whispering, repeating, as if he knew her.

Wait. Her father was holding *her* back? "It's okay, Gwennie. It's okay."

She turned on her father. "It's not okay! Stop saying everything's okay!"

Her dad tried to take the packet of noodles from her fist, but she would not let it go, so instead he reached for the last on the shelf and handed it to the thief.

Gwen gasped, high and pained, as the bastard ran off with her noodles.

She glared at her father, nostrils flaring, no more tears. She wanted to beat the ever-loving-shit out of him. How had she become a person who wanted to beat the ever-loving-shit out of a person, let alone her own father?

He caught both of her arms, and the ramen noodles shook in her fist. "This is what happens. It's our contribution to the community."

"The community?" she cried. "Now I have to feed the community, too?" Jerking away from him, she threw an arm in the direction the man had gone. "He can't afford a packet of *ramen noodles?*"

"He's homeless, Gwen. He's taking a packet of ramen noodles because it's the cheapest thing in the store. Because he doesn't want to take anything, but he will not only be homeless, but also hungry, if he doesn't."

"If he's homeless," she seethed, "how's he going to make ramen noodles?"

"He's going to walk next door, and Mae will have a bowl of hot water waiting for him."

"*Waiting for him?* Does this happen every day?" She couldn't breathe. She was all mixed up inside, her heart and lungs morphing and pushing and doing the wrong things—her heart trying to think, and her lungs trying to beat, and her brain trying to breathe... Doubling over, as if she'd run a marathon, she tried to get her body back to a reasonable place.

"Not every day. When Mae has old bread or soup, they go there first-"

"They?" she whimpered.

"They aren't faceless," he said gently, placing a warm hand on her shoulder. "You went to school with that kid—Blake Tessenderlo, remember?"

She squeezed her eyes shut, not wanting to remember. His parents worked for the big cleaning company in town. The one that got all the contracts for the vacation homes. The one that shut down in the winter. He kissed her in fifth grade. She'd been in sixth. She loved the velvety fringe of his hair and the thrill of being kissed for the first time, but he smelled like lemons, and not in a good way but in a disinfectant way, so it ended there.

That's how close to him she was, though. Their lives, nearly interchangeable. Her family, in the same boat as his. It could be them, homeless and hungry. It could be her.

She tried, one last time, to alleviate her growing sense of responsibility. "We aren't the homeless shelter."

"They can't keep up, Gwen, and Blake needs it more than us."

Gwen stood, bracing herself on the shelving next to her, and let her father guide her to the office, where he motioned for her to sit.

"How 'bout I run to Mae's and get you a sandwich," he said. "Food will make you feel better."

She shook her head.

"Come on. You're gonna say no to a turkey and coleslaw? Or a pork and apple on English muffin? BLC?"

Bacon, lettuce, and cherry chutney—it did sound good. "From now on, if I eat lunch at all, I'll pack it. And you should start eating at home when you're done with your three hour shift."

"I don't mind running next door," he said. "It's easy."

"It might be easy, but it's not cheap."

"Mae doesn't charge me, mostly."

"Mostly isn't good enough," Gwen snapped. "Mostly could go towards Mom's five grand."

He dropped his gaze with a sigh, propped himself against the front of his desk and nodded. "I go to the bank every January, take out a loan, and pay it back in June. They expect me. We just have to squeeze by until then."

She stared at him. Hands folded in front of her, she forcibly relaxed her shoulders. That was, at least, a plan, and a more effective one than what she'd been operating under.

"They'll give you enough to cover everything? Grandpa's funeral and debt? Mom's Christmas? On top of what the store needs?"

"They've never turned down an Aaldenberg."

"They better not, or you're on your own." There it was, Gwen cutting him down to his knees. Her father. It shouldn't have to be like this. "I won't let you dump it on Betta, either. I won't let her come into the same mess I did. Not after what she did for this family."

He studied her for a minute, his expression tired. "That's why you decided to stay?"

She snorted. "Why the hell else?"

* * *

Christmas Eve gave Betta a headache every year. So much chaos in the kitchen, so many people packed into the living room.

She loved it for mom's sake, and this year especially, as her mother was nearly teary with joy. Everyone was there.

Gwen, Betta and James, Van and Kate, Esmerelda and a tall boy with a mousy face—Gavin or something? This year her mom's sister made it too, and her daughter, and her three grandchildren who were playing chase around the house, ducking and weaving and nearly toppling everyone over. Old lady Phoebe from across the street, who'd outlived everyone her generation and the one behind her, and George—the homeless guy who spent winters sleeping on the pews of their old church, who could always be found on the beach when it was warm, no shoes, one bag, and music in his head.

Christmas made her mom happy. People filling her house made her happier. Feeding them all made her happiest.

Gage arrived last, hours past dinner, having driven through a snowstorm. After greeting Gwen and everyone else he passed, he found Wanda in the kitchen to give her the small poinsettia he'd brought. She set it on the counter and kissed both of his cheeks. "You gave us quite the fright."

"I'm an excellent driver."

"Yes, well, you stay until it blows over, okay?"

The sea had been frantic with anticipation earlier that day, but it wasn't snowing yet. Betta stood at the window over the sink, having cracked it open to breathe in the crispy, fresh air.

Gwen and Kate were catching up in the corner, and the littles were crawling all over Van. As Wanda opened the fridge to make Gage a plate, Ez appeared with boyfriend in hand, sliding up next to her mother to pick out of the containers with her fingers—mashed potatoes and corn, cranberry-pomegranate sauce, wild rice and sweet potato casserole.

"Don't forget the protein," Van yelled from the floor as he crawled by, a horse now instead of a tree.

James slid his arms around Betta's waist and tugged her tight to him. Scruff against her cheek, he whispered, "Up for a little basketball?" This had been a thing since the days of James and Gwen. Every time there was a holiday dinner, Van, James, and herself ended up outside. For being so athletic,

Van was piss poor at shooting, and for being not so athletic, James had quite the aim. Betta, though she had no experience, had the talent but not the height. She preferred an actual game, where she could speed around them on light feet and bump into people when she was frustrated with their towering hands, to H.O.R.S.E, which James always voted for.

"Van looks like he could use a break," James muttered.

"He loves it," she admitted, though it looked painful, all that weight on his knees. "Actually, maybe we should take the kids sledding."

Pushing away from James' embrace, she shouted, "Who wants to go sledding?" To her surprise, it wasn't only the kids jumping up and down with hands in the air, or her brother, playing along with them, but also Phoebe and George.

Gage shoveled food into his mouth, and they donned mittens and hats and scarves. Van challenged them to race for the park, a warm-up so they were ready to climb the hill when they got there. At the top, Betta took a moment to gaze out across town, almost to the sea. It was cloudy, the sky blending through and into the water so you could barely tell where one ended and the other began. Mostly, she felt its looming presence, bigger than all of them and their problems put together.

The air was brittle, with a sharp, frozen smell to it, the wind rough and unforgiving. They took turns on the old sleds, two by two, and as they stood at the top of the hill for the last run, Betta crossed her arms and looked out over the soft purple of the evening snow. Clumps of people here and there, kids screaming as they dropped, George racing on foot after Phoebe in the sled, fists in the air—Betta hoped he didn't trip—and her sisters tumbling over at the bottom.

"We could bring this party to Shelby's," Van said from next to her, when they were the only two left up top.

"The store's closed," Betta reminded.

"At the same time, it's always open."

Betta gave him a look. She didn't even want to know.

He snickered. "She told me to stop by, if I was lonely-"

Betta put a hand up. "You do know Kate would be coming with, right?"

Van chuckled, threw out a "Three's never a crowd," and Betta pantomimed a gag, making his chuckle turn into something bigger. Wrapping his arms around her, he swallowed her in an embrace. "Those books Shelby pulled out for me that day? I spent hours pouring over them. So don't think she can't be my platonic friend too."

Betta tried to maneuver out from beneath his overworked football muscles, but instead he got her in a headlock until she punched him in the thigh.

"I'm starting an internship after the holidays," he said, after releasing her. "Thanks to Shelby's books."

"You found a job?" She squinted at him. "A real job. Here? In December?"

"I'm working for free to start, it was all he'd offer me, but that means I'll be trained by the time construction starts up again in the spring. Electricians make good money, and I don't need to pay to learn it. Win, win." He elbowed her. "You should look into the trades. Doing something for free is better than what you're doing now."

"I'm not going to be a plumber or an electrician," Betta muttered, gazing below at where their family was waving them down.

"What about offices, though? Have you looked for reception anywhere, or only checked retail shops?"

She rolled her eyes to him. "First," she pointed to her scar, "And second, their receptionists have been working for decades. They're not going to replace them."

"Decades means they'll be retiring soon. That lady who works at the dentist has got to be over a hundred. You get yourself in there before anyone else, that's what you do."

Betta turned her attention back to the sea-sky with a frown. What she wanted was to work reception at their store.

"Anyway, it's Christmas," Van said. "Shelby's alone, and if you haven't noticed, we're the party."

She smiled. He was right, and that was nice—nice, that after Pops and how the store played out, her family was still knit together. No matter if most days didn't feel like it. No matter if her sister had snatched Betta's life out from under her, as if she hadn't taken enough off the top of the world as it was.

Noticing the fat flakes drifting through the purple sky, Betta tilted her head back. Staring straight up at them both dizzying and mesmerizing. Soon the snow would cover everything, weighing the world down. Weighing them down.

Soon, they'd be engulfed.

JANUARY

Christmas was over.

Wanda tried to push her holiday mood into the new year, but it dried up before the first. Actually, it dried up Christmas morning as soon as the presents were opened. All that money and the fun of shopping for her family, and it brought them three minutes of joy. Well, it brought Betta, Van, and Esmerelda three minutes. Wanda did not detect even one second of joy from her eldest or her husband.

What a waste.

Winters were always a drag, so opposite from the energy and abundance the summers brought. But this year, not only her husband but also her daughter were watching her with distrust in their eyes, as if she would do something to dig their hole deeper. She could not stand to look at them, and she could not stand to look at herself.

So she stayed in bed.

The lights stayed off and the TV on, while she tried to push through via the contrived happiness of her soap opera characters. All those beautiful people on the little screen were persuasive, but she still wasn't convinced there was anything to live for.

Esmerelda checked in from time to time, Van spoke to her from the door, and Harvey held her hand at night, but Betta's visits were the ones Wanda grew to look forward to.

Betta was not fearful of the room, the mood, or her mother, and Betta did not tiptoe around carefully. She walked in, opened the blinds, and if it was exceedingly warm or stuffy, she'd crack a window. She always brought something for Wanda to do, and if Wanda didn't feel up to it, Betta worked on the crossword herself. If Wanda didn't want to play cards or read a magazine, Betta played solitaire or read aloud. And on days when Wanda was particularly listless, Betta told her about the family and what they were doing— what they were eating even, if it came to that.

"Is this how you got through the years taking care of Pops?" Wanda asked her one day. In that she meant talking to herself when the other party was listless, cleaning and scrubbing and keeping busy as the world moved on around her, playing solitaire, doing crosswords, reading novels out loud as if one small kernel deep inside the patient might be holding on and listening.

That kernel was inside Wanda somewhere, though she hadn't yet been able to find it or root out it, to water and grow it until it prompted her out of bed. Even so, it was there. It listened, and sometimes it roused her—after midnight, when the house was silent and Harvey was sleeping so soundly he seemed quite dead, when she herself could not sleep for the worry and anxiety and sadness that took hold like quicksand to strangle her. It roused her to flip on her lamp and open the novels Betta left bookmarked on her nightstand.

Looking over from the armchair at Wanda's bedside, Betta shrugged. "I guess."

"Do you like your eReader?" Wanda asked, nodding at the hardcover in Betta's lap.

"Oh, I love it." Betta flipped the book closed and ran a hand along its cover. "I was just in the middle of this. Maybe tomorrow we could shop for eBooks together, ones we'd both want to read."

"Gwen didn't seem very happy with her laptop."

"Gwen doesn't seem very happy with her life," Betta muttered.

"I thought Christmas might fix things," Wanda said absently, almost as if she didn't say it.

"Fix what, Mom?"

The heavy sadness everywhere and all around. Across Gwen's shoulders and in Harvey's intentional oblivion. Esmerelda's twisting and turning and general hormonal adolescence, and Betta—Wanda dared a glance to Betta's face—disappointment and idleness etched about her.

Rolling over, Wanda pulled the covers up over her shoulder. She'd heard once that a mother was only as happy as their least happy child, but she felt an accumulation of all of them, and then so much more.

She felt her own sadness twisting and turning, her disappointment and idleness. It was the perfect storm.

Celia watched Esmerelda closely, waiting, but Ez didn't need the oversight. She knew how to slip things out of their place and into her possession, even if dirty underwear was a new low.

Funny, though.

They'd skipped out of class for a 'bathroom break' at a predestined time in order to sneak into the locker room, because Celia said what her birthday party needed was someone with a little daring. She'd stared at Esmerelda and waited, so of course Ez admitted she was daring—she snagged things from her sister all the time. Thus, a test.

Ez felt a little bad for the girl who was going to be pantyless the rest of the day, but it wasn't like she was taking her bra, which someone might have noticed, or her jeans which would have screwed her completely. Plus, this girl did have a stick up her ass, Celia was right about that.

Furthermore, Esmerelda knew what it felt like, and it wasn't so bad, for Celia had commanded their lunch table to go commando the week before, one at a time to see who could pull it off. By all accounts, Ez had been the only one.

Georgia couldn't stop complaining about the seams bothering her, which caused Celia to wear a skirt, which meant she was terribly preoccupied with keeping her skirt down. The other girls walked in varying degrees of strange, and one found a crazy pair of phenomenally loose, calf-length culottes at the resale shop, which disqualified her. Ez, however, committed one-hundred-percent, had taken it upon herself to play the part.

If Celia wasn't going to let her be in the play, she would still have fun playing a part.

Ez scratched her head as she neared the targeted pile of clothes. She shouldn't be so nervous. It was mid-class, and everyone was in the gym. They'd come from algebra and English, so no one would suspect them, and it was true, she did have practice at least with this.

Without a glance toward Celia—Ez was doing this on her own—her free pinky snaked out to catch the panties, and as she hit the corner, she dropped them in the deep, black hole of a garbage can. As she swung back around the corner, Celia appeared from the other end, a smile like she'd just eaten someone's soul.

A covert high five passed between them, and the two girls left the locker room side by side. A team.

"You did *what?*" Christine's disapproval was clear when Ez told her about it, back in the same locker room later, during Esmerelda's assigned gym hour.

The girl had wiggled past them in the hall with a pinched look on her face, and when Ez couldn't stop giggling, she explained. "Everyone knows you should hide your underwear during swimming if you don't want to lose them." She pictured the girl's walk again, and her giggles turned into full blown laughter.

Christine put her hands on her hips, which wasn't all that intimidating, considering she'd just changed into a swimsuit. "So she has to go all day without underwear?"

Flipping her hair into a pony, Ez raised her eyebrows. "You've never gone commando?"

"Is this all CeCe?"

"Please." Ez shot her a look—*are you an idiot? I can think for myself.*

"Listen, I was the funny one until I wanted to be taken seriously. Then I was the joke, until I decided I didn't like being laughed at. Then I was nothing."

"What's your point?" Ez didn't need a mother. She had one. Albeit stuffed up in a stale cardboard box, but still.

"My point is you will fall. Everyone does." Ez rolled her eyes, but Christine continued anyway. "You have me. You have the play. You have Gavin. You don't need Celia."

"I do need Celia," Ez corrected. "I need an invite to that party to get my locket back."

"It's not worth it. If she invites you to that party, it'll only be for some shitty reason you won't know about until it's too late."

Ez crossed her arms. "I can handle Celia."

"Tell me you won't go if she asks. Tell me you have a little self-respect."

"It's not about self-respect." Esmerelda wanted to remind Christine that they were only gym partners. She couldn't admit that an invite to Celia's party would be a solid win. Celia made her work for it, and though it might still be all about Gavin and keeping an eye on Ez, if Ez got in—if she truly got in—then however it happened, it was Ez's victory. "I'm going to that party."

Christine frowned.

"Whatever I have to do," Ez added, throwing a towel over her shoulder. Because what she knew that Christine did not was it might come down to giving up the play.

She didn't want to, and she was playing both hands, but if it came down to it, she'd pick Celia.

There was no contest.

* * *

Gwen stared at her dad, and he stared back. He'd stepped between her and another customer—a real one this time— and though she refused to admit it out loud, she knew she'd been a little snarky to the patrons lately.

Because they kept asking for things the store no longer had in stock.

What was she supposed to say? *Sorry, check back in June— my parents can't manage their money, so I'm not letting my dad fill inventory.* Her only choice was to order items as they were asked for, and she wished the customers would stop looking at her like she didn't know what she was doing, like *she* was the one who'd run the store into the ground.

Sales were the same as they were last year this time, maybe even up due to Gage loading his car with supplies when he'd been there last.

An after-hours shopping spree—he'd said he always wanted to. Of course she knew it was baloney, but it was sweet just the same. Then, at the checkout, he'd presented her with a jewelry box.

She'd panicked for a minute, thinking he wasn't actually going to pay for the cartload of toilet paper and laundry detergent, but he did after she opened it—another locket. Finding it now with her fingers, she anchored herself to a better place, a future she had to keep an eye on.

"We have an appointment with the bank next week," her dad said, pulling her back to the time and place she so desperately wanted to escape. If it were true, if he got a loan every year, he certainly wasn't comfortable with it yet, the way his eyes wouldn't focus on anything for more than a second when he spoke of it.

Her eyes went wet, from pure mental exhaustion or actual fatigue, she didn't know. "I'm sorry I'm not handling this more gracefully," she said.

Betta had handled their grandpa gracefully. Gwen was trying to live up to that, but now she wondered if she shouldn't have just let Betta deal with the store too. Growing up, everything came easier to Gwen, but all this shit hitting the fan? Maybe Betta was the stronger one.

Her dad patted her shoulder. "Have a little faith. You'll get us to May, and then think of how accomplished you'll feel."

Accomplished? Really? Like she was building an empire?

"Listen, why don't you take the afternoon off?"

"Are you sure?" she asked, not that they didn't work the store plenty on their own, but because it felt like a responsibility shift—him letting her go, as if he were the one in charge.

Gwen snorted. They both knew that was a farce.

With a smile, he nodded, so she grabbed her coat and purse and booked it out of the store, almost running into Mae and nearly toppling the platter of cookies she cradled in her arms.

Gwen caught it on both sides, a lovely antique tray piled high with potato chip cookies, her father's favorite.

"So sorry," Mae said into Gwen's frown, ducking around her and hurrying down an aisle.

Straight to the office, as if she had a meeting. As if she'd been there many times before. As if she were welcome and part of the family.

All the times he went to Mae's... maybe it wasn't only about the food. And Mae, how often she was here in the store. Gwen tried to remember—did she buy something each time, or was she only there to visit with her father?

What had he said? That Mae didn't charge him "mostly." Could he be sleeping with her for free sandwiches? Worse yet, what if he'd sent Gwen home because he knew Mae was on her way over?

That was ridiculous. Except, should she not leave them alone? No, that was even more ridiculous. What'd she think they were going to do, have sex on her desk?

Maybe, Gwen surmised, instead of sex, they were only sharing food.

Did she even care?

She knew she *should* care, but all she could think was that there was more money for the store if her dad was eating what Mae brought in—be it inedible treats along with the edible—because that meant he was no longer eating off the shelves of the grocery aisle. Besides, she wasn't going to be her father's keeper on top of everything else. She did not have the time or the energy to guard his store, his finances, *and* his soul.

With a shake of her head, she brushed it off her shoulders and hurried home, straight to the bathroom to strip and slide into the tub. After it filled, the scent of eucalyptus and bubbles surrounding her, she hung herself over the edge by her armpits and called Gage.

He would make her feel better. The sounds of the city behind him when he opened his windows for her, that would make her feel better.

Only, he wasn't home of course. It was the middle of the day.

"I can't get caught on the phone during tax season, Gwen."

"It's *January*, Gage. Tax season is April."

"Tax season, my love, is as soon as clients start sending in their stuff. Some people are very on top of things. If I don't keep up right away, I'll be drowning by mid-February."

She heaved a heavy sigh and closed her eyes, wishing he had a window in his office. He could set the phone up, she could listen, and he could work. "When will you be home?"

"When I'm finished," he replied gently, his voice at least a soothing rumble over the phone. "You know I won't have much time in the next few months, right?"

"Yes. You've warned me, like, a million times."

"I know, but until you live it, I'm not sure you can really know."

"Sort of like this damn store?"

"Let me look at the books."

"They're so bad I don't want you to see them."

She could hear his smile through the phone. She knew which one it was, because it had an airy quality about it. This soft, compassionate smile came on the slightest of huffs—amused, though, not irritated. "You keep saying that, but they can't be the worst I've seen."

She'd cut as many corners as she could and put off as many debts as the creditors would allow. Plus, her dad said *she'd* get them to May. What if this January loan thing didn't come through? What if the bank laughed at them? "Fine," she agreed. "Help."

"Good."

"When?" she asked.

"Yeah. That." His chair squeaked. "You can send me an accountant's copy, but it's going to have to wait until I have a minute, which could be May."

Not helpful. "What about the next time you're here? It could be a date. After hours, in the office…" Her words went dry as she realized this was possibly what she'd left her father and Mae to do. She swallowed the thought as Gage's chair squeaked again, but no reply. "You don't think you'll be here again until *May?*" she asked.

"Job gets priority during tax season, Gwen. I'm sorry, there's no way to know when I'll have a minute, until I have a minute."

"Stupid job," she muttered, referring more to hers. Oh, when they only had one to deal with—when she could be there, in the city, waiting up for him.

"Listen, whatever happens, your parents will understand."

"Not when they can't buy groceries, they won't." *Ugh.* Being an adult was the pits.

"Your dad's a reasonable man. Just talk to him."

"He's not reasonable!" she cried. Not now that she'd seen inside. "He keeps telling me to have faith."

"Well,"—a teasing lilt—"you're comfortable with faith."

Gwen didn't care if he was trying to lighten the mood. She didn't appreciate where he'd decided to go. "What's that supposed to mean?"

"Nothing, just that-"

"Just that you might visit more if we had sex in my childhood bedroom, my family within hearing distance?"

"I can be quiet," he said with an impish lilt, meaning a different smile—his sexy one.

"Gage!" She closed her eyes to squeeze it out. "This is not helping me right now!"

There was a sigh from the other end of the phone, and Gwen knew she was being a total downer. Burying her face in the crook of her elbow, spitting out a few bubbles, she mumbled, "Maybe I *can't* be quiet."

He chuckled. "That's more like it."

"It's too cold to do it in your car." Suddenly she was aware of her breasts pressing against the side of the tub.

"And you wouldn't want the locals to gossip about how we checked into a hotel."

"Not Gwen Harriet Louise Aaldenberg." Gwen scoffed. "She wouldn't dare."

"I couldn't get away for a whole weekend anyway, not till

after April."

Gwen ignored this. "I told you I might want to wait." It had been a test. Was he okay living how a person should? Except look where shoulds had gotten her. She was about done with them.

"Then you tried to take me on our first night together."

She grinned, sitting in those memories. "Guess what I'm wearing right now?" she asked, a hand pressed flat over the gold heart hanging around her neck. Her heart rose in her throat, thrilled and ready for promise—*your locket, and only your locket,* she would breathe out on a whisper.

"As much as I'd love to, I really can't." His tone all business again. "I have to get back to work."

Gwen clutched the necklace in her fist, heart tumbling to her gut where it made her sick. For one, fleeting moment life had again felt like a whisper, light and soft and promising. One moment inside a desert wasteland of time stretching out on either side of her.

She needed to find that somewhere—a night, a something—where she could remember how thrill and promise felt. If she didn't, if she didn't drink from an oasis soon, she might not make it out alive.

* * *

Gwen stood at the counter while her dad ordered a cup of coffee like another man might order a beer. They'd been to the bank, asked for what they needed, and were waiting nearby for the answer.

He was in a suit and she in a dress, in order to look and feel as respectable as possible when asking for someone else's money. Heels, jewelry, perfume. Like she was planning to date the banker, if that's what it took.

She'd pulled her most ignored perfume bottle from the back of her drawer, because she wasn't sure she'd ever smell it the same after this. Even if they got the loan, this moment was the epitome of failure: the whiff of lilies on her neck and wrists, the smell of coffee wafting from the pot, the sizzle of bacon and its odorous call, her crisp-pressed dress—the iron-scented heat of it beneath her coat and the warmed smell of her sweat.

Her dad stooped his shoulders closer to the steaming mug like it might hold some answers.

"Is this how it usually goes?" she asked, wondering if she should leave, walk back home to change before the store opened, or slump down next to him and wait. Six months ago, she never would've considered wallowing in misery alongside another person. In fact, she'd made it a life habit to not wallow, ever. She sidestepped that crap as soon as she spotted it, forced herself to keep going, and focused on the road ahead.

That being said, she was starting to realize that she was no longer who she thought she was—who everyone thought she was.

"They usually approve it right away," he admitted.

Gwen shrugged out of her coat, hotter now than she'd

been at the bank. "So it's not going to happen. What are we going to do if it doesn't happen?" She'd put off creditors with promises about tax returns, but there were no tax returns coming. Her parents paid in as little as they could get away with—imagine that—and so, based on the history she'd gotten off her dad's bank statements—yes, that was a fun night—they paid it in full come April. Only, there wouldn't be money in April. Unless there was a loan.

She wished she could collect on all the non-profits her mother donated to. You only had to ask her, anyone knew, and so they asked. The Aaldenberg name was a pillar in the community, her parents always said, and pillars were meant to be charitable. Gwen grew up thinking they were generous, but now wondered if it was for show, a way to pretend everything was all right, for everyone else's sake as much as their own. Gwen had a habit of doing that herself; she must have learned it from somewhere.

Sliding onto the cold metal seat, she nodded for the waitress' attention. Did they serve alcohol at this diner? Gwen glanced around at the locals she'd known her whole life. Not that she cared any longer what they thought of her. She would be leaving soon anyway, God willing.

Her dad slid a warm hand over hers, closed his eyes, and began to pray.

Praying in public. That's where they were at. Well, she'd been thinking of Him too.

A roiling turned her stomach, and Gwen clutched the metal rim of the counter. No, it wasn't going to subside. Running across the old, scuffed floor—Gwen felt old and scuffed and had to remind herself she was twenty-two—she launched herself into the bathroom, losing her two bites of breakfast and the water she'd sipped at the bank to keep her from screaming. All of it down the toilet, same as her life.

No more bacon and coffee, but her lilies mixed with the barest hint of sewer water as she sat propped against the black stall. In her nicest heels and sexiest librarian dress, she was on a stained and sorrowful bathroom floor.

She was doing it for her family. She was doing it for Betta. She was doing it for herself—for freedom.

Please, please, please, please, please, she chanted, as she climbed up the toilet paper holder and handicap bar. Please *please*, as she rinsed her mouth and wiped her lips and studied the bags under her eyes in the hazy, bent mirror.

She needed cucumbers for them, and a facial. A spa in the city. Something, anything that was for or about her, and her alone.

Okay, so again, this was where Betta had been a few months ago. It was why she—Gwen—took this all on.

As her heels clicked back along the diner's sticky floor to her stool, she kept up her mantra. *Please God, pleaseGod, pleaseGodpleaseGod.* Her chant flowed from discernible syllables into one word into nonsense.

Gwen took her seat, her chest tight. Her father's phone sat on the counter, screen up. No, it wasn't only her chest that was tight, but all of her. She was still. Waiting. Begging. *God, please.*

"Mae might help us out," he said, softly.

"What?"

"You asked what would happen if they don't approve it."

"Mae has that kind of money?" The sandwich shop went on the same cycle as the store.

"She's only supported herself for a long time now."

Gwen tried to swallow the knot in her throat with a huge gulp of lukewarm coffee. Taking money from Mae might save the store, but at stake then was her parents' marriage.

Oh, God.

Maybe that was the key—only supporting yourself.

Oh, God, please. She stared at the phone set between them. *Do this one thing for me, it's all I ask.*

Soon, it lit itself up.

Her dad snatched it and hurried outside. Gwen tucked her hands beneath her thighs and held tightly onto the stool, unable to make herself follow, unable to witness it, if the news wasn't good.

He paced and nodded and talked and paced.

Pleasegodpleasegodpleasegodplease.

When he hung up, he closed the phone between his palms, and turned to her with a thumbs-up.

Gwen rushed back to the bathroom before the sobs of relief overwhelmed her. She slammed into a stall and locked it, sat on the toilet, head in her hands, and wept with exhaustion and hope.

Perhaps she could turn this around. Perhaps freedom was right around the corner.

* * *

Betta read her mom to sleep. The first time she chose one of her own books, instead of something with promises of sex on the cover, and her mom fell asleep.

There were things you found out about people when you took care of them that you'd rather not know.

Betta hadn't wanted to know that her grandpa's favorite movies were tit flicks. Tit flicks disguised as eighties movies, of course, for the humor—*sure, Pops*. She hadn't wanted to know her mother's attention could only be held by the kind of romance that ended in payoff. And payoff again. And maybe one more time for good measure in the den with open windows blowing rainy mist onto naked bottoms.

Now she had all these images in her head she never asked for—the price she paid for taking care of people.

So Betta found her way to the kitchen for something to poke her eyeballs out with. When the doorbell rang, she was considering a pretzel stick while Ez spooned SpaghettiOs into her mouth directly from the can.

The sisters looked at each other. No one rang the doorbell.

"You should get that," Ez said, around a mouthful.

"I'll get that," Betta said. She peeked out the window before opening the door, in case she needed to put her guarded face on for a traveling salesman, but it was Mae.

"Mae?" Betta opened the door with a touch of surprise.

"Hi, dear. May I come in?" She held the biggest casserole dish Betta had ever seen, definitely not a size that could be purchased at Aaldenberg Hardware.

"Oh, of course." Betta moved aside, and Mae bustled to

the kitchen. She shoved the dish in the oven, slid a glove off to turn on the heat, and set the timer for twenty minutes. "It's a roast, and probably still warm enough, but in case it cooled on the way over."

Why was this woman bringing them food?

Mae shifted her feet and slid her glove back on. "I heard about your mother's flu and wanted to do something to help. Have you all enjoyed a good meal since she took ill?"

Betta and Mae both looked to Esmerelda, spoon hanging from her mouth and empty can in front of her.

"Nothing home cooked," Betta admitted.

Mae pointed to the oven. "Freshly home cooked. Enjoy!" Shooting out the door, she hurried back around the side of the house for her backyard.

"Everyone thinks Mom has the flu?" Betta wandered to the rear of the kitchen to look out the back door. Mae slipped into her house via her sliding glass patio.

Ez shrugged as Betta turned back around. "Better than them knowing the truth."

"That's disgusting, by the way." Betta nodded at the can Ez tossed into the recyclables.

"Hey. A girl's got to do what a girl's got to do."

"At least finish it off with an apple."

Ez stuck her tongue out, but snatched one from the fruit bowl. "Okay, *Mom*."

Resting against the counter to face the oven, Betta crossed her arms. If there was a family meal—one of her mom's favorite things—maybe she'd join them. Betta was so used to sitting at Pops' side, knowing there was nothing she could do to stop the decline, that it was how she met her mother's depression. Not that Betta thought there was an easy answer; she knew there wasn't. Still, she hadn't been showing her what there was to live for either.

As Betta set the table with her mother's favorite placemats, dishes, and centerpiece, Van slammed in through the front door with a green carry-out bag. He dropped it next to Ez, where she was leaning against the counter eating her apple down to its core.

"Real food," he said. "Because, to be honest, I'm surprised to see you ingesting fruit."

"Betta made me," she admitted.

"You bring me any of that?" Betta asked, rummaging through the sideboard for the napkins her mom liked best.

"Sorry." He wrinkled his nose. "Ez is still growing. Next time, okay?"

Betta waved him off and lined her cell phone camera up to take a picture of the table, planning to text it to her mom with the menu and the guest list, once she knew who would be home.

If Betta could get her out of the bedroom for one hour, it would be a start.

* * *

Esmerelda should've been at Celia's birthday party, instead of waiting forty-five minutes for her mom to pull herself out of bed and join them for dinner. Forty-five minutes before they gave up and ate without her, which was okay with Ez because then she didn't feel like she had to stuff a roast into her mouth, as she was still full from her SpaghettiOs, apple, and the hunk of sandwich Van brought her only a few hours earlier.

She sat through it anyway, Gwen and Betta ignoring each other while Van chatted with each of them in turn. College basketball with their dad, Gage with Gwen, Shelby and James with Betta, and Gavin with Ez. Gavin and Van really hit it off on Christmas eve, and sometimes it felt like all she talked to either of them about now was what the other was doing.

Van helped Gwen do the dishes since Betta cooked—only she hadn't, not really—and Ez wiped down the table and counter. Betta left to meet James, Van took the car to the train station to pick up Kate for the weekend, and Gwen wandered out to meet her friends. Her dad and her the only ones left. They looked at each other and retreated to their rooms, early for a Friday night, even considering such a late dinner.

She'd told Gavin she couldn't hang out with him today because she wanted to leave herself open for the invite whenever it might come. Only then it never came. In case she found herself in this position, Ez had stopped by the store after school to load up on Skittles and Starburst. It was her store, pretty much, so it wasn't really stealing. Plus, her parents did it all the time.

The moment she gave in to wallowing and ripped all the Starburst packages apart to sort by color, her dad stuck his head in her room and told her some Celia girl was on the phone.

She scrambled for it, unable to believe her luck. Considering Celia went to the trouble to get her home number, it was the perfect excuse to exchange cells. By the end of the night, Ez promised herself, she would be in Celia's phone.

"Hello?" Ez aimed for a tone that said *I've been so unconcerned with your social media posts, I have the boyfriend you want, life is good, don't you want to be my friend?*

"It's Celia."

"Oh, hey. What's up?"

Celia scoffed a little. "You know what's up. Are you trying to tell me you don't know what's up?"

"Your birthday? Happy birthday, by the way." As if she hadn't been thinking about it.

"Yes, thanks, so why aren't you here?"

"Um." Had she missed the invitation? No. She wouldn't have missed the invitation.

"Bad girls show up to parties they're not invited to, I thought you got that."

Oh.

Oh.

Esmerelda wanted to pound her head against the wall. All this daring bullshit, Celia had been molding her as the bad girl who did what she wanted when she wanted.

Test: failed.

Ez glanced at the time; it was after ten. She wasn't allowed to walk the streets alone after nine, Van wouldn't be back for hours, and she was not about to ask her dad to walk her to a sleepover. "Shit, Celia, my parents will never go for it."

"I mean, your call, I guess. Friends aren't friends if they don't make your birthday party, you know?"

Right, of course. Another test, which honestly Ez didn't mind. She liked fun, obscure tests that were unclear and difficult to pass. She just needed to start paying more attention. After chewing on her lip a bit, she decided, "I'll sneak out. Not a big deal."

Except it was a big deal. Her mom might not leave the bedroom for a hurricane right now, but her dad hadn't had his bedtime snack yet. Not to mention, how would she sneak back in tomorrow morning when her sisters were there?

"Perfect," Celia said. "Hurry up, yeah? It's a little boring here without you."

Ez grinned. "Give me ten minutes."

Hanging up, Esmerelda threw a change of clothes and toothbrush into her backpack, then slipped boots over her pajama pants. Music on and lights out so everyone would think she was asleep, she tiptoed through the house. About to grab her winter coat, she heard her dad in the hall upstairs and slid into the living room, heart beating against her ribcage so loud she was sure he must hear it.

She hadn't done anything yet, though. Taking a deep, forced breath, Ez dropped her backpack and waltzed into the front hall as if she hadn't been thinking of going anywhere. Her dad would know nothing.

Except, her boots.

Standing on the entry tile, looking down at them, straining

to hear where her dad was headed, she considered slipping them off. She could go without a backpack, and she could go without a coat, but she couldn't go without boots, and she couldn't not go.

"Harvey?" her mom called. His footsteps turned back.

"Yeah?" he asked, moving further toward their room, in the back corner of the house.

Now or never.

Ez swept up her backpack and yanked her mittens and scarf from the arm of her coat, leaving it behind on its hook in case anyone might notice it missing. Quickly, quietly, she opened the front door only as much as she needed to sneak out, and used two hands to close it gently and controlled behind her.

Then she flew, to make up lost time and keep warm. A light snow fell, the snowflakes sashaying down the deep navy sky and past the glow of the streetlights. She danced and slid along the slippery remnants it left on the sidewalk. She had snuck out. She was roaming town after nine. What was there to be scared of anyway? She knew everyone in this town, and the tourists with whatever bad intentions weren't around this time of year. Besides, she was almost an adult.

Really, it was amazing. She should walk after dark every night, on her own, tempting fate and feeling alive. It was so cold her fingertips might freeze and break off, but it was *great*.

Esmerelda thought about knocking on Gavin's window as she skipped by his house. They were next door neighbors, Gavin and Celia—Gavin said they used to have tin cans strung from their bedroom windows. Ez wondered what kind of naughty things they might've done, windows facing each other, if Gavin actually liked Celia back.

Stopping in front of the clapboard house next to Gavin's, Ez noted the faces lined up in the front window, waiting: Celia, Georgia, and three other girls from their lunch table. That meant Ez beat out four; she was no longer the lowest on the totem pole.

Celia opened the door for her, a finger to her lips, and the girls tiptoed down to the basement where they landed in a fit of giggles on a thick, shag rug. Sleeping bags were lined up between long couches in the finished basement.

"How'd it feel?" Celia asked, Gwen's locket glinting at her collarbone in the low light.

Ez shrugged. "Same ole, same ole."

"You've snuck out before?" Georgia asked, with enough appreciation and awe to allow Ez a feeling of belonging—or even better than belonging. Just plain *better than*.

Ez smiled. "To see Gavin when we can't keep our hands off each other." A reminder to Celia who had what, even if such a thing had never happened. He was, as Christine foretold, still roaming the landscape from atop her shirt. "So, got anything to drink?"

Due to the wickedly pleased smile from Celia, Ez knew she'd done something right. If she could get Celia a little drunk, maybe she'd pass out and not notice if the locket slipped off her neck.

Celia put a scary movie on and gave each of them a word. Random words, like *anyone, sorry, light bulb, and butterfly*. Whenever your word was said, you were to drink. Ez was careful to take the bittiest sips—control, control, control—and after the movie, Celia launched them into a game of truth or dare.

"Esmerelda," she said, drawing out her name as if it were made of marbles, "Truth or dare?"

"Dare." Of course.

"Kiss me."

Ez was careful to keep her forehead smooth so as not to show any thoughts or reservations, but would Celia turn on her later and tell Gavin she cheated on him?

She was sure it was another test, and the thrill of what seemed to be an endless string of dares—don't wear panties to school, take her panties, do what you want and not what I say—made Celia worth it. Thrill felt like moths in her chest, loose and wild, beating their whisper-light wings in a flurry against her organs. Excitement and promise and a giggle waiting to burst from her throat.

Christine didn't offer that—Gavin barely offered that. So Ez leaned across the circle and waited for Celia to meet her halfway, then planted her lips on the other girl's mouth the same way she would if it were Gavin in front of her. With her eyes closed, it didn't seem much different; Celia smelled nicer, and her lips were softer.

She imagined Gavin throughout, to help her play the part, to make it real, and then, like he did sometimes, she slid one of her hands up along Celia's neck. The delicate chain of the locket under her fingers, the clasp—yes, that's right, it was a lobster clasp. With some pressure, she'd only need one hand to take it off.

Fingers clamped down on Esmerelda's wrist, and Celia jerked back, looking, if Ez did say so herself, a little stunned and quite impressed.

Yes, she did know what she was doing, thank you very much. Gavin taught her well.

The rush of it all continued to thrum along Esmerelda's breastbone, and her heart beat in satisfaction—the buzz from the alcohol, the secret of the low lights, the sneaking out and being someone no one else was, the danger of skimming so close to Celia, the dance, the game.

All that was left was getting the locket in her hand, and Ez would be the final, ultimate champion.

She made sure to maneuver her way next to Celia's sleeping bag, for easy access once she was asleep, but later, as the sky first began to lighten and they were finally settling in, Celia whispered her name. "Esmerelda?"

Ez flipped over, both of them on their sides, face to face.

"I'm glad you came," she whispered.

The thrum came back. This was the hardest win, blatant acceptance. "I'm glad I came too."

Celia sat up and put her hands behind her neck. Before Ez realized what she was doing, the locket was dangling in front of her. "Quit the play, and I'll give you your sister's locket back for good."

Ez tried to say it, *yes*, but couldn't work her tongue. For Celia had admitted it; it was her locket. Or did she care about the play more than she thought? But this was *the locket* up for grabs, not to mention maybe even Celia herself. Everything Esmerelda had been working for.

Auditions were next week. She and Christine had read lines together, had recited them in the halls, texted the dialogue back and forth. All that work for nothing, and she could see her name in lights, the attention and the applause...

But the decision had been made long ago. She'd committed to this, what she was here at this party for, and she wasn't a girl who went back on her lists.

Ez nodded, her mouth dry and tongue like lead, but she nodded.

"Say it," Celia demanded.

"I'll quit the play." The words felt like sandpaper coming out, forced and scratchy, whittling down something inside her, she didn't quite know what.

Putting her hand out, Ez willed the locket to drop. She could feel it—taste it—already in her hand.

Celia didn't let it go. "Quit Christine, too."

With the pang such a demand came in on, Ez realized Christine was more than her gym partner. Things were easy with her, how they were supposed to be with a friend. But Ez wanted more of the thrill, and Gavin's friends were Celia's friends, and Esmerelda was so close, so close to Celia. Plus, the locket. It was beautiful, glinting in the moonlight, a promise wrapped up inside.

She felt she'd worked for it, like it was due her.

Ez swallowed hard, whatever pride and loyalty and integrity she had left flushing away with her saliva. "Christine who?"

Grinning in triumph, Celia dropped the locket into Esmerelda's palm, then promptly fell into a snoring, satisfied sleep.

Esmerelda, on the other hand, lay awake for a long time, stunned and churning, chewing on the conversation again and again, worrying over whether it could have gone a different way.

As it was, the victory stung and pierced, opening a package of regret and disappointment inside her she didn't know she'd been carrying.

* * *

Gwen poured herself a cup of coffee. On second thought, she grabbed a bigger mug. Not bothering to sit, she leaned against the kitchen counter and took a sip.

The snow swirled in the street, and she faced a lonely Sunday at the store—more biting because Sundays were so busy during season, one of the more common days for tourists to stock up for the week. The emptiness of the weekend now felt like iron fingers clutching her throat.

Her hand went there, to her second locket, as Betta shuffled in and nodded a good morning. With a sigh, Gwen moved over so her sister could get to the coffee pot, wrapped both hands around the mug, and inhaled the scent that perhaps did more to wake her than the caffeine itself.

Esmerelda barged in the front door, only to freeze once inside, glancing around as if she were taking in a situation. Gwen, with direct line of sight through the open archway, raised an eyebrow and checked her watch. It was barely nine.

Betta turned. "Ez? What are you doing?"

"In your pajamas," Gwen pointed out. "What are you doing coming home, at this time of the morning, in your pajamas?"

Betta's mouth dropped open. "Did you sneak out?"

"No! Of course not! Someone called me this morning and said they found the locket—I went right away." Dropping to her knees, she rummaged through her bag, checking zippers here and there.

Gwen laughed. She couldn't help it. Of course she'd snuck out. No other explanation for the huge eyes and flapping mouth.

Esmerelda straightened, something clutched tight in her fist. Gwen shook her head. It couldn't be. Ez opened her hand, revealing the delicate chain and gold heart, and Gwen could no longer do or think anything but set her coffee down and collect it for herself, once again.

Cold, it was so cold, where the one on her neck was not. She put it on, the hearts clanking against each other, the same length chain—that wouldn't work, not for good. She smiled anyway.

Ez must have seen her opening, because she grabbed her bag and ran up the steps.

Betta sat down at the table. "She totally snuck out."

Gwen slid into the seat next to her. "Yeah, I'm actually kind of surprised you let that go."

"Me? You're the oldest."

"You're the one standing in for Mom."

"I'll trade you," Betta whispered into her coffee, reminding Gwen of their dad at the diner.

Gwen realized they hadn't been alone since she told Betta she wanted the store, since she broke Betta's heart. Oh, how she wanted to tell her. *I'm taking a bullet for you. Be patient. You did your duty, now I'm doing mine. Then we can both be free.*

Betta turned to her, as if she could read her mind. "Tell me you want the store."

Gwen could barely bring herself to look her in the eye. "I want it."

"I don't believe you. What's going on?"

"What do you mean?"

Betta closed her eyes, the liner there still strong from the day before. "What about our plans, Gwen?"

"What plans?"

"You and the city, me and the store."

Gwen let out the start of a laugh. "We were kids. *Babies.* Van thought he was going to be a professional football player."

Turning back to the window, the snow, and her coffee, Betta frowned. "Our plans meant something to me. I guess I thought they meant something to you too."

"Yeah, well, what about James? You think he didn't mean something to me?" Betta shot a glance at her, and Gwen rolled her eyes to get out of it. "No, that's not why I took the store. I shouldn't have brought it up."

A car rumbled by.

"The traffic, Gwen, in the city. You're always talking about how exciting it is—the noise and excitement of a place that never sleeps. Where there's always something to do or see or a new corner to discover. You could map this town on the back of your hand, and you're *bored*. Don't try to tell me otherwise."

Gwen took a slow sip of coffee, swallowing down the truth of Betta's words. Was there anything worse than being bored? "Plans change."

"So I guess I'm moving to California then. Or going back to school." Betta stared at her, and Gwen felt this was a dare. "Then, when you come to your senses, I won't be around and you'll be stuck with it forever."

Damn.

Steadily as she was able, Gwen continued sipping her coffee. She hadn't much time with the loan money yet, to see how far it stretched, how much more it might take to get clear of the red that had been chasing her since September. Ultimately though, she did want Betta to have it. She did want their plans to play out.

"Don't do anything drastic, okay? Just let me get my life sorted."

"That's not fair!" Betta cried. "That I should have to wait around for you to get your life together before I can even start on mine?"

"I'm a year older than you," Gwen snapped. "By the time you're my age, we'll both be sorted."

Betta stood, nearly knocking her chair over, and strode to the kitchen sink. Gwen couldn't look. Couldn't watch her react. Couldn't bear to break her heart. But had to. She was so close. And she'd promised her father not to drag Betta into it. It was almost over. A few more months, five at the most.

"I still can't believe you let that go with Ez," Gwen muttered, thinking a change of subject was the only way out.

"I'm not her mom," Betta said, through what sounded like clenched teeth. "And I'm done being the things I'm not meant to be."

Gwen bit down on her tongue. If only it were that easy.

* * *

Her dad was futzing with the register drawer when Betta walked into the otherwise empty store. She'd sat at Shelby's most of the afternoon, hoping and praying it would be him closing up, and as soon as she saw Gwen leave, she headed over.

Their conversation that morning, hearing from Gwen's mouth again that the store was hers and she wanted it, had spurred Betta into action. It was a new year, and she was tired of waiting. If she had to put up a fight for the store, then so be it.

"How's my girl?" her dad asked with a smile.

Slipping into an aisle to take a deep breath before she betrayed her sister, she trailed her hand along a row of chips. There was a similarity to how James smelled after the garage, old metal shelves versus the metal of cars in the old garage. The hardware aisle, especially, held the faintest scent of the oil James couldn't scrub out of his pores.

She would go to him next, no matter what her father said.

She would hold his hands, nails blackened, and run her fingers up the ropey muscles of his forearms. She would tell him, even if the store was not hers, that she was staying forever— never California.

How much easier to wait for the store than to wait for him. How much quicker she'd known it was that which she wanted to build her life on.

Right. So. She came back up the detergent aisle, an altogether different smell, bright and cheery. "Dad?"

He opened and closed the drawer, seemingly satisfied that it was working. "Yeah?"

"Is Gwen really doing a good job here?"

"Of course she is."

Betta rested her hip against the customer side of the counter. "The shelves are half empty."

"Oh." His gaze flittered over them. "Well, we're waiting until after Christmas to do another restocking."

"It's after Christmas."

"Until January."

"It's January."

He opened and closed the drawer a few more times.

"She's not, then."

"I didn't say that."

"I'm happy to take over anytime."

They stared at each other. Betta couldn't read him.

"I want the store, Dad. Gwen doesn't."

"Maybe she wants to make sure she and Gage are a sure thing before she does anything drastic," he said.

"Not fair that I'm waiting for my life to start, due to her

needing a security blanket."

He wound his way out from behind the counter, righting items on the display that didn't need righting. Then on to the nearest shelf, spacing items so it looked less bare than it was.

"I have a year and a half of business classes that Gwen doesn't."

"No Aaldenberg has needed a degree or any fancy classes to run this store."

Betta swung around the endcap to face him. "Maybe she does, if she can't keep inventory on the shelves."

"She's cleaning house. It's a good time of year for it. They teach you about that in your fancy Boston college?"

"No, because there's *no such thing*."

Harvey moved on to the next section, turning his back to her.

"Remember when I reorganized the service desk?" She'd been fifteen. Christmas break. There'd been decades of paperwork and binders spilling out from every crevice.

His hands stilled. "Yeah, you've always been good here. I'm not saying you weren't made for the place."

See? She wanted to jump around him—*see, see, see?* Crossing her fingers behind her back, she made her next move. "Gwen's never done anything like that, because she doesn't care like I do."

"She's reorganizing the shelves and the back office, Betta. She's done a lot you should be thankful for."

"*I* should be thankful for?" The affront in her tone slipped out before she could catch it. "I should be thankful she's stealing my life and brainwashing you to buy it?"

He spun around faster than she remembered he could move. "You're still a kid, and there are things you don't understand. When your sister is ready—when you're ready—it will work its way out. Have a little faith."

How it might work out for everyone else was exactly what she was afraid of—how she might be left behind.

Stuffing his hands in his pockets, he sighed. "You're taking care of your mom, yeah?"

Betta figured he'd bring that up. Would he have if she and Gwen weren't bottlenecked? One life, one option, and two girls. Betta was starting to think that waiting meant giving up and giving in, getting seconds when there were no longer seconds, getting left with nothing. And this, after fifteen years thinking of no end game but the store.

"I have to get a life, Dad. I can't be the one always taking care of people." She heard James' words, from long before— *maybe you should start taking care of yourself.*

"Let's get your mom through this. Then you can worry about the store."

Of course she wouldn't shirk taking care of a loved one, but nursing people wasn't what she wanted to do with her life. Did anyone see her as anything else anymore? What about who she'd been, who she was turning into, and who she wanted to be?

She was losing grasp of it herself.

"Maybe the timing will be perfect," he said, squeezing her hand. "If you just let it."

But Betta was sick of letting it. And she couldn't see how that had gotten her anywhere. "So to be clear-"

"To be clear, Gwen is in charge of the store until she deems otherwise."

It hurt just as much to hear him say it, as it had that morning. She felt like she was falling. Falling from grace, from favor—if she ever even had it—and from sanity.

Everything was wrong, and it seemed there was nothing she could do to make it right.

* * *

Ez spent the week wondering how to ask Gwen for the locket. It didn't seem right Gwen had two and Esmerelda none, not after what she had to do to get it back.

She wanted to wear it to school for everyone to see— Georgia, the carbon copies at the lunch table, and Christine.

"It's our four month anniversary," Gavin said, breaking into her thoughts as they headed up the walk to his large, covered porch.

Four months of a first boyfriend and a first kiss. She'd actually have a Valentine this year. Standing straighter, squaring her shoulders and letting it fill her, she almost stepped on the huge crack on his front steps. It was the only one she cared about anymore, because it was massive. The entire corner of the stair might fall away if she hit it wrong, and then what would become of her mother?

"You hungry?" Gavin asked as he opened the front door.

She shook her head, *not yet*, and slid past him to the stairs, dropping her backpack at the bottom before he grabbed her hand to stop her.

They always went up to his room. Monday through Thursday were about making out, Friday for friends (now that she had some), Saturday for talking, Saturday night something bigger was usually happening, like a football game or party or everyone went to the movies, and Sunday he kept for family. Esmerelda loved that their relationship was so easily compartmentalized.

So she turned with a frown, wondering if Celia had told him about their kiss at her birthday party. If she told anyone and it got back to him, he might think Esmerelda cheated on him. He might be mad. He might break up with her.

"I have something for you," he said.

She came down a step so they were the same height and bit her lip for good measure. In response, as she'd known he would, Gavin kissed her quick and sweet, the slightest dart of his tongue.

"Don't distract me," he said, with an eighth of a smile.

Esmerelda loved how his smiles worked in fractions. She liked measuring them, what made them pass a quarter to a half, and what kind of seriously fabulous business pushed him to three-fourths. She'd thought three-fourths was all he had until she showed up at a football game she hadn't thought she'd make. The first full smile happened when he noticed her, surprise being an important factor, and ever since, she wondered what kind of bigger, better surprise might push him further.

He would get her full smile, Ez thought, if he was holding

a jewelry box behind his back—a full and a half if he bought her a heart-shaped locket.

Oh, how she wanted a heart-shaped locket. She didn't care if it was silver, or so cheap it tarnished and left fake jewelry dust on her chest. But all he handed her was an envelope.

Furrowing her brow, Ez took it. A gift certificate wasn't very romantic, and he didn't seem the poetic type. With what she hoped was a confused frown and not a disappointed one, she slid her finger under the flap.

"Tickets?" she asked. "To the play?"

He nodded, but his grin was not as enthusiastic as it had been—only at a sixteenth. "I didn't mean to scare you off being a stupid fanboy about it before auditions." He looked down to his feet. Thirteen people he'd readied to cheer her on. She never could have gotten that kind of crowd on her own. "Thought you'd want to check it out. Maybe you'll feel better about not doing it-"

"I don't feel bad about not doing it," she interrupted. Had she said that?

"Or be excited to try out next time."

"I'm not a theater geek."

His face fell normal again, serious. "They're artists, Ez, not geeks. Is that why you didn't do it?"

"Of course not."

He pushed past her on the stairs, and she followed him to his room. "I also thought you might like to support your friend."

"What friend?"

"Christine?" He narrowed his eyes at her. "What's up with

you?"

Esmerelda checked herself. Her boyfriend of four months thought she wanted to do the play, and that Christine was a friend of hers she'd want to support. "Christine didn't get a part."

"She's an understudy. You never know. Plus, I hear set design's a lot of work."

Ez crossed her arms from where she stood in his bedroom doorway, while he looked around like he didn't know where to sit. There was the bed, where they always sat, or his skeletal desk chair. He sat in the desk chair.

Was this their first fight?

"She didn't tell me she was an understudy," Ez muttered.

"Did you ask her?"

No. She hadn't. Because she'd been trying to make it clear they were only gym partners. Especially after Celia's party.

God, she'd been kind of a shit.

Ez walked over and slid the envelope on his desk. "I have to tell you something."

He blinked up at her, unreadable.

"Celia dared me to kiss her at her birthday party. A real kiss."

"That's why you're being weird?"

She shrugged. Was she being weird? His gift was thoughtful. She supposed she could act like it.

"Do you want to break up with me?" he asked.

"No!" She wanted to touch him, but he'd chosen a chair meant for one. "It was truth or dare. I wasn't thinking about anything but getting the locket back. It meant nothing. I'll never let it happen again." Resting her knee against his, she whispered, "Forgive me?"

She leaned over and curtained their faces with her thick hair, blocking out his stinky sock boy room.

Gavin pursed his lips for a moment. "We never talked about kissing other people of the same sex, but let's not."

"Of course." Esmerelda straddled him on the chair, thank goodness it didn't have arms, and the thrill came thrumming back to her. "I'm sorry if I was being weird. The tickets are perfect. The best four month anniversary present I've ever gotten." The only, too, but he didn't need to know that.

Sliding his hands against her lower back, he nudged her a little closer. She scooted up his lap, and he kissed her.

It was their four month anniversary, and she hadn't bought him a present. Plus, the thrum was waning. To solve both these problems, she reached behind her for his hand and brought it up not only under her shirt, but also her bra.

Thrill on thrill on thrill felt a little like danger on danger on danger. But Ez was a girl good with control, and his fingers washed her mind clean, crowding out the nagging thought that he might be right about her—that Christine was her truest friend, and that she actually *did* want to be an artist.

Because if he was right, then she was doing it all wrong.

FEBRUARY

Betta left her coffee and eggs on the table when she heard the knock at the door.

James stood on the porch, wrapped in his orange army jacket, fingers drumming his thighs. No hello, no kiss, no *may I come in?* Instead, simply, "I'm leaving for California."

The February cold surrounded her, rushing into the house with his words. A light snow fell, a dusting of which he brushed from his hair. At the curb, his car was full of boxes and seemingly anxious to go. With the snow drifting past, the sidewalks white and untouched, and the picturesque house across the street, the scene was a postcard of a goodbye.

"Wait. For good?"

"I want you to come."

Her heart sped up to meet the rhythm of his fingers, so perfectly she imagined she could feel them on her breastbone. She settled a hand there, but it wouldn't be soothed. "I can't just *go*. You haven't given me any warning—no time to pack."

"If you want to come, I'll wait."

"I don't understand. How could you not have mentioned this sooner?"

"I've mentioned it."

"I mean, that you were actually going. That you actually picked a date."

"February's the worst, Bets. I don't want to do it anymore."

She stared at him and tried to decipher what he didn't want to do anymore—the winter or her.

"I am sorry. I've tried to tell you, but I didn't want to ruin the last few weeks."

"*Weeks?*" He'd known he was doing this for weeks? Betta struggled to keep the tears from exploding on the world outside, but when he pulled her to him on the chilly front steps, she lost it. He held her and kissed her hair, one arm folded tight around her neck, the other searching for her hand.

"I was afraid we'd fight about it until I left, and I couldn't bear to have that be our final time together. I love you, Betta. Please don't forget that."

She didn't understand. If he loved her so much, why was he leaving? Ugh. Fine. She knew the answer to that. She'd essentially told him she'd pick the store and this town over him and California. How could she hold it against him that he'd picked California over her and this town?

Wrapping her arms around him, she pulled a few more heated kisses, her tears wetting both of their cheeks. It was cruel, riding up at the last minute, and crueler to leave in such a way, but she wanted the final moments, all of them, all of him, every last drop.

Resting her nose against the skin of his neck, she inhaled soap and oil and metallic garage. "You aren't coming back?"

"Not for a while."

She wiped her cheeks and nodded. "So that's it then."

He rubbed her chin with his thumb. "Maybe I won't be able to stay away."

She reached up to knot her fingers in his hair one more time, and his face twisted. Swiping a hand to his nose, he stepped off the porch backwards, stalked to his car, and drove off without another glance.

Still in her pajama pants, slippers, and sweatshirt, Betta sat on the frozen porch steps. The last few weeks of her and James's life together fell into place. The last few months—the marriage proposals she never took seriously, the talk of California and how he thought *she* needed to move there.

He'd loved her and held her, and she closed her eyes to remember this as she sank against the wooden railing, aching for the cold to seep in and freeze this moment so she wouldn't have to feel it.

Lonely.

Alone.

Left.

'People come and people go'—she saw it all the time, it shouldn't surprise her. The tourists were a never-ending cycle of relationships, picked up for summers only to be gone come fall. Even those who wouldn't dare leave your side, Pops for instance; fate and life eventually left them no choice in the matter.

'People come and people go.' *And after they go,* she thought, staring into the empty space where his car had been, *all you're left with is you.*

* * *

Gwen sat back and stretched. She was at her desk with a hard-earned smile on her face. Sure, her computer was still in the red, daily speaking, but the loan money had gone a long way.

Pops' credit cards, paid and cancelled.

The bill for the funeral, burial, and wake, including the most ridiculously priced coffin she could imagine, taken care of.

Her mother's Christmas, check.

Inventory her dad placed before she shut the orders down, paid for in full.

On top of that, she set aside the last of the loan to cover her parents' income tax come April, then separated the store finances from her parents' personal finances, taking their names off everything.

The transition of ownership paperwork was drawn up, and she forged Betta's signature, putting herself as a minority partner so she could get her dad's name off the business checking. That would ensure he wouldn't take any more draws for last-minute needs at home. Their house was paid off, so if he needed to he could take out a mortgage, but he wouldn't ruin Betta's store.

All that was left was seeing the daily through from red to black, then hopefully she'd feel okay leaving Betta to save up summer excess for future winter lows.

Now that the bulbous pimpled head of the stress was over, Gwen relaxed back into herself. As best she could see, it was time to celebrate.

Digging into her savings, she booked the honeymoon suite at her favorite local inn. Favorite from the outside anyway, due to its reputation and the owners, because of course she'd never had cause to splurge before, let alone book a room in town. She chose it with hope for the future—only a city accountant's wife would book such a room, and she no longer cared who knew what might happen there, not even what her parents might think. Certainly not her dad, whatever the hell he was up to, and not her mom either. Gwen was no longer a child. Another thing the last few months had taught her.

She dialed Gage's number.

"Hello?" An absent-minded greeting. He must be in the middle of something.

"I have cause to celebrate, I miss you, and I have Sunday off."

Gage groaned, but not the kind of groan she'd been hoping for. The other kind. The kind that wasn't enthused, or ready, or on board. "Gwen."

"Gage," she clipped. "Surely you're coming to town for Valentine's Day."

"We have a huge account that's turned into a complete clusterfuck, and we have to get it sorted by Monday. I can't promise anything."

"It's our nine month anniversary this weekend."

"I have something special planned for our year." His stress of *year* made her feel childish that she cared about any other.

The best kind of celebratory night she could think of at this particular point in her life, and he wasn't going to be there. Considering she couldn't fulfill her plans without him, that pretty much left them a bust. Plus, the room was nonrefundable.

Figures.

She was so stupid. As stupid as her parents. She should have checked with him first.

But it was Valentine's Day. Who would have thought for a moment he wouldn't take time for her on Valentine's Day?

"I could come to you, then." At least they'd be together.

"It's not worth the trip, Gwen, if I'm swamped and can't leave work."

She could tell him what she wanted, what she'd paid to set it up, but then she'd be the nagging girlfriend who didn't understand responsibility and how sometimes you had to do what you didn't want to do, which she would not be. Not after what she'd just been through.

"Fine," she said. If he didn't want to make love to her on Valentine's Day for their nine month anniversary, if he didn't want to help her celebrate the only thing she'd yet done in her life that truly felt a feat worth celebrating, then maybe she'd stay at the inn by herself.

"I'll make it up to you," he said. "I promise."

Gwen kicked off her shoes and put her feet on her desk

with a frown. That's where they were now, after a measly nine months—to the point where he had to make things up.

* * *

Betta squirmed in her chair while reading aloud an excruciatingly vivid sex scene from a novel written by her mother's favorite author. Betta felt the scene building, sensed it coming, and asked if she could skip it, but Wanda insisted she needed the whole picture in order to understand the characters better.

As Betta forced out the phrase "heaving package of bulging man meat" with some difficulty, her phone chimed out a text notification.

Oh, thank God! She looked up to heaven to make sure He knew she wasn't using His name in vain, that she was actually professing deep and heartfelt gratitude, before checking it: *Made it to Eddie's. Well, home really. I made it home. Feels weird. Thought of you the whole way.*

The tears came unexpectedly, as if she were a faucet someone turned on. She tried to cover them, hands to her face, but the sobs would not subside.

"Honey, what's wrong?" her mom asked, more emotion in her tone than Betta had heard from her the entire last month.

She struggled it out, that James was gone.

"Oh, baby, I'm so sorry." Getting out of bed, Wanda wrapped her sour-smelling self around Betta. She knelt down and pulled Betta to the floor to hold her tight. Betta rested her head on her mother's greasy hair and sobbed until it was wrung out of her.

Tissue after tissue after tissue, until they knelt on the carpet inside a sea of clouds.

Grandpa, her friends, the store, James—all the things lost.

James and California was a door she refused to walk through, yet now that it was closed, she felt an overwhelming sense of regret that she'd never truly considered it. "I've lost everything," she whispered.

"Sometimes it's the best place to be," her mom replied, hand on the bed to hoist herself up.

Betta studied her. Her words hadn't been hard, but what an awful thing to say. Wanda sat on the bed in her robe and month-old pajamas—goodness, Betta hoped not, perhaps she should've been paying more attention.

"At such a point, there's nothing left to do but rebuild."

A person couldn't rebuild a relationship out of thin air, though. Or a dead relative. And her friends, well, she missed them, but they'd still judge. Plus, she was handcuffed to her mom now, per her father's wishes, and it sure didn't look like *she* was taking any steps to rebuild.

So where would Betta even start?

* * *

Gavin and Ez headed out the front doors of the school when

Celia skipped up to them and linked her arm through Esmerelda's free elbow. "Hang out with *me* today," she said.

Ez glanced at Gavin, who shrugged. For one moment, Ez worried about upsetting him, as the kiss confession hadn't been too long ago. But Celia never asked her to do anything, not just the two of them.

"Sure," Ez replied, cool as she could manage.

Jerking Esmerelda forward by the elbow, Celia broke into a run, stopping only when they were a solid block ahead of Gavin.

Esmerelda glanced back but was too far away to read his expression.

Ducking her head near Esmerelda's, as if they were the type of friends to share secrets, Celia asked, "What do you think he's going to get you for Valentine's Day?"

Ez nearly stumbled as they turned the corner. Had he saved the jewelry for Valentine's Day? "I thought we'd get ice cream or something."

"Didn't he already give you a gift for your anniversary?" Celia let go of Esmerelda's arm, and they were separate beings again. "Tickets to that stupid play, yeah?"

"Yeah."

"So why wouldn't he get you something for Valentine's Day?"

Esmerelda looked at her. "I don't..." *I don't have any money.* But Celia had to know what it was like. Winter was tough on everybody. Gavin's house needed a new roof, and that cement step was crumbling. He wouldn't get her two presents in one month, would he? Except, either way she was already behind. "Shit."

Celia veered across the street. "Let's go shopping."

"No, I-" Ez stopped in the middle of the slushy road. She tried again but could not admit that this time of year was hand-me-downs and scraping by.

Tilting her head, Celia studied Ez from head to toe. "In that case, what about a makeover?"

"How is that a present?"

Celia's smile grew into something dangerous, and Ez had to admit she was intrigued. "A sexy photo shoot. The present being the pictures."

A car turned onto the street, and Celia guided Ez back to the sidewalk. There, Celia's grin met Esmerelda's reservations, because how sexy was Celia thinking exactly? Very, if one could judge by the look on her face. Esmerelda focused on what it might feel like—naughty enough for her skin to go electric, but not naughty enough she'd find herself in any serious predicament—and when she thought about it long enough to overcome her reservations, she grinned wide. "I could send them in the morning. A Happy Valentine's text."

Celia linked arms with her again. A reward, Ez thought, for the right answer.

Without discussion, their pace quickened, then quickened again, until they were racing up Celia's front steps, laughter carrying down the street. Exploding inside, they charged up to Celia's room and collapsed on her bed.

It felt good to really laugh with someone, hysterically and for no reason at all. Ez vowed not to stop until Celia did, and when they were quiet, on their backs gazing up at the ceiling, the smiles on their faces lingered as proof it actually happened. Ez wasn't about to ruin that either, but Celia sat up.

"I'm going to gather some things. You stay here and work on your sexy face." She pointed to her dresser, a forgotten antique almost as beautiful as Gwen's.

Ez scooted off the white bedspread and sat in Celia's chair. Celia didn't have her makeup spread out on her dresser like Gwen did, but she had an earring tree, which Esmerelda spun as Celia's footsteps stomped down the stairs.

She could take a pair Celia never wore and hide them in her underwear drawer, by her lists. Setting her fingertips on a pair of small hoops, however, the thrill did not thrum in her chest. If she wanted that, she'd have to take one of Celia's favorites.

With a glance to the hallway and Celia's open bedroom door, Ez snatched a pair of rose gold studs with a rougher, rockier face. Slipping them into her backpack's smallest, most secret pocket, she turned on her sexy face in the mirror. When Celia slipped back into the room, she dumped a pile of randomness on her bed and turned to Ez with hands on her hips.

"A fur coat?" Ez asked, eyeing the pile.

"If you're going to be wearing nearly nothing, don't you want a fabulous coat to hide the goods with?"

"I'm going to be wearing nearly nothing?" Esmerelda swallowed. Her throat was dry. She needed a drink of water.

Celia began picking things out. "An old pair of booty

shorts my mom won't let me wear anymore. Her fanciest bra—we can stuff it if we need to. Her sexiest lingerie—maybe a little too weird. Or," Celia turned on Ez with a raised eyebrow. "What are you wearing under all that? Better he knows it's your stuff, as long as it's not grandma panties."

Folding her arms over her stomach, Ez willed the electric buzz back. She was not confident enough to strip for Celia and stand in front of her to be judged without it.

Celia plopped down on her bed. "Not up for it?" She delivered this casually, but Ez was no idiot—she heard the bottom line: *We're friends if you're exciting.*

Esmerelda assumed hair and makeup would happen first, but maybe she needed to sit in Celia's chair and get comfortable almost nude. Maybe *being* that girl would make her so.

Quickly, she undressed—sweater, jeans, shirt, socks—and with Celia's nod of approval, Ez stared at herself in the mirror while Celia turned her flat iron on.

* * *

Esmerelda woke the next morning and scrolled through the pictures on her phone.

OCD to the rescue, for her bra and panties always matched. The peacock blue was faded but looked amazing under Celia's mom's white fur coat.

Why she owned a white fur coat? Celia had rolled her

152

eyes. "In case there's ever a gala."

A pair of cream heels, and in the few pictures they dared without a bra, a long necklace from Celia's collection, drawing down the expanse of Ez's bare torso. The fur covered her nipples, of course. Celia was super on top of keeping it tasteful, and Ez had ended up loving every second of it.

Choosing her favorite few, she attached them to a text: *A secret gift, from your Valentine.*

Propped low on her unmade bed, she tapped her heels into the frame and stared at her phone, waiting for Gavin's response. The anticipation was worth it, the beating of her heart and the airy quality of her gut—floating and morphing and squeezing and bouncy.

She ignored a few other notifications, caring only about the ellipses that would tell her he was typing a reply.

Her bedroom door flew open with a bang, and she startled, dropping her phone to the floor.

"What the hell is this you're tagged in?" Betta asked, phone outstretched in her hand, one of the shots Ez had *not* sent Gavin blown up on the screen.

Ez picked up her cell which was quickly accumulating more notifications, but no reply from her boyfriend.

Celia had taken them on Esmerelda's phone. No one else had access. Unless, if Celia texted them to herself while Ez was changing, she could have deleted the text from Esmerelda's phone so she wouldn't notice until it was too late.

Blinking through tears, Ez clicked on the first notification: *Celia Walker tagged you in a post.* A post titled: My bff is the hottest. Agree or disagree?

That, and a ton of likes, plus new friend requests from boys in her class and even some sophomores and juniors.

Tears brimming, Ez scrolled through:

Agree.

Agree.

Agree.

Meh.

No one is hotter than you, Celia.

Agree.

Disagree—you're the hottest.

Agree.

Give me some of that.

Give me some of that? Ew. Her stomach turned and Ez swallowed hard to bite back tears. It didn't work.

All in a hot minute, too. Like everyone woke up and checked Celia's social media first thing in the morning. As if the entire town waited around for her to do something.

Betta snatched Esmerelda's phone out of her hands. "Are you that stupid?" she asked.

Ez wiped her cheeks, the perfect makeup from last night surely running in black, blue, and gold streams. "How was I supposed to know?"

"How were you supposed to know taking pictures of yourself, unless you want them plastered online forever, was stupid?"

Her phone rang. Esmerelda reached for it, but Betta hid it behind her back. "You do not get this back until I talk to Mom and Dad."

"No! Please! It wasn't like that!"

"You're grounded. For at least today. I don't even-" Betta shook her head. "Until I figure out what to do about this." Betta left the room, slamming the door behind her, and Ez slid off her bed, hands to her face.

She and Gavin had plans. What would Betta say if he showed up at the front door? She was a loose cannon, more than the rest of them, and clearly pissed.

Scrambling for her Christmas tablet, Ez pulled up her apps. She tried to ignore how many more agrees and disagrees there were, and especially the I'D DO HER, HOOK US UP in all caps—a demand as if Celia were a pimp. Ez wanted to scream as she fumbled over the touch screen to get to messages.

Esmerelda: They were supposed to only be for you. I'm so sorry. I'm grounded and I ruined Valentine's Day. My sister saw and she took my phone and I suck it's all my fault I'm sorry.

She bit her lip and gnawed on her nails and pinched the skin on her wrist because she made a terrible mistake and that's how long it took him to respond. She knew he was there and the app told her he was typing, but then he wasn't, and there was nothing, and then he was typing and then not and still nothing.

Of course, no one in this situation would know what to say. She'd ruined their day, and he probably hated her, and he was trying to figure out how to break up with her via social media.

Gavin: You're beautiful. The most.

Then: Happy Valentine's Day.

I'm sorry Celia sucks.

You should be careful with her.

Have I not told you that?

Esmerelda flopped backward against her soft, cozy, unmade bedding, and breathed a quarter sigh of relief.

God, how she needed a half-smile from him right now. That might actually make her feel better, but she sure as hell couldn't ask him to send her a picture of his face. He might think she wanted more, something in kind, and she'd be mortified if he thought that for even one second. Or sent something gross, which would totally ruin everything.

She should be basking in his words—*you're beautiful, the most.* Instead, she felt tarnished and dirty—*I'd do her, give me some of that.*

Covering her ears and rolling over with a groan, she realized how stupid she actually was, if Betta only knew. Here, while Ez thought she finally had the upper hand, the in and the skills to play the game, Celia successfully orchestrated what Esmerelda was to be in high school. To top it all off, Gavin was giving her a play-by-play of the conversation he was concurrently having with Celia. Because of course she swooped in, talons ready and outstretched, aiming to sink them deep into his heart.

What do you have planned for Ez today?

Oh, no! She's grounded?

You need some company then?

What a total, despicable bitch. A little seed of pure hate nestled deep into Esmerelda's heart. She nursed it. It would make her stronger, and it would make her smart.

Hopefully, it might even make her dangerous.

* * *

It was Valentine's Day, Gage had indeed not shown, and Gwen was drunk.

She sat at the townie bar of townie bars on Main Street, which her friend's family owned. Sara was an only child, so there was no one else to inherit and no one else to help.

This, Gwen felt, would be even worse than how she had it.

"You better slow down, Gwennie." Dana, the other bartender and her other friend, set a hand on Gwen's wine glass. "That's almost an entire bottle you've gone through."

All winter, Gwen had been too stressed to lose control, and too busy, and hadn't really wanted to take her anxiety out for a stroll. Now she was ready to celebrate—finally she'd found some space to breathe—and they were giving her a hard time.

Sara made a funny face, likely a reaction to the sour one Gwen was giving them both. "Get David," she muttered to Dana, hand on the tap as she refilled a glass. "Have him bring her home."

"David's here?" Gwen perked up and scanned the bar. He'd been Sara's on again/off again high school boyfriend, but he adored Gwen. A veritable puppy dog, one of the many who'd followed Gwen around back then.

Gwen didn't do puppy dogs. She liked the ones who stood on two feet and met her confidence with their own. But no one minded being adored.

Dana swung around the bend of the bar, and when she came back with David, he met Gwen's grin with his own. He held himself differently, shoulders back and chest proud, smile almost arrogant. Not much of a pup anymore. Gwen was impressed.

He opened his arms to her, and she stood to meet his hug, appreciating his checkered button-down shirt and slick pants more than she cared to admit. He looked completely out of place in a way that sparked her itch. She'd been trying to drown it in alcohol, but it was there, and she squeezed him extra hard for it.

Splitting, they sat on neighboring stools.

"Gwen Aaldenberg." He tapped the neck of his beer bottle to her wine glass. "How in the hell are you?"

Gwen could not answer truthfully, so she asked instead, "How are you? How long's it been?"

"Too long. Which is all the more obvious after reacquainting myself with your lovely visage."

Gwen snorted, a real snort, thanks to the wine, and covered her nose with a hand. "Wow, city spiffed you up, huh?"

A smirk and a shrug, past confident and on to cocky. The city must be treating him well.

Sara rolled her eyes and elbowed Dana. Dana waved a hand in front of David's face. "Can you run her home?"

Except she wasn't going home. She was going to the inn.

By herself. Lonely and alone. To celebrate. The key was hard in her pocket, a reminder of what she planned to do, what she couldn't do, what she wanted so badly to do.

Her phone vibrated against her chair, and she pulled it out to see if it was Gage. It was.

It was?

He wasn't here, though, so she ignored it.

David tipped his beer bottle to his lips. "Important as always, I see."

"David," Sara snapped. "Can you bring her home please?"

"I'm not ready yet," Gwen said. "But I do plan to drink enough that I'll likely require an escort home."

David let out a huge laugh, but with a glance to Sara, sighed and stood. "If you want an escort, I'm afraid it's going to have to be now." He put a hand out for her, and she stared at it. "Can't piss off the ex-girlfriend if I want to stay welcome at her bar."

"Go, Gwennie, please?" Sara asked.

Gwen looked to Dana. "Am I really that bad?"

"Honey, you just undid three buttons on your blouse."

Gwen looked down. She could see cleavage, because of her vantage, but doubted anyone else could. Not really. "I'm hot," she said, unbuttoning another. There, now they all knew what she wanted.

"You're hot because you're drunk," David said, helping her up. "And for other genetic reasons." He gingerly redid her bottom button, and she stumbled into him, pushing her hair back off her face. Now that she stood, she did feel awfully uneasy. And a little sick to her stomach. David grabbed her purse and guided her out to his car.

Oh, much easier to lean against him. Yes, that was better.

She told herself he wasn't holding her up while they stood at the curb and he unlocked the door. That his hands weren't out and waiting to catch her as she slid into the seat.

"Oooh. New car smell," she muttered, running both hands along the sleek leather, back and forth and back and forth.

Her buzz and the sexy car and Valentine's Day. Where the hell was Gage? She deserved to celebrate. To *celebrate* celebrate, she no longer even cared where. In David's car even, down at the far, far end of North Beach Street where the sand gave way to a tall, grassy field.

"Oh!" she cried as David pulled away from the curb. "I'm staying at the inn tonight."

He raised an eyebrow and drove her home instead, even though she kept insisting. She pulled out her room key, she could've walked actually, why was she in his car? Giving up, she rested her cheek against the headrest and watched him in the light. Bright, then not, then bright, then not, as they passed the street lamps.

She'd always liked David, and she was sick of playing it safe.

She didn't get out when he pulled up across the street from her house, because she was considering running a finger up his thigh. He'd kiss her. She knew he would.

If her father could play around with Mae, why couldn't she play around with David?

Not that she knew for sure what was happening with Mae, but David wasn't the type to kiss and tell, either.

Better yet, she would run the room key up his thigh, he'd know what that meant; she wouldn't have to say it. He adored her, and he'd adore her in bed, and he was comfortable. A perfect first if your boyfriend was going to ditch you on the night you'd planned, someone who suddenly had swag and arrogance and the sexy vibe of city all over him and his car even. She deserved a celebration and she would get it, one way or another. God, she was hot. Fingers on her button, David stopping her, his hand closing around hers.

"That your boyfriend?" he asked.

Gwen peered over him, and sure as shit, Gage sat on their front steps, flipping a small box around and around in his fingers.

Why was he sitting outside? Their house was never locked. Wasn't someone home?

He tried to call.

Shit.

Gwen scrambled out, using the hood of the car for balance and nearly tripping across the street. As Gage noticed her, he caught the box in his hand.

A jewelry box.

He always wrapped the jewelry boxes. This one wasn't wrapped, and she was completely toasted.

She touched her neck. Undone buttons. Quickly, she did them up, smoothed her blouse, and cleared her throat.

David's footsteps behind her. "Your purse, Gwennie."

She turned. Took it. Clutched it to her chest. "Thanks for the ride, David. If you're heading back, you can tell Sara and Dana I'm home safe."

David stuffed his hands in his pockets and crossed the street slower than molasses. What the hell was he waiting for? Her boyfriend was here, she didn't need him, *go, little puppy, go*.

When she turned back to Gage, the box was gone.

"Are you drunk?" he asked.

She waved it off. "I wanted to celebrate, I told you."

"Who was that?"

"Sara's boyfriend." A little lie wouldn't hurt. It wasn't what it looked like anyway. David wasn't her type. "What'd you have in your hand before?"

"Not important."

Gwen knelt in front of him, the concrete cold through her black pants. "It is important. Please don't let me ruin anything."

He studied her for a long moment, then pushed her hair behind her ear. "I almost left."

"I'm so sorry." She put her palms to his knees. "I had no idea. I would've waited had I known."

"Waited to get drunk?" He laughed a little. "I didn't know if I'd make it or not. They called it a night at seven, and I have to be back by ten tomorrow morning."

He wasn't mad. It wasn't the state of her that bothered him. With a grin, Gwen stood and offered a hand. "So we celebrate?"

"Will you remember this in the morning?"

"I'm not that drunk," she lied, because she could still see, and hear, and touch. Touch was the most important part, she could touch.

He stood up into her, catching her arms as she stumbled back, then lowered himself to one knee. Gwen's head cleared the rest of the way. In the light of her porch, in front of the picturesque Aaldenberg home, with the lightest, most delicate glow of the moon above them, Gage took her hand and gazed up at her.

"With me working so much, I didn't want to waste any more time. I also wanted you to know, without a doubt, that it will never be like this again. You mean so much to me, even if it might not always feel that way, because, well, because of work." He ran his thumb along her skin. "Our busy times do not coincide, which is unfortunate, but we'll fix that, okay? If you marry me, we'll fix that." He squeezed her hand. "Gwen. I love you. Please be my wife."

She nodded and cried and told him about the room and handed him the key, and asked him to take her right there, on the steps, she didn't care. He said things she couldn't understand, but she got that the steps weren't a good idea, and he nearly carried her to the car and she was so, so ready that she unbuttoned the rest of herself on the way, which meant he had to rebutton her to get her inside. The suite was beautiful and huge and she lay on the bed, soft and fluffy, and she tossed the pillows and spread out and for goodness sake, the damn buttons, they were so hard to get undone and with fingers on the last, she took a break, she was so tired, and Gage was in the bathroom anyway.

Probably he was too much of a gentlemen to have sex with her in such a state, knowing it was her first time, but it didn't matter, because at that point, she fell asleep.

* * *

What pissed Esmerelda off the most was that she couldn't look at the pictures, even though she totally loved them, because when she looked at them, she realized she never had a chance. All she'd been to Celia was a bee to keep the tip of her toe on, just in case.

Well, Celia's plan backfired, to some extent, because Ez had never wanted to sting someone more.

She didn't know if Celia had tried to call or text her because Betta had her phone, but Celia couldn't have cared too much, or she would've stopped by. At least Ez knew Celia hadn't spent Valentine's Day with Gavin, like she tried so desperately to do, because he spent it chatting with Ez. Thank God for tablets.

What Celia did do was smile at her in the halls that next Monday, as if they were still friends and the weekend hadn't changed anything. *Of course I shared them*, Ez overheard her saying, *why wouldn't I show off my best friend?*

Best friend. Now, finally, after utter humiliation. Was that what made a best friend in Celia's mind? Complete control? Maybe.

Ez stared a little too long at what she'd begun to think of as her table. She'd hung back to wait for Gavin instead of hurrying to get in the lunch line with Georgia, and all the girls were seated, one spot open and saved next to Celia.

She'd earned a saved spot right where she wanted, and all it took was complete and utter annihilation.

"Sit by me," Gavin said from behind her.

Yeah. That would be good. Following him, she didn't dare look at Celia as they passed, lest she be swayed by the crown on her head.

"Ez!" Celia cried, once they'd sat. Gavin blocked her view, but Celia came over, hands on her hips. "What are you doing?"

"Nothing." Esmerelda cut her hot dog, starting in the middle, then each half in two, and in two again.

"I saved you a seat."

"No, thanks."

"Are you mad at me?" Celia must have been standing directly behind her; Ez could feel the heat of her body on her back.

"I am," Gavin interjected, twisting on the seat to face her. Ez forked one-eighth of her hot dog. No ketchup. Ketchup was messy.

"Beauty is meant to be spread around."

"I'm not yours to spread," Ez snapped.

"So you are mad."

"More like, beyond pissed."

The boys at the table muttered out some jokes and snickers, one low whistle, and hopes for a girl fight on their table—*in fur coats and nothing else*. Gavin shot that kid a look, and he quickly shut it, but it was said.

That's what she was now, to the entire school—a bra and panties in a white fur coat. Those pictures let each of them

165

feel like they owned her, like she was theirs, in their room, for their sake alone with which to do or say anything they wanted.

With one arm over her chest, fingers clutching her opposite shoulder, she shoveled hot dog into her mouth as fast as she could. Thank God she'd cut it in pieces and wasn't trying to eat it whole—imagine the commentary then.

"You can't be for real," Celia said. "Look at me."

One hot dog was enough to get her through the day. It was lodged in her throat, but it was sustenance. Standing, she exposed her chest to grip her lunch tray with both hands and stepped over the bench as if Celia wasn't there.

"So, you're done then." It wasn't a question, but a statement: *you are done then. I will end you.*

Ez didn't care. She *was* done. The only thrill she was after now was the thrill of revenge.

Stupid? Maybe. But no one could say she wasn't a quick learner. And no one could say she didn't have enough fuel.

MARCH

Wanda felt a bit better since she heard about the proposal. She meant to talk to Gwen about an engagement party, but was trying to figure the right time, considering finances were usually tight in March.

Unless Gwen turned things around. It was possible. Gwen did have a magic touch.

It was *for* Gwen too, so Wanda hoped the spending would go down a little easier, not get her yelled at like it had back in the fall.

Anyway, Wanda hadn't thought it pertinent enough to get out of bed and find her. Perhaps she'd start by mentioning it to Betta, who'd brought her baked macaroni and cheese with, what was that—lobster? Wanda sat up a little straighter.

"What is this?" she asked.

Betta flipped through the latest book they were reading, trying to find where they'd left off. "Mac and cheese."

"With lobster."

"Yes."

Betta hated lobsters. She'd eat any fish on the planet and

many strange sea creatures, but she would not fight a lobster into a pot. And this was fresh lobster, Wanda could tell. "Who made this?"

Betta looked at her curiously. "Mae."

"Mae?" Wanda snapped.

"Yes."

"Not you?"

"You thought I was making all this?"

With Wanda's affirmative nod, Betta let out a large laugh. "I burn toast."

"This isn't on her menu."

"Word in town is that you have some crazy flu, so she's been bringing us food."

Wanda was well aware Mae did not have a husband, and she was well aware how miserable she was making hers. He sat in bed with her and watched TV on Valentine's Day, for goodness sake. They'd eaten casserole on TV trays—*had Mae made their Valentine's Day casserole?* "Every night?"

Betta found the spot and stuck her finger between the pages. "Maybe four nights a week."

Wanda set the bowl on her night table and meditated on this for a minute, then swung her legs over the side of the bed and headed to the bathroom.

"You're not going to eat it?" Betta asked.

"Does she sit at our table with my husband?"

"Mom." Betta's intonation suggested Wanda was being silly.

She peeked out from the bathroom. "They dated in high school, you know."

"This is *Dad* we're talking about," Betta said. "He's as likely to do something sketch as Gwen."

Wanda showered, blow-dried her hair, did her make-up, and on second thought, pulled her most expensive heels out of the back corner of the closet, all while Betta sat in the chair next to that godforsaken mac and cheese.

"Wow, Mom." Betta closed the book and crossed her arms over it. "You look… alive."

"What month is it?" Wanda asked.

"March."

With a nod, she stomped into the hall. She hated March. There was nothing that could make her get out of bed in March. Nothing but her husband's ex-girlfriend trying to take her place.

Wanda would throw the biggest engagement party for Gwen this town had ever seen. Proof to that little tart this was *her* sparkly family, and there wasn't a damn thing she could do about it.

* * *

Christine was waiting for Esmerelda before gym. Swimming made it hard to talk as much, and the team sports kept them busy and apart. That's how Ez spun it in her head anyway, rather than that Ez had flat out been ignoring her.

Ez slipped past her into the locker room. Christine hadn't commented on the pictures, but no doubt she'd seen them.

Everyone had. The looks she got in the halls—impressed to disgusted to approving to creepy—well, now she knew what people thought of her.

Except Christine. She didn't know what Christine thought of her. She was harder to read than everyone else. Maybe she thought Ez was behind it, or, at the very least, okay with them being plastered online. Maybe some people did think that, the less observant ones who hadn't noticed Ez was no longer sitting at Celia's lunch table.

Probably didn't do much for her reputation to now be sitting at a table of boys.

Shrugging out of her tee and into her gym shirt, Ez finally allowed a glance in Christine's direction.

"What happened, Ez?" she asked. "Did I do something wrong?"

Christine was her own person, and Ez had been trying to fit into a mold; that's what happened. That's what was wrong. Ez sighed. "You were right about Celia."

Christine collected her hair into a pony. "She put those pics up without you knowing, then?"

They fell into step together, following the crowd to the gym. "Yeah."

Ez didn't regret them—they'd forced her into a corner where she could no longer care what people thought about her. Or maybe it no longer mattered since it wasn't anything she could, at this point, affect or change.

Not after those pictures.

All she could do was put her head down and move on. Celia thought she'd broken her, thought she was grooming a workhorse, tame and domesticated, but really she'd made her stronger, more wild. And she'd cut her free.

That was when Ez remembered the earrings, tucked in her backpack in her locker. Esmerelda would put those earrings on as soon as she could, and she would march around school with them. She would march around town. She would never take them off.

"She's a total bastard," Christine said.

"She really is. I'll never doubt you again."

At Christine's smile, Ez felt everything skew back to normal. No more wondering what Christine thought, she knew Ez better than that.

She knew Ez better than that?

Huh. She kind of did.

As they lined up to count off for teams, Ez snuck a person between them, so they could be together again.

* * *

Gwen stood at the front foyer window of the event hall. Her engagement ring spun a dizzying array of spots on the floor. She felt ill.

Her mom scurried about behind her, arguing with the event planner about details she insisted she'd explained clearly. It was a rush job, and Gwen wondered if you had to pay more for that.

She put a hand to her stomach.

The engagement party was in full swing, but she needed a moment. Space to breathe. Then a van pulled up and a group of guys spilled out, musicians judging by the one with a guitar.

Gwen had thought the equipment in the corner was from someone before, or for someone after. She figured live music cost a lot, and she'd told her mom, *nothing that costs a lot.*

Her dad's hand landed hard on her shoulder. "Gage is about to do a toast, honey."

She should be at her fiancé's side for a toast, but all she could think of was, "Where are we getting all this money?"

"We've pulled in some favors, Gwen. It's okay."

He'd fed her that same sentiment before. "I said no band." They came in rowdy, nearly skidding past, a burst of noise in the quiet front hall.

"Gage pitched in too. We wanted a night you wouldn't forget."

Knowing her mother, the wedding would have to top the engagement party, which a year ago, Gwen would've been all over. It was how she'd planned it honestly, but now she only wanted it done. Easy. Simple. She could see more clearly what she needed now, and it wasn't much. Quality over quantity, value-added over pomp and circumstance.

Now, the fabulous she used to crave only stirred her nausea. Regardless, she would put one foot in front of the other and take her spot next to Gage and smile like she was expected to. Like she should.

When had the *shoulds* stopped feeling safe? When had they started strangling her?

Focusing on her heel clicks, she made her way past the

many guests milling around cocktail tables, up to where Gage stood on the platform. With a squeeze to her hand, he tapped the mic. The room applauded in cheers, but he shushed them with his hands. She hoped she wasn't expected to say something next, because she wasn't sure she could orient her brain toward any toast-worthy thoughts. Not while money was being spent so unnecessarily in front of her.

Dana handed her a fresh glass of champagne with a wink. So there was that—she and Sara were bartending, and they'd do it for free, for her. Maybe her dad was right. Maybe this night wasn't setting them back again.

"Thanks for coming, everyone," Gage started. "You've truly made this a special night. Thank you for welcoming me with open arms." He glanced over at her and cleared his throat. "It's been especially important to me, not only because I want to be part of Gwen's family, but because I want to be a part of your lovely town too." A huge, satisfied smile spread across his face, and he thrust his glass up for a toast.

Wait. She put a hand on his arm. He was speaking metaphorically, right? He went back to the mic, this time speaking to her instead of the room, glass still in the air. "I'm moving. Next month."

"You're moving where exactly?" she asked, close enough to the microphone that her words echoed around the room. She shrunk at the tone of them.

"Here," he whispered, with a small, secure smile, before looking back out at the crowd and trying again, "To permanent residence!"

Nearby, Betta coughed, sputtering out a light spray of

water. Van lifted his glass. "To Gage and Gwen!" he cried, breaking the suspension of everyone's disbelief.

"To Gage and Gwen!" the room chorused.

Gwen could not. She simply could not. Nearly tripping on the raised platform, she caught herself on the nearest table, tugging its tablecloth enough to knock over a glass or two. Water and champagne and white wine.

She was disoriented. Lost. Confused.

Reaching the back hall, she spun in a circle, held her hand to her stomach, and forced her heaving breath to slow before she hyperventilated.

Gage appeared.

"What kind of game are you playing?" she asked, through the sweat and the heat and the suffocation.

"What do you mean?"

"You're moving here?"

He grinned, pleased with himself. "Fantastic, right?"

"No! We're supposed to live in the city!"

"You didn't like me working so much. You wanted more of me. You complained about my job-"

"My being there would've been more of you!"

He frowned, but she didn't care. Hadn't she said? Well, maybe she never *said* said, but she for sure said, 'I'll move with you to the city.' He said, 'Either way works.' So no, she hadn't said 'I'm moving to the city with you for fucks sake I can't stay here I'll die,' but also, he'd never said, 'I really love it here, can we stay please, please, pretty please?'

"This will be better than the city, Gwen, I promise. The pace of life, especially for a family. Tax season won't kill me like it did this year. It won't kill *us*."

Gwen's anger cracked, and a desperate sadness welled through. Her eyes filled, and she wiped them violently.

Gage's frown deepened. "I don't understand. You were making all those excuses to stay."

"Excuses?" she echoed.

"Having to stay for Betta's sake? I mean, come on, she's a big girl. Then needing to get the store through the winter, like you were afraid to tell me you didn't want to leave, like you thought I'd care, which is silly. You know I've always loved it here. All you had to do was ask."

"I did all that so I wouldn't have to come back." Her hand fluttered to her chest. She patted it there and walked in a circle. "I'm trapped here, Gage. You are trapping me."

"That seems a bit melodramatic."

"Did you grow up here?" she yelled. "Do you know?"

"Shh." He stepped in toward her, moved to grab her hand but didn't connect. "You can still hand off the store to Betta. Or don't, but you won't have to make a dime—you won't need to worry about it hemorrhaging money. Trust me, I thought of everything."

Except for her. He'd thought of everything except her. She blinked and stood taller. "Take it back."

"I put in my notice and sublet my apartment. We can't have what we want there."

"*You* can't have what you want there, maybe, but I for sure can't have what I want here."

"Frank hired me already. My work load will be half of what it was, and that's full time to him. A normal schedule—

a normal life, Gwen."

Her nails dug into her palms, and she tightened her fists. She wanted to punch his lights out.

He crossed his arms. "Can't we talk about this?"

"Oh!" She laughed, rather hysterically. "Can't we?"

"Gwen, please. You really don't know what it's like. I worked through Valentine's weekend, didn't sleep so I could be here like you wanted me to, didn't sleep so I could propose. What happens when we have kids and they're sick, and you're sick, and you need me, and your parents aren't there to help, and mine are in Maine for the summer?"

"There are people you can hire in the city."

"No." He shook his head. "It's not what you think it is. You have to trust me."

"I did." She stared at him with everything she had left in her, which was nothing. No warmth, no hope, no light.

"If you only trust me when things are easy," he whispered, his words tight, "then we aren't going to get very far."

Betta swung around the corner, hand on the wall as she looked back and forth between them, likely trying to gauge the situation.

The situation was that Gwen thought she picked a man who wanted to buy her fancy shoes and bring her somewhere to wear them, when really he wanted what he wanted and could make a convincing argument to himself about how that was what she wanted too.

They were a unit now, she and Gage, and if he was determined to stay here, then she should too. She should want it, she should listen to him—more than listen, she should believe him. It was what couples did for each other, believed in each other, sacrificed for each other, trusted each other. It felt like that was only going one way right now though, and the thought of those shoulds had her blood boiling.

She knew her face was twisted. She tried not to look at him so he wouldn't think it was about him, even if it was about what he'd done. He must have got the point though, because he strode down the hall and brushed past Betta, back to the party.

Betta walked toward her. "What's going on? You okay?"

Her sister, of all people, should know what was going on. The fact that she didn't, that she might actually think Gwen was on board with this, meant Betta really believed Gwen wanted the store, that she'd take the one thing everyone knew Betta had always wanted. What a shit sister she'd be if she did that; what a shit sister Betta must think her.

"I am very much not okay," she admitted.

"Want me to sneak you out of here?"

Gwen bit her lip. Hard. "I can't. Can I?"

Betta shrugged. "You probably shouldn't."

With a visible, disgusted shake, Gwen marched forward. "Then let's go get a drink." Or as many as it took to pretend the night had gone in a different direction. The way *she'd* planned. The way she'd wanted.

Whether or not she should get wasted drunk for all of town to see, she no longer cared.

* * *

As Betta sat in that ballroom, listening to the aftermath of whispers when Gwen rushed out of the room, all her hopes and dreams imploded in her gut.

There was no other choice now but to walk away from everything she'd planned and start over. And in whatever she decided, she would move forward confident and sure.

She admired that about Brennan, how it came off even in his stance as he informed her about the sale of the house going through. He'd caught her at the start of the engagement party, excited to let her know it was final. She hadn't been able to look at him after Gage's announcement, of course, because she felt like a liar.

She wanted what he had—to know what she was doing, to have plans she made happen, to know she'd done good things. Not quiet things like usher people to death or through darkness, but tangible things.

All of this she chewed on, working it out for days, until she found herself standing on the sidewalk in front of his offices.

With as much fortitude as she could muster, she pushed open the large glass door with the kind of surety and confidence he would, only to find him standing at the unmanned reception desk rifling through some paperwork.

Okay, so she thought she'd have a little more time to compose herself. *Stand tall, Betta. Pull it together.*

He glanced up and smiled. "Morning, Betta."

"Good morning, Brennan." She stood unsteadily before him, rocking a bit on her heels, and folded her hands in front of her to keep them still. Having dressed the part, she was in a pencil skirt and one of Gwen's blouses, hair twisted into a bun. "I'd like to work for you. Free as an intern if that's all you have."

He blinked, his only show of surprise—because she was an Aaldenberg, and in this town, Aaldenbergs did one thing. Only, of this generation there were too many, and Van already had the sense to branch out. He was learning something new, *doing* something new, but still doing it here, still something for the town with roots deep and important. Yes, of course she might like to work for Brennan. He shouldn't be surprised.

"I could use a hand, yeah." His smile still held one corner of his mouth. "That why you're all dressed up?"

Betta looked down at her outfit, feeling a bit silly now that he pointed it out. Reaching behind her, she let her hair down, running a hand through a few times to loosen it up. He was in slacks, but no jacket and no tie. For some reason, she'd thought he wore a suit to work every day.

"We're pretty casual around here," he said, smile lifting further. "Forward-thinking, too. You only have to wear a skirt if you're comfortable in it. Otherwise, pants will do." He moved toward the back offices, stopping to turn when she didn't follow. "Well, come on. I'll show you around."

* * *

Best Gwen could tell, there was no financial trace of her

engagement party anywhere near the store's finances, so she'd gone ahead with the inventory order as planned. The first one she'd allowed in the calendar year, and the shelves were nearly bare for it.

Up side was they'd be easy to wipe down, clean as new, in the next few weeks while the products rolled in. Then, come April—the very slow beginning of tourist season—the place would look not only stocked, but spotless, as if it hadn't been through hell and back.

So, for a third attempt, Gwen was going out to celebrate. The first attempt being the night Gage proposed, and the second being the night he ripped the rug out from under her. Both, she now realized, had been dependent on his cooperation. This time, for better odds, she took him out of the equation. He was not invited. It was tax season anyway; she was sure he wouldn't have been able to make it.

Gwen tipped her glass toward Dana, implying she wanted another—no wine this time, the harder for Dana to judge how much she had, and if she needed to stop.

"Already paid for," her friend said with raised eyebrow, sliding her another Moscow Mule and nodding to where David sat.

She could read Dana's eyebrows very well after the last twenty years, but Gwen didn't see what it mattered that their friend's ex-boyfriend bought her a drink. Sara and David were as old of news as she and James—not that Betta and James hadn't pinched a bit—but it didn't matter, Gwen was engaged. Anyway, she couldn't help it if David still had a thing for her.

"Back again so soon?" she asked as he stood to join her.

"Unfortunately, yes."

"Problems at home?"

"Just birthdays."

His chestnut-tinted blond hair was brushed back in a swoop, and he smoothed it as he set an elbow on the wood. "You only look better, every time I see you."

Gwen rolled her eyes. "You're my friend's ex-boyfriend, David. Don't get any ideas." Except, as she said it, she got enough for both of them.

Okay, maybe Dana's eyebrows were telling Gwen to be careful, that she was already drunk and might not be in the state to make good decisions. Maybe they'd been a warning: *be careful.* Not that Gwen saw what being careful had to do with anything. It hadn't prevented any of the last year from happening, so maybe careful and good were just as overrated as should.

David smirked. "Not 'I'm engaged, don't get any ideas?'"

"He's moving here in a couple weeks."

"That's rich, Gwennie. You getting hitched to a local."

"He's not a local."

Snickering, he nodded. "He is now."

Gwen frowned into her glass, then downed it. She stared at him, and he motioned Dana to bring another before sitting down next to her. The city had definitely changed him, sanding his awkward corners smooth and sharpening his soft, dopey look to something hard and sexy. He gazed at her as if he had the upper hand, arrogant in a way he'd never dared be in high school, all of which made him more alluring. She shouldn't care though. She shouldn't have noticed. She shouldn't think the aura of Boston on him was anything special.

Fuck *should*, though. That was her new motto.

They caught up on the years between then and now, reminiscing through a few more drinks. At that point, Gwen couldn't see what it would hurt, getting a little taste of the city she'd so desperately been waiting for. A few years older, he was a freshly minted big city lawyer sure to do big things, judging by his brain and what it accomplished in high school. If Gage refused to help her out, well, maybe David was a better fit anyway. He always wanted out too, they shared that.

When he asked her to come back to the inn he was staying at for a nightcap—they had a pretty sweet set-up, a whole bar right next to the TV in his room—she figured one more drink couldn't hurt. Even if it led to a little heavy petting.

Gage hadn't given her one thought throughout the many steps he'd taken to plan his move, so she wasn't going to give him a thought now.

A one-night stand didn't count if it were an old friend, right?

It's not like they were married yet.

As the door closed behind her, she realized she'd never imagined David the type to do this—to so easily ask a woman back to his room.

Was there anything else a nightcap in a transient hotel room might mean? She laughed. Oh, how people changed.

"Something funny?" he asked from the tiny bar.

Gwen dropped her purse on the floor. "Have you turned into a dog, David?" Not that she cared; she wasn't marrying him. Stepping backward toward the bed, she squinted. The wallpaper was fuzzy. Confirmation she didn't need another drink. What she did need was celebration, long overdue. Or better yet, *satiation*. Unbuttoning her blouse, she watched his face as he followed her fingers.

Setting the glass and tiny bottle of alcohol down, he walked forward, matched her button for button. "I can bring something to the table, if that's what you mean." Said as if *she* could, and had always been able to. He must assume she wasn't a virgin. Then again, some people had different definitions of virgin, so okay. Regardless, she wasn't going to complain if he had enough experience to make her first time memorable, considering she was cheating on her fiancé.

Her fingers faltered.

This should be Gage. She should be sober.

On the plus side, David was comfortable. He was steamy, delicious, and new. But old, too—new and old—this mix of who he'd become and the puppy she'd known.

Okay, but she was doing this. She'd accepted the invitation, and her blouse was gaping open. Her breath was slowing, deepening, shameless, rather than the panicked gasps that told her she was in the wrong place, doing the wrong thing.

"You're sure about this?" he asked, sliding out of his shirt.

She sat on the end of the bed and splayed her fingers against his stomach. If he was a dog now, he was a polite one. She smiled, and he leaned down to kiss her.

Insistent. Demanding. Sure.

And that was all her.

David lifted her from her armpits to slide her further onto the bed, then slid himself on top of her. She went for her pant zipper, but he caught her hand, moved it above her head, and held it there as he kissed softly down the length of her side.

Thinking of her, not himself; taking his time, not rushing his pleasure. If he was a dog, this was what had them coming back for more. She supposed she should enjoy it.

There was nothing not to enjoy, but for her impatience— the itch turned insistence that she could no longer rein in.

He moved slow and smooth, so smooth she barely noticed the condom—perhaps he'd gotten it on when she was overwhelmed by the skin, all at once both of them bare. Her insistence in that moment screamed along her epidermis, so much she would've missed Gage walking into the room.

As such, she should have considered it karma that her phone started buzzing at the same time she did—a barrage of cell phone intrusions while David was inside her.

"Want me to grab that?" he asked, a whisper in her ear.

"No. Never. Leave it."

It needled at her, though, keeping up a nearly constant distraction while the mess of jazzed wire David had found inside her vibrated and sung and then calmed to shuddered shakes. As he collapsed on top of her, she reached over to turn it off, her finger lingering on the button, because could she black out that in such a rapturous minute, Gage called three times and texted twice?

"The fiancé?" David asked. When she didn't answer, he

added, "You probably shouldn't call him back naked in my hotel room."

"Is that you kicking me out?" Gwen's eyes narrowed as she pushed David off her, his watch clinking on the nightstand as he stretched out on his back.

Naked but for jewelry. Her engagement ring—she twisted the diamond in to her palm—and her second locket, along with the diamond earrings her mom bought her for her eighteenth birthday. She squeezed out this fact of her mom and Gage in bed with them, and focused on David's watch instead, remembering how the cold metal of it brushed her skin during. Yes, focus on the now. She did not want to face reality yet. She wanted to stay here, with David and his watch.

"Not kicking you out." He turned on his side and slid a palm over her thigh. "Do what you need to do."

What she needed to do was celebrate. She needed to be free, or at least feel like she could be. Gage had proven piss-poor at that, so she turned her phone off and reached for his wrist.

Unlatching the watch, she put it on herself and snuggled in.

She didn't know how long she would stay, or at what dark hour of the night she would pick up her shame and walk out, but for now, she was cozy. David had delivered, and she wanted to sit in that for a bit, wanted to sit in the person he saw her as, the one she'd been before life happened, the one she wanted so desperately back into that she'd do anything for it.

Anything, like sleeping with someone who knew her only as a memory.

APRIL

"Why are you in running shorts?" Wanda asked as she scrubbed the empty store shelf next to her husband. It had bothered her all morning, but they'd started on opposite ends of the store, where Gwen had put them.

All hands on deck lately, to shine the store new before shipments were ripped into and displayed. The first boxes sat in the back room on steel storage racks, which the family plus Gavin had spit-shined last week before their arrival.

"Because I plan to run later," Harvey answered.

Wanda did a double-take. Yes, he looked serious, and yes, up close, the shorts looked even more like sausage casings. "You're going to *run?*"

"I need something now that I'm nearly retired."

"Now that you're nearly retired?" she echoed. "This is solely because of excess free time?"

"What else would you think it about?" His arm was deep in a shelf, and he wouldn't look at her. "Come with if you want."

Wanda thought that was a rather weak invite. "What about

our walks?"

"Running isn't going to stop me from walking."

What Wanda heard, though, was having Mae isn't going to stop me from having you.

If he was even having Mae. Wanda shouldn't jump to conclusions. Perhaps Mae was simply being a good neighbor. Perhaps Harvey wanted to lose weight for some other reason.

Leaving her towel and spray bottle, she checked the time and wound through the aisles until she found Gwen—blonde hair up in a pony, getting dirty in a blouse and slacks. She was the only one technically punched in, and the type who was going to look the part no matter what the task.

"I'm going to get us lunch," Wanda informed.

Gwen straightened to wipe her forehead with the back of her arm, exposed because her sleeves were rolled up. "Betta packed us sandwiches."

"Then I'll grab drinks."

"We sell drinks here." Gwen slid an arm and shoulder back between the shelves to scrub some more, then added, "Cheaper drinks."

"Cookies. We deserve cookies."

"The store isn't paying for cookies."

Wanda put her hands up. "Fine. I'll buy my family some cookies."

"I closed our account over there," Gwen called after her.

In that case, she'd have to swing by the office for her purse. That was fine. It would give her more time to think of what to say. She'd start with a thank you, of course, but how far would she take it? How close need she get to root out whether Mae had been cooking for her neighbor or her ex-boyfriend?

Walking past Harvey on her way out, she refused to look at him or his sausage shorts.

As Wanda pulled open the door to the sandwich shop, the bell dinged to announce her arrival. And Mae, from behind the counter, had the gall to cry out, for everyone to hear, "Hi Wanda! So glad you're feeling better!"

The woman sounded like a wind-up toy wound up too tight, not like she meant it. Clutching her purse strap, Wanda gave her a tight-lipped smile and waited in line. It was long, always during mealtimes. Winter wasn't as rough on Mae as it was on Wanda.

"What can I get you?" Mae asked once they were face to face, the counter between them.

"A half dozen white chocolate Craisin cookies." Wanda pulled her wallet out and counted exact change. Mae took the money while the youngest Samuelson girl gathered them from the bakery case. "Also, I wanted to thank you, Mae, for the food this winter."

"Anytime, Wanda." Mae handed her the receipt. "Harvey came in for food so often it was clear something was going on—you being such a good cook and all."

Wanda shook her head, both at the receipt and Mae's confession. Harvey came in so often, and now he was running?

"Do you run, Mae?" Wanda asked, remembering she had in high school, and she had when her husband died. Wanda hadn't seen her chasing the streets in awhile, but then again,

Wanda had been in bed.

"I'm training for a 5k, actually."

Wanda nearly choked on her own spit. She'd come in here to assuage her suspicions, not—well, not to verify them. "I must repay you somehow," she decided. "Could I take you out for coffee?"

Mae laughed. "I get too much of that already!"

Stuffing her wallet back in her purse, Wanda tried again, "A drink then? I'd really like to show my gratitude." A drink might loosen her tongue, get her to slip up if there was something to slip up.

"Completely unnecessary." Mae's eyes skipped to the next person in line while Girl Samuelson handed Wanda her bag of cookies. "What can I help you with, Sally?"

Wanda clutched the bag and didn't move. "Lunch then? You must eat."

Mae studied her for a moment.

"I won't take no for an answer."

Mae nodded, "Okay," then went back to her line, effectively shutting Wanda out.

If that's what she was trying to do in her marriage, she had another think coming. Wanda was awake now, and she would weasel her way back in, if that's what it took.

Harvey was her husband. He'd built a life with her. Mae had her chance; she'd made her choices. Now, she best back off.

* * *

Betta's job was mostly filing papers and taking calls, sometimes catching meetings that had been erroneously scheduled concurrently in the one conference room, and she'd taken it upon herself to reorganize the reception area.

Come to find out, the front desk at Mas Properties was generally staffed with teachers during the summer and empty during the school year. Thus the backlog of filing and reorganization that was easily filling her days.

Brennan asked her opinion on the town and its developments, more and more until his lunches often had them in the ancient, dry leather armchairs that sat by the front window—lunches which could stretch for up to two hours if they really got into it. The history of the stone library and how anyone could consider tearing it down, the massive new condos going up across the highway, the restoration of the quaint movie theater in the face of the big multiplex being built halfway between town and the next coastal tourist hub.

As if her insight was worth hearing. And she never felt like an afterthought, not even when the other employees walked in—the realtor on staff, the lawyer and accountant, even the designer Brennan consulted with on occasion. They all greeted her at the reception desk to ask what they'd missed. Like she was the one who'd know. And she did, actually.

It was a nice change, compared to how she'd been shuffled to the side at the store, and she often found herself smiling into it.

Now even, as she oiled the leather armchairs with a conditioner she'd picked up at the furniture store a few blocks down. She must look like an idiot grinning out at the sea.

Then again, who didn't grin at the sea like an idiot?

She glanced over as the door opened, and Brennan walked in. He tossed a set of keys on her desk. "What are you doing?"

"Oiling your chairs."

"We have oil for chairs?"

"They needed it." She finished the last spot and flipped the cap shut. "Desperately."

"You took money out of petty cash?"

"Of course not. It wasn't on the list of reasonable expenditures." She'd used her first paycheck. It had been years since she'd gotten paid, for real, and twenty five dollars seemed far worth what she was getting in return.

"Make sure you put the receipt in the box and take out what it cost, okay?"

She shrugged. "Okay."

"Okay. So." He nodded at the keys sitting on her desk. "You're heading up this reno, yeah?"

"This... what?"

"The saltbox by your store?"

She slid the leather conditioner and the rag in the cabinet behind her desk. She'd bring the rag home to wash it, then tuck it back in the closet by the cleaning supplies where she found it. "Heading up the renovations?"

He winked. "Let's see what you can do, huh?"

"Brennan, I'm just a secretary." To prove it, she sat in her chair. Behind the desk. In reception.

"You're not just anything, Betta." He tapped a finger on the corner of the desk as he moved past it. "Let's see how great you'd be in the development world."

She spun her chair to face him. "I haven't proven myself yet."

"This is how you do that." He stood in the narrow hall beyond reception. "You know the town, you believe in what we do here, and you have great insight. All those conversations we've had, they were me picking your brain to see if you were ready. If it goes well, there'll be a full-time job waiting for you when you're done."

The fact there wouldn't be a full-time job for her at the store hung over them, a hazy mist.

"Tell me that's not why," she muttered, almost hoping he didn't hear. Yet she needed to know.

"Tell you what's not why?" he asked, meeting her mutter with his lower rumble—she'd noticed it replaced his more polished tenor when he was unsure, when he was being careful.

Forcing herself to look him in his eyes, she elaborated, "Tell me you're not doing this because you feel sorry for me—because of the store and my sister."

"Honestly, I've thought of it as your house since that day on the street. If you don't like the process, or if I don't like what you do with it, well, part-time reception will still pay its rent. Otherwise, I've always wanted a designer in house. Madeline refuses me every time—she likes those big city homes and the money they can throw at her more than she likes what we do here. I'm guessing you'd feel the opposite. So even if you like that part of it…"

"I have no design experience."

He motioned around the foyer. More than rearranging,

she'd added books on the tables, brought a plant in that was too big for her room—it had been transplanted from Pops' apartment—and unrolled a rug she found in the storage closet. Everything was clean and clear, yet still homey and comforting. He'd complimented her on it in the middle of a deep conversation about the town's pier situation the other day (he thought they should be redone; Betta felt they illustrated so much, piecemealed together as they were.)

Betta held herself still for a moment, as she faced this new life on a platter that he was offering her. A house, a career—at Mas Properties there wasn't one spot, but many. As many as you wanted. As many as you could make happen.

She could take it all the way. She could quit the store and move out, be her own person. As long as she could stomach the fact that it would feel like quitting her family.

Her family. Betta checked her watch and cringed. "I said I was going to cut out a little early today?" As if that didn't look awful on the heels of such a conversation.

"Right." He cleared his throat. "Of course, go."

"I'm so sorry, Brennan, I know it looks terrible. Gwen's got the whole family working to get the store ready for the season-"

He put a hand up. "You're not a slacker, Betta, I know. Honestly, go."

"I'll research over the weekend what to do with the house." She stood to gather her things, and he stepped back so she could get around the desk.

"You don't have to make up for it."

"Oh, no, because I want to. Why wait to get started?"

Brennan crossed his arms with a chuckle. "I'll pencil you in, then, my first meeting Monday morning."

"Perfect!" She shrugged into her parka and hopped to the door. Flashing him a smile and a wave, she pushed through to the world outside. Her world. The one she was taking over.

* * *

Gwen couldn't believe Esmerelda made it to the store before Betta did. What the hell did Betta have to do all day?

"Where've you been?" she demanded, rushing up to meet her sister the moment she stepped through the door.

Betta raised an eyebrow, her liner moving with it. "I have a job, okay?" She slid past her down the center aisle for the office. Gwen hurried after her.

"I said everyone was needed today. Gage-" Every time she said his name, her gut punched her in the throat. She'd forced herself to answer his calls, at least half the time—the times she wasn't thinking of David's hands on her. Gage's hands had been on her too, she needed to remember.

Thank God she hadn't had to face him yet, not in person. Tomorrow, though... how could she be normal with him after what she'd done? This was something she hadn't considered. But she had to be normal; she had no choice. "Gage is moving tomorrow, and I have way too much to do before tourist season to help him as it is. Had you actually been here all day, maybe I could've taken some time off tomorrow night to go see his place."

Hanging her purse on a coat hook, Betta turned to face her. "I'm sorry, Gwen. I'll work for you tomorrow and tomorrow night."

"Is that my blouse?" It looked good with jeans, actually. Maybe she could start wearing jeans to work and still look like she ran the place.

Betta looked down and smoothed it. "Yeah. Sorry. I only grabbed the ones in the very back of your closet I didn't remember you wearing."

Gwen waved her hand. "It's fine. It looks better on you." Then it hit her. "Wait. You really have a job?"

"I don't work weekends, so I can still help out during tourist season, and tomorrow."

"I don't want your help tomorrow." What did that mean, though? If Betta had another job and Gwen wasn't moving to the city... She put a hand to her throat. "You'll quit though, right? Of course you will."

"Why would I quit?"

"To take over the store."

"But you have the store."

"I don't want it."

"Yes, you do. You've been saying all winter you do."

"How can you, of all people, think I want this goddamn store?"

They stared at each other. So that was loud. Probably everyone heard it. Gwen closed her eyes and walked to the office door. She didn't have to look. She didn't have to look to do anything here, that was part of the problem—rote motion got old. Closing it, shutting the two of them up in the office, Gwen turned to rest her back against it and decided it was time. "The store will be yours."

Betta only blinked. God, what was she going to do if Betta didn't want it anymore? Had she shot herself in the foot? Van was through his apprenticeship and a full time electrician, Ez had three more years of school. Could Gwen do this for three more years?

She slid to the floor, focusing on Betta's heeled boots as she explained, "You were exhausted. The store… the finances were a mess. Mom and Dad, they spend before they have it. I mean, hopefully not anymore, I've cut them off so at least the store's safe. Then there were all these other expenses, and I didn't want you to have to come into that after the last few years with Pops. Not to mention, you didn't make the situation any easier the way you handled his bills. I figured I had enough time to fix things, then you'd be recuperated and ready, and I could leave, move to the city and know everything was okay here. That I wasn't abandoning you and leaving you to deal with all this shit alone that was my responsibility, as the first-born."

Betta opened her mouth to speak a few times as it all sank in. Gwen imagined that looking back, a girl as smart as her sister could easily connect the dots. Finally, Betta sank to Gwen's level, settling on her knees. "Why is Gage moving then?"

Gwen let out a bitter laugh. "He convinced himself it's what I really wanted. That all this was me making excuses because I didn't want to leave. He's talked himself into this town as a better choice—a better way of life."

"Shit, Gwennie." Betta breathed out a heavy almost-whistle, and Gwen read understanding there—Betta could see how his actions might be a deal-breaker, and Gwen wanted to sob with relief that finally someone might get it. Everyone else thought love should win out, what was the big deal?

The big deal was Gwen's heart was breaking. Maybe she loved the city more than she loved Gage. Or maybe she loved herself more than she loved Gage. Was that so awful to admit? It might mean there was a better match for her, or it might mean she was healthier than everyone who thought love should trump all. Call her selfish, fine. Different life philosophy was how she chose to look at it.

"Bets, please tell me you'll take this store. I was only trying to get you to June, when the money would be flowing and you could save it for the winter—you have to save it, you can't spend it. Summer pays for the entire year. Do you understand me? Mom and Dad were always behind. The bank loans them money every year to get around it, but please be smarter. Be frugal this summer, always save, and you'll be set for life."

Betta looked pained, but she nodded. It was enough for Gwen. She would take scraps; she would take barely. It's what she'd been living on anyway.

"I'll work for you tomorrow," Betta said. "I'll do all the things you were going to do. Leave me a list. You should be with Gage."

The thought of helping Gage move in made her tear up. She bit down hard on her tongue so she wouldn't lose it.

Betta squeezed her hand, and Gwen composed herself. "I'd rather you help him for me, to be honest."

* * *

It was a beautiful April morning as Betta wrenched open the cab door and hopped into the moving truck. Almost as if the world agreed Gage belonged in town.

Gwen was inside getting ready for work. Betta had listened to her side of the phone call. She'd told Gage that because Betta was now working all week—not completely true, as it was part-time—she couldn't make her work all day Saturday too—also not completely true, because Betta didn't feel like the store was much work. Without giving him any time to respond, Gwen then offered Betta to stand in for her and help him unload. Plus, she'd asked Van and her dad to swing by at some point too.

"Congrats on the new job," Gage said, staring past Betta to the house where Gwen hid.

"Thanks." She glanced over at him, at his subsequent frown. He pursed his lips together in a way that pulled his broad chin apart from his smooth cheeks, and Betta wondered what he'd look like if he ever let himself get a little messy. A little hairy. A little rough.

They rumbled over the streets, past the lovely chocolate saltbox and up the climb into the neighborhoods further from the ocean. He turned at their old church, the steeple white and glossy amidst the green flowerets of the trees behind it.

He'd picked the small apartment complex Betta and James used to pretend they'd live in together someday, and she braced herself for the pang she knew would come when they pulled into the parking lot. On one of their anniversaries, he'd driven her there and they'd sat in his car, decorating the place and making plans.

James called her once, after he left, but it was too soon to answer. She'd still been raw and sore. After, he began sending her notes on California weather, and she told him about her new job. In the last text she received, he asked if it were really over between them. Betta hadn't replied.

It had to be over, if he was there and she was here, yet she couldn't set that into type. Couldn't commit.

"You really don't think she's going to show?" Gage asked as he turned off the shuddering giant box they were inside.

Betta shook her head, grabbed his keychain from the cup holder, whipped open the door, and headed for the apartment.

After propping the doors open with rocks, she met him at the back of the truck. He wrestled with the hinge, and she helped him heft the door up, putting her hands on her hips as he surveyed the contents.

"Three college buddies helped me load it."

"I can do the work of three college buddies."

Gage's eyebrows drew neatly together as he studied her head to toe, and she flipped up the collar of her charcoal chambray shirt. It wouldn't stay because she always left the top few buttons open, but nonetheless she felt it meant business.

"How soon till Van gets here?" he asked.

She shoved at him, the way she might shove her brother, and he snickered. They pulled down the ramp, and Betta climbed up first, sliding a box off the closest column and stalking past him.

"You're so fancy," she teased, the first time they slid by each other, him with a box, her with empty arms heading to grab another.

"Fancy?"

"An apartment of your very own." Turning around, she set a hand to her chest. "Most of us can only dream."

At the next pass, his eyebrows furrowed. "What do you mean?"

"Rent's not cheap, Gage. You must be bringing in some serious money."

"I'm an accountant. I do okay."

A few passes later, he still wore a frown. She stopped in front of him. "I was teasing."

"Maybe, but you're not wrong."

"Well, what other choice did you have? You move in with us, and my mom hovers over you twenty-four seven."

His other choice was staying in Boston, but neither of them said it.

"What's your new job?" he asked, a bit later.

They'd stuck to a good rhythm, catching each other at the door to open it wider when the other needed it.

"You know the local developer?" There were signs on the way into town plastered with his motto: *Building a bustling tourist haven while ensuring the integrity of our past.* "I'm reception, and I'm starting a reno."

"A reno?"

"A renovation. He's letting me lead one on an old house I love. We'll see. If I'm awful..." If she was awful, she was back to the store.

She wanted it, of course. She was supposed to want it; she'd always wanted it. Yet when Gwen told her it was hers the night before, her insides hadn't reacted the way she thought they might. No relief. No excitement. No *finally*.

She was in the middle of figuring something else out, something she was excited about. Enthused. Her brain churned with ideas, her fingers itched to get access to the internet, to start planning and brainstorming. Everywhere she looked she was inspired.

But the store.

But the house.

If Betta wanted a chance at that house, she couldn't pass up the project. That's how she'd explained it to Gwen. They stayed up late, talking and working their way through a glass of wine like business partners or adults—like friends. All of what Betta held in her head, what she'd been so sure Gwen thought of her, and where Betta placed herself in relation to her sister, it all seemed silly after last night.

The whole time Gwen had been trying to save her, keep her safe, give her a minute to breathe. So now that's what Betta was doing. Helping Gage so Gwen could have a minute to breathe.

Both of them were at an impasse, straddling a before and

an after.

Gage stood in the doorway so she couldn't pass. "What if you're awful?"

Betta shrugged. "Gwen and I will figure it out."

He squinted a little, a wince almost, and she realized too late that he and Gwen had more to figure out than she and Gwen did. "What do you want more?" she asked. "Gwen or a slower life?"

He stared at her, blank.

Yeah, life was a bitch. Always making you choose between the people you loved and the life you needed to live for your soul's sake. She sighed it out, all the heaviness of the conversation and Gwen's absence, which was hanging over them.

"Listen," he said, forcibly light-hearted. "You've been putting all the office boxes in the master and all the master boxes in the office."

"No, that is most definitely the office." Betta pushed past him through white space after white space and into the white hall, stopping at the doorway of what she was certain should be his bedroom. "All the trees here will block the sun in the morning and keep it private at night for, well, never mind." She set the box down and pushed him out of the way, leading him to the second bedroom. "The sunshine here—wouldn't you prefer to work with natural light and sleep in the shade of the pine trees?"

He let out a grunt. She wasn't sure what that meant.

"Otherwise, you're trying to sleep in but it's too bright, and you're trying to work but it's too depressing. Dark isn't depressing in a bedroom—it's relaxing. Dark in an office is depressing. And-"

"Okay, okay." He threw his hands up. "Honestly, you had me at 'well, never mind.'"

She blushed. At least on the inside. "Let's take a break, wait for Van and Dad before we do the furniture."

"I'll get the small stuff, you take a break."

Betta took that as a challenge though, and soon they were rushing back and forth, keeping a tally of who brought how many pieces in—if it was awkward, it counted for two, or maybe they should base it on how many pounds...

Gage was trying to wrestle a rather foreboding dresser on his own when Van showed up. He hoisted himself up without the ramp, took one look, and laughed along with his sister.

"You two better be careful, or I'm banning you from the wedding."

Betta opened her mouth, but before she could remind him of their current score—she was winning—Gage and Van were yelling at her to keep an eye out, that they didn't hit anything with the bedposts.

* * *

Gwen was locking up the store when her phone rang.

She'd expected Gage to call all day. Of course he was preoccupied, busy moving, but she figured when he got to town, or when they stopped for lunch, or because she wasn't there and should be.

Frowning, she snaked her phone from her back pocket, then stood in the dark store, alone, watching David's name scroll across her phone.

Did he call all his women? It probably made him come across as the sensitive type. Gwen wondered if this was on purpose, or a vestige of who he'd been, leftovers from a more romantic version of himself he couldn't kick.

Even so, she wanted to hear his voice, wanted to close her eyes and pretend they were back in that hotel room. A few moments with him would wash her mind clean. In fact, his body on hers had taken her mind completely out of the equation, and though there was guilt, so much that she'd sent her sister to her fiancé in her place, there wasn't exactly regret.

Ignore.

She couldn't entertain anything more with David until she faced Gage, and she might as well rip that Band-Aid off. He hadn't called her, but she hadn't called him either, and he knew what time the store closed. If she didn't go to him, what more would that say?

Too much more, when she should be saying it herself.

Out the back door, she headed up the back alley to the street. As she climbed the hill, passing homes she knew by heart, Gwen recited the names of everyone who'd lived in them in chronological order. In the quiet of almost-tourist season, with the sun at half mast, Gwen peered into the windows as if she were peering into souls, mining her memory for their secrets.

They all had them; it was about time she did too.

Perhaps she'd known, subconsciously, that after David she couldn't go back to Gage. That she'd have to tell him, and that it would force them apart. Unless Gage forgave her. Did she want him to forgive her?

He opened the door to his apartment seconds after she knocked, and Gwen read relief in his eyes. Throwing herself at him, she pressed her cheek to his chest, the force of her movement propelling them both inside.

Betta cleared her throat. She stood a foot away. "We were heading to Shelby's, because, have you seen Gage's library?"

Gage shoved her shoulder like Van would, if she were teasing their brother. "It's a collection," he said.

"No. It's a library. You have a *reference* section." Betta fished three novels out of her purse. "Look, Gwen. I've already checked some books out."

Gwen stepped back from Gage and scanned the living room, then the kitchen which was in view over the half wall. Furniture in place, only a few boxes on the counter, and books already unpacked. "Wow."

"Yeah." Gage put his hands to his hips. "We got a lot done."

Without you, is what she heard him say. "Sorry I had to work."

He shrugged. "I get it. I've been there."

She eyed him. Because did he? Could that be what he really thought? Not that she was avoiding him?

"Well, I'm gonna go to Shelby's," Betta said. "You two are staying here?"

Gwen nodded and Gage smiled at her. "Thanks, Bets. I owe you."

"Not a problem."

"Really, pizza or something, I promise." He turned to Gwen. "I was going to feed her dinner, after all that."

"After Mom and Mae's spread, I couldn't eat anyway."

"Mom and Mae?" Gwen asked.

"They were at lunch or something. Mom told her we were moving Gage in, and Mae insisted they bring us nourishment—that's what she kept saying, 'nourishment.'"

"Was Dad here?"

"Yeah. He didn't stop to eat, though. Thought he was going to have a heart attack how fast he moved today."

Or, Gwen thought, because his wife and mistress showed up together, not to mention *after having lunch*. Staring between her fiancé and sister, Gwen fumbled for the couch to hold herself up. *She* had a wife and mistress. She'd scorned her father all winter, and now here she was.

Gage's hand slid over her neck. "You okay?"

She nodded. "I'll see you at home, Betta."

"You can stay here tonight," Gage said. "I'd thought you'd stay here now."

Betta slipped out as Gwen was hit with the innuendo in Gage's words.

She was to sleep there. They were to sleep together.

Could she? Maybe she should try. Maybe being with the person she should have been with in the first place, no matter how angry she was at him for tying himself to this town, maybe it would right things again. Maybe if they were the kind of intimate she'd been with David, maybe they'd be even, and things would feel normal again.

Stepping forward, she placed her fingers on the waistband of his jeans and unbuttoned his pants.

"Gwen." He said her name in a new way—a warning, a chiding rejection—and ricocheted away from her onto the tiled squares leading from the front door to the kitchen.

"I know." She scrambled after him. "I should've been here today."

"Yeah. You should've." Back to her, he filled a glass with water at the kitchen sink. He chugged it, then set it down. "You've been avoiding me—*lying* in order to avoid me. There's no way Betta wouldn't have worked for you today. Or your brother. Your dad. Your mom. Ez!"

She pointed at him. "You made *life-altering* decisions without me!"

They stared at each other. She should say the rest of it, too. Right now while they were confessing, before they made up and it was too late. *I cheated on you. I slept with someone else. You thought you'd be my first, but nope. That's not what you get when you piss me off.*

She bent over, hands to her knees. She had been awful. That was awful. How childish of her. How short-sighted.

"I'm sorry," he finally said. "You're right. I'm sorry."

She looked up.

"I want to start over," he whispered. "Let's try starting over."

How, when she'd done what she'd done?

"I'm here and you're here, and for now that's all that

208

matters."

"Meaning we ignore Boston and try it your way?"

"If it doesn't work, we'll, well, we'll worry about that then."

If they started over, then David didn't matter. It was worth a try.

She slid closer to Gage and set a palm on his chest. Her nails looked nothing like they used to when she took care of them. Chipped and torn, they were different jagged lengths. She curled them into her palm, unable to face the proof of her unraveling. "I love you, Gage."

"I love you, too." He moved his hands to her sides, palms flat and unsure. She'd taught him to be unsure. She'd instructed him to be cautious.

Stripping her shirt over her head, she stared into his eyes as she unclasped her bra. Only, as soon as his hands were on her, his mouth too, like it was coming home, she felt what she'd done.

She felt as if she were someone else's, when she should've been his.

Covering her chest, she blinked through tears. "I'm sorry," she muttered. "I'm sorry, I can't."

"It's okay, we can slow down. I'm in no hurry." All while she spun and searched—for her clothes, for her courage, for her soul.

Once dressed, she blotted her face with the back of her hand. "I slept with someone else."

She forced herself to watch him absorb this. The pursing of his lips, the jut of his chin, the furrow of his brow. "What do you mean?"

Right. Because he couldn't comprehend it, not of her. No one would comprehend it of her.

"I mean I had sex with someone else. And I'm moving to the city." There. It was out. All of it. She didn't feel better.

He stumbled past her and sat down on the couch. "Was this on Valentine's Day? That guy? Before my proposal?"

"No, Gage, of course not." She sat down next to him, but he slid away from her. Tears pricked her eyes, and she clutched tight to her knees.

"Are you moving to Boston with him?"

"He has nothing to do with Boston. It was a stupid one-night stand. I'm so sorry. I don't deserve you." In those words, she realized it was true. She didn't deserve him. He'd been patient and careful with her, making sure to do everything right because that's what she wanted. Thoughtful, sensitive, taking all the cues except the one—the big one, the one that mattered—and she betrayed him. He never would've betrayed her.

Regardless, she didn't want this life and she didn't want this town, and if all that desire and desperation had her making awful decisions, then she'd move along and get to where she wanted on her own.

"Does he live in Boston?" Gage's attention was on his hands, clutched white-knuckled between his knees.

"It doesn't matter, I'm not moving to the city for him. I'm moving to the city for myself."

He blinked. Opened his mouth. Shut it. Clutched his head in his hands, elbows to his thighs. "I shouldn't be surprised."

"Shouldn't be surprised I slept with someone else?" She scoffed, slightly offended.

He dropped his head to look at her. "Your first time? Really? A one-night stand?"

Gwen stiffened. "An old friend, not a stranger."

"Doesn't make it better," he muttered.

"I didn't come here to be judged."

"No, just to break off our engagement."

"Unless you want to move back to the city."

He laughed, but it was high and painful. "I sure as hell do not."

"Shouldn't be surprised what?" she pressed. If there was an insult here, she wanted to know it, whatever he could throw at her. It was what she deserved, and it would make her feel better. Plus, if he was going to be nasty while she was in the middle of being broken, then she could hold that against him later, when the regret seeped in.

"How I didn't see this coming. You've been weird for months."

"I tried, Gage."

He snorted. "Tried what, Gwen? I don't see how you've tried much at all."

"Tried to come to terms with staying. I'm sorry you gave up your life-"

"I didn't give up anything." He looked at her. "Moving here was me picking my life."

"Moving here was you picking yourself," she snapped, blinking so the tears would stay put. "Picking what you wanted, when if you would have searched your soul, you would've known it wasn't what I wanted."

"And the fucking someone else? What was that?" He stood and walked to the door with a clip. "Goodbye, Gwen."

His jaw was set and his hair messy, long sleeve t-shirt shoved up to his elbows. She seldom saw him in a t-shirt, and it made him look vulnerable. She loved him and she would miss him and there was no hope of going back, not now that she'd told him.

Not that she wanted to go back, but why did it have to end like this? Why had she chosen something that left them no choices?

She couldn't beg him to not hate her either. Because facing him, the truth propped up between them like a mirror, she saw into the ugly space she created for herself, and she hated her, too.

MAY

"Richard Jacobson is perfect for you, Mae," Wanda twirled the landline cord around her finger as Harvey got up from bed to storm into the bathroom.

Was it that he didn't like Wanda having lunch dates and things to do, or that he didn't like her spending time with Mae?

"Remember at lunch, how he kept inching his chair closer to our table? That was for you."

Mae laughed. "He's ten years older than me."

"Ten years is nothing at our age. Plus, he has a full head of hair—all the old ladies are chasing after a fistful of that."

"Are you calling us old ladies, Wanda?"

"Yes, there's no point in denying it any longer. Want to get coffee this afternoon?"

"Only if Richard won't be there."

"Oh, no. I'll set you up for this weekend. Coffee will be just the two of us."

"Sure, sounds good."

Hanging up, Wanda tried to ignore Harvey's looming

presence in the bathroom door.

Nope, not possible.

"Going for a run?" she asked innocently.

"Yes," he growled, sitting on the bed to put his socks on. Maybe it was that he didn't like running as much as he thought. Then again, it was the same mood he'd been in when Wanda arrived, Mae in tow, at Gage's new place last Saturday. He'd conversed in grunts and hadn't stopped to eat with the rest of them. Ignored them both, really.

Well, too bad for him. She hadn't liked whatever the hell it was they'd been doing, and now it was her turn. Besides, her lunch with Mae had been rather delightful. Both of them agreed they should have done it a long time ago.

It was fresh air to have someone to commiserate with, instead of only a husband who told her how she should be thinking about a situation. "We've been caught up in the kids and the store for so long; I forgot how nice it is to have a friend."

"So nice," Harvey muttered as he stood. And without a glance in her direction, he strode out of the room and down the stairs.

* * *

Ez was hungry. She was always hungry after she and Gavin made out. Maybe it was the time of day—hours after school and dinner looming on the horizon—or maybe it was that she wanted more, wanted to fill herself, didn't want to stop.

It was what they did, though. They made out and then they stopped.

Gavin followed her into the kitchen but didn't move toward the pantry as usual. "Hey Ez?" he asked, palms flat on the butcher block island.

"Yeah?" She'd been here every afternoon for six months. She could get her own chips.

"I've been thinking..." Looking down, he rubbed his finger along the wood grain.

It was unlike him to not make eye contact, to not be brave. What would embarrass him so much that he wouldn't meet her eye? She ripped open a fresh bag of chips and set it in front of him. He wouldn't ask her to sleep with him over a snack, would he? Yes, of course he would. If anyone was going to be straight up about it, it would be Gavin, and they'd slid by their six month anniversary without any more progression. Ez had thought about what came next—not sex, of course—but if she were thinking about it, he must be too. He was fifteen-years-old and male.

"It's okay, Gavin," she said. She was ready for something. Shirts off maybe, or his hand somewhere else, her hand... both their hands...

Ez kicked at one of the wheels on the small island. She got it now; it was hard to look someone in the eye when you were thinking of doing things to them. Private things you'd barely read or heard about.

"You're feeling the same way?" he asked.

"Feeling the same way about what?" she asked, because he

might also have an idea for revenge on Celia. Ez was happy wearing her stolen earrings for now, but he knew she'd been thinking about it, that it was impossible not to when she got at least a comment a week, offers for private photo shoots or *let me see a little more, huh?*

"A little space. A break."

Ez leaned toward him, sure she'd heard him wrong, but leaning toward him meant leaning into the island, too far, and it slid his way. "*What?*"

Gavin stepped back from the assault. "You know, break up for a bit."

She glared at him. "For a bit? Are you kidding me?"

He shrugged.

"How long have you been thinking this?" She checked the time on the microwave. "Seven minutes ago your fingers were on my nipples!"

He frowned. "That's harsh."

"Yes, it is!" she agreed. "So tell me what this is about!"

"Maybe for the summer, you know, make sure we miss each other, that we're right for each other."

Esmerelda laughed. She laughed and she laughed, because otherwise she'd start crying and hell if she'd do that in front of him. For the summer. Of course. She should've known. All the afternoons and Saturdays, all the talks of life and futures and school and Celia and Christine and what it was like being an Aaldenberg, working the store, dissecting Van's football career—which she'd entertained completely for his sake—and he'd never liked her enough to keep her over the summer.

She should have known. She was no more important than any other girl, no more important than Christine, who he'd dated all of eighth grade, dumped for the summer, and crawled back to at the start of freshman year.

Same story.

Spitting the rest of her laughter out, bitter as it was in her mouth, she set her face with narrowed eyes. "You'd rather be some city girl's vacation treat?"

"Come on. It could be fate, you know, like your sister and Gage. What if I'm with you and miss that opportunity? What if you're with me, and you miss yours?"

"Your *fate?*" She let out the longest, most exasperated *ugh* that she could muster.

He squirmed. At least she'd managed to make him squirm, cool and straight-forward that he always was.

"I'm sorry," he whispered, studying his stupid lobster socks.

She stared at him for a long time, wondering what to do and fighting the sadness that was welling up inside her. From her knees, to her waist, and if she didn't get out soon, it would be coming out of her eyes.

How much time did she have? Could she talk him out of it? Could she beg him to love her?

He'd never worked that way, though. If there was one thing Gavin didn't do, it was waver. What he decided was what he decided.

Anyway, Ez was pissed. If he wanted to break up with her, why had he mumbled to her an hour ago that her lips drove him crazy? A person didn't do that to another person.

Well, apparently they did.

"Screw you, Gavin," she seethed, throwing the open bag of chips at his face. Shoving the island toward him for good measure—it didn't get to him, but felt satisfying nonetheless—she spun toward the front hall, swept up her backpack, and stomped out of his house, pausing for a moment on the porch to compose herself. She wouldn't give Celia the satisfaction, if she were home and looking out a window, to see Ez upset, wonder what was going on, and throw herself at Gavin in the name of comfort.

Actually, she should. She should text Celia right now and act like a jealous ex-girlfriend, like Celia was why they broke up. Whatever happened would hopefully give them both a little just dessert. It might be Esmerelda's last chance to use him for revenge, which she no longer felt so bad about doing.

Ez: Thanks a lot, Celia. Your plan all along?

Ce: What are you talking about?

Ez: Gavin broke up with me. How'd you weasel your way in?

Ce: Oh, no! I'm so sorry! That's awful!

Esmerelda snorted. So. Fake.

Ez: I'm sure you are. I'm sure you're sorry while you're running over to his house to comfort him.

Ce: I'm not even home.

For good measure, Esmerelda planted some seeds: *Fine, so you're sending pictures to cheer him up? Same thing.*

Ce: Ugh, you're still mad about those?

A little water to help them grow: *If they're not a big deal, why haven't you put up any of yourself?*

Ce: Maybe I will.

Sunlight so they bloomed: *Maybe you know they won't be as good as mine.*

Ce: Oh, they'll be as good as yours. They'll be better.

Esmerelda hoped they were. If it meant she wasn't the only one with sexy pictures being circulated around the school, she'd be happy for it. She hoped Celia made a total fool out of herself with Gavin. She hoped Celia cried.

As for Esmerelda, she raced her tears the rest of the way home and straight to Gwen's room; she didn't care who saw her, and she didn't care which cracks she stepped on. Dropping to the soft, shaggy rug next to Gwen's bed, she cried her eyeballs out until her cheek was nearly stuck to the fibers.

When her sobs slowed and she wiped her eyes, she noticed the locket lying forgotten under Gwen's bed: discarded, uncared for, and lost.

It reminded her why she used to come here, into this room—to take some of the magic that was Gwen and sprinkle it on herself, a shield against the world. And here, on her worst day, the locket that should be hers. No more sprinkling; she would douse herself with it, hide it under her sweaters for awhile, but what did Gwen care? It was on the floor, deserted the way Ez was deserted. More proof it was meant for her.

Her fingers closed on the chain, and as she pulled her arm out from under the bed, she felt stronger, more deserving. Gavin was an idiot to do this to her. Everyone wanted a piece of Esmerelda after those photos. Not necessarily the types of pieces she wanted to give, but there had to be one or two in the mess who'd like her for who she was, who could see past the object Celia had presented.

Standing up, chest out, Ez strung the locket around her neck and marched out of the room, feeling both broken open and newly armed.

It felt like a dangerous combination.

* * *

A few weeks after Gwen broke up with Gage, he walked into Shelby's.

Betta went herself most days after work. Flooded with ideas for the house, she'd rest back on the familiar couch, close her eyes, and sort through them with better focus than she could at her desk.

She hadn't forgotten Gage's massive pile of books and was working through the three she'd borrowed. In fact, every time she opened one, she thought about how he needed the bookstore in his life. Still, she hadn't contacted him since she'd walked out of his apartment the night he moved in. Betta felt for him, that he was alone now in a town where loneliness was felt triple-fold, for the locals had known each other forever, were comfortable with each other like family, and picked up wherever they'd left off at any given time.

It was glaring when you weren't one of them.

Added to that, the town where he'd found himself stranded believed Gwen could do no wrong and spread news like wildfire. He must have gotten the cold shoulder more than not.

Now here he was, looking as lost as she imagined he felt. She waved him over.

Catching sight of her, he smiled—relieved and over-eager, if she read his expression right.

Shiny shoes, smooth cheeks, pressed clothes, no wrinkles. The only tell he'd worked all day was the Oxford shirt rolled up at the sleeves. Dropping a snazzy briefcase at her feet, he sank down into the couch next to her.

"Shelby's," Betta said, motioning about.

"This is where you were going to take me, right?" Glancing around, he took it all in, peering through and around the dusty, swaying stacks of books.

"Yep."

Shelby appeared in front of him with a coffee cup. "Need some happy hour?"

"Excuse me?"

"She spikes the coffee for her regulars," Betta explained.

He looked at Betta. "You're a regular?"

"The most regular," she admitted. Since there was no James, since she'd been on a schedule, since Shelby was on her way home from work, the list went on.

"Happy hour at a bookstore?" Gage took the cup. "Can I be a regular too?"

Shelby and Betta caught each other's gaze. Betta raised an eyebrow: *no, not him, you should not try to sleep with him.* Where Shelby's face wondered: *That too weird for you, if he's a regular?*

"Sorry." Gage ran a hand through his hair. "Clearly

desperate for friends over here."

Betta elbowed him. "You should've called. Or Van. We're your friends—you have friends."

"I should've," he said. "I owe you dinner still."

She waved him off and took a sip of her coffee. "This'll suffice."

He sank back into the couch, and Betta shifted a little, to be farther from falling into him and to face him better. Gwen was doing okay since the breakup, better than expected, but she had a one-track mind for the city. Did Gage have a one-track mind for the town, for a life here? Was it helping him get over her?

Betta wanted to ask him if it was worth it. She wanted to know if James thought it was worth it, leaving her for a place, and she wanted to know if maybe she should've picked James over everything she'd always wanted.

"You seem good," she said instead.

"I was miserable for a bit, I'm not gonna lie. She tell you what happened?"

Betta shrugged. Him moving to town would've been a deal breaker to her too, if she were her sister, same as James' leaving had been.

Gage closed his eyes. "I like it here, Betta. I like my job, and I want to forget everything else."

Betta rifled through the stack of books on the side table, books Shelby kept there for her, adding to them on occasion when the pile got low. Choosing the most masculine cover, she handed it over.

Books and spiked coffee were a great place to start, if you

needed to relax. If you wanted to forget everything else.

She'd been there. She could help.

* * *

The guilt gnawed on Gwen in the quietest moments, in corners she didn't know she had.

Still no regret exactly, but looking back, she couldn't believe she'd turned into the type of person who'd do what she'd done. If she were going to make such a rash decision, she might as well have broken up with Gage on the spot, when he first made the announcement.

Unless she and David were meant to be. More than being the girl who cheated on her fiancé because he made his own decision, maybe she was the girl who found true love at an awful time in the messiest of ways.

It would be redemption.

Gazing up at her ceiling, Gwen took Gage's second locket off her neck and spun it around her finger, weighing her options. She promised Betta she'd stay on at the store through the house renovation, but if it got delayed, like most construction projects, September was Gwen's deadline. Her go/no-go. Her line in the sand.

She refused to stay another winter. She'd done her time.

That meant she had four months to feel David out. To see if they might work, if he'd grown up like she suspected—if he was the man she'd wanted that night, sexy and slick and confident. If he still wanted her as genuinely as he had in high school, when he'd settled over and over again for her best friend. Or if she'd fooled herself with alcohol because she was in such desperate need for an escape.

It could be she was only a trophy, and once was enough to prove whatever he'd needed to prove. He'd called her after though, and she'd ignored him, another message she'd sent without really thinking about it. Which meant it was up to her, the next step.

Dropping the necklace onto her stomach, she reached for her phone and dialed his number.

"Come home this weekend," she insisted, not even giving him time for a hello. She wanted a man who could stand on his own two feet and also bend to her beck and call.

"I'm sorry, who's this?" a woman asked.

Gwen's fingers tightened on the chain. "An old friend David happens to be sleeping with. Put him on the phone."

She could hear hushed conversation, a little tense but nothing like the screaming she would've unleashed if she were living with someone and heard that. Then, his chuckle. Closing her eyes, she let the noise travel down her skin, from ear to hip, the way his mouth had when they'd been together.

"Gwen?"

"Are there other old friends you're sleeping with?" she asked. "That you can't be sure it's me?" Another chuckle, but her feathers were ruffled; her plan derailed before it began. "That your girlfriend?"

"No. No girlfriend."

So he was a dog. A polite, sensual, romantic dog with

many tricks. Well, maybe she could salvage that, if she still had pull and wasn't only a trophy. "Come home this weekend," she said again.

"I can't."

"Because of her?"

"Because of work. You and the fiancé having problems?"

"I broke up with him."

Silence. No soft arguing on the other end of the line with the other woman, so it wasn't that he was distracted by anything but the news. The news had shut him up. "Because of me?" he finally asked, tone low and hidden.

"No, for a multitude of more important reasons."

"More important than me?" he teased, righting the conversation before she'd been able to get a handle on how quickly it had tipped.

"Hard to believe, I know."

He chuckled. Then, more serious again. "I called you."

"I know."

"You didn't answer."

"I was sorting through some things. Did you need something?" Then she panicked—did he have some nasty disease he felt obligated to tell her about? *Calm down, Gwen, he'd used a condom.*

"No, just checking in."

"You do that with all your women?"

"It's not like I have a new one every day, Gwen. You didn't answer, I moved on."

Gwen wound the locket chain around her pinky tight, until the tip was deep red. If she'd have thrown him a bone in high school like she did in that hotel room, he wouldn't be so easily deterred by a missed phone call. Fine, she didn't mind working it a bit. Less pathetic of him too, which she appreciated.

"If I'd have answered," she asked, "then what?"

"I'd have invited you to come stay for the weekend." Tone soft again. Not the confident man he seemed to have morphed into. So strange, straddling this line with him. Mostly, she liked it.

"I have to work this weekend," she said. "That's why I want you here."

"Same," he replied.

"Another time, then?" she asked, casual and cool. Picturing herself in high school, she would have played it off with a toss of her hair, but now she squeezed her eyes shut and crossed her fingers while she waited in a silence that hung like a fog.

It nearly suffocated her, his lack of response, and nearly washed all hope of redemption away, but then, soft and serious and heavy, loaded with weight and promise, he said, "Anytime, Gwen. You're welcome anytime."

This should make her feel better—a step in the right direction. Aside from asking to crash at his place until she got a job in the city or begging her way into monogamy, this was as good as she was going to get. What more did she want? A sure thing?

Gage had been a sure thing, and look how she'd messed that up.

One step at a time, slow and steady to make it real, to assuage the guilt. She felt better already, that David wanted her still, that she hadn't disappointed him that night, that she had a hold on someone, even if he was a dog. "I'll see you, David."

"I hope so, Gwen."

Dropping her phone to her side, she tossed the locket across the room. She'd made her bed. She was willing to lie in it. Might as well get comfortable.

* * *

Ez stood in the hot lunch line behind Georgia, who was effectively blocking her out. If Ez moved into Georgia's line of vision—even her peripheral—Georgia spun for something in the other direction.

Ez had been sitting with Gavin at lunch since the photo shoot incident, but this was new. This meant Ez was banned from existence, which meant Celia believed the texts, which meant Celia had done something that resulted in humiliation.

The thought alone made her so happy that she didn't care she might be banned from existence. She didn't care it was the Monday after her boyfriend broke up with her, and she had to find a new lunch table. She only cared that she had successfully speared Celia with a sixteenth length of the spear Celia had been gutting into her side for months now.

Esmerelda scanned the crowd for where Christine sat with the other kids from the play, and decided she had to follow Georgia past Celia and Gavin, or it would be too obvious she was avoiding them both.

Swallowing hard, Ez forced her feet, one in front of the other, half a foot by half a foot. It should have kept her stable enough that she didn't trip when Celia stuck her foot out in front of her, but it didn't.

She went down hard—tray skidding across the floor to meet up with Gavin's feet—and landed on her elbows.

Standing, Ez brushed herself off and turned to face Celia, who nodded, as if in acknowledgement that yes, she'd tripped her on purpose.

Ez tried very hard to control her rage. She wanted to scream like a crazy person, a string of obscenities or one very, very long F word, but no way she'd give Celia the satisfaction.

Celia wobbled, as if shaken out from an invisible hand attached to a string, or like she were an apparition, going suddenly unsure. Straightening, she peered up at Ez, a new twist to the scowl on her face. "Are those my earrings?"

"What are you talking about?"

"Those are my earrings!"

Ez was unable to control the smirk. "How do you know they're yours?"

"Because I do! Give them back."

Twirling one in her ear with her now free hand, she lied. "I got them for my birthday, Celia." Her mom had bought her older sisters diamond studs for their eighteenth birthdays, so it didn't feel like that much of a stretch. Anyway, these weren't diamonds.

"Esmerelda." Celia spoke through clenched teeth. "Those are my earrings."

"Sorry, Celia, they're not."

She stood. "Where did you get them then?"

"I told you. They were a gift." A gift from your dresser, thank you very much.

Ez spun away. She was not about to let that bitch get close enough to rip the earrings out of her ears. Gavin was holding her tray for her, milk upright and hamburger back in one piece, green beans lost and scattered on the floor.

He must not know Esmerelda was behind whatever Celia had done. Or he knew and didn't care. He had been as angry as Ez about the Valentine's Day pictures. Or he finally felt bad for playing with her nipples one minute and breaking up with her the next, the bastard. Or he wanted to keep her buttered up for when he wanted her back once summer was over.

Oh, how she'd love to ask him what happened. But she was not speaking to him, and so would have to live off the fact that Celia was clearly destroyed enough to try and destroy her again.

Without a word, Esmerelda snatched her tray from Gavin and stalked over to join Christine.

* * *

Betta led Brennan toward the front foyer of the half-demoed saltbox that she could only hope would someday be her home. She'd led him through room by room, pictures in hand of where she wanted to go with it.

He didn't care so much about the wall of built-in bookshelves in the master bedroom, but she knew Gage would. When she worked on it at Shelby's, he was always peering over her shoulder, and when she'd flipped to that picture, he'd slapped his hand on the page, taking her whole binder to get a better look.

For Brennan's tour, she focused more on the master bath, particularly the antique copper casement she wanted to bring in for the countertop. It was already on hold with the antique barn out on highway M.

Betta could tell Brennan liked her kitchen the most—the slightly vaulted, beamed ceiling was a perfect frame for handmade wooden cabinetry, all original. A metal smith was looking into refurbishing the chandelier that had been lying in the corner of the mess when she'd first walked in. She'd bring in a new industrial stove for the over-sized island, which they were redoing with wide wooden slats painted a deep but neutral green. The floorboards were worn and faded, but bespoke of a white and black checkerboard pattern she was insistent on recreating, once the floors were refinished.

"White walls, all of them," Betta said, as she and Brennan stopped near the front door, at the base of the stairs. "A blank canvas for the checkered floor, and the fat, darker slats in the living room," she motioned that way, "the green island in the kitchen, the red cupboard in the pantry alcove, and the vintage rug I have in mind for the bedroom."

He grinned, taking in the little galley workspace off the front entry, opposite the living room. "Take a breath, Betta."

"I'm not sure I can until you tell me what you think."

He scanned the stairs—oh, and the steps she would do with reclaimed barn wood, the banister white also. She might have already mentioned that on the way in.

"It sounds very authentic. You've put a lot of thought into this."

She tucked her hair behind her ear, forgetting about the pencil she'd lodged there. It tumbled to the floor and she shot down for it. "Thank you."

"Rugs aren't in the reno budget. They're in our interior design budget, which we only have for bed and breakfasts, not rentals or resale."

"Right. Of course."

He was smiling though. She was unsure if he was laughing at her, so green and eager and overachieving, or if he was that pleased.

"Impressive organization, also." He nodded at her binder of pictures. She hadn't fumbled once going through, showing him what her plans were. "But back to the vintage rug."

"They're expensive, I know. I was just dreaming." She opened the door for him, and he stepped onto the front steps, which needed to be redone. The cement was crumbling, chunks discarded at the side.

He opened the little gate and closed it behind them. The picket fence was not original, and it would be going. "You have proven yourself enough that a raise is in order."

"Oh, I wasn't fishing-"

"I know."

"And I haven't proven anything. The project is barely started."

Brennan tapped her binder. "The raise is for this, Betta. There'll be another if this turns out as great as I think it will— a pro job on your first try."

Betta hugged the binder to her chest and tried to spit it out, that a raise was wasted on her if she was leaving.

She felt she was leading him on. She should say something about her sister leaving in September. About the store that was a part of her she could never cut out. He had to know, though, the way news traveled. Was he pushing her so she'd say something, so she'd admit it?

She clutched tight to the binder until its edges left imprints on her skin. This job fulfilled her like nothing else yet in her life, but the store was a foregone conclusion—a legacy tracing her roots back through generations, honoring her father and grandfather, an intrinsic tie to the town and its history, a heartbeat through the bloodlines of her very life.

It was no contest. There was no choice.

JUNE

Gwen chose to walk up the thirteen floors. If she started breathing heavy when she saw David, at least she'd have an excuse.

The weekend after Memorial Day, one of the busiest of the year, she'd rewarded herself by paying her entire family to work so she could escape to the city.

She'd thought of David every day since their phone call, sorted through her guilt and grief over the breakup, and told herself making David a real thing didn't fix what she'd done to Gage. Even though it sounded good, it sounded scared too, like she couldn't face the world with a one-night stand being her first time unless it meant something. It didn't have to mean something. Though, she did want to see him again. She wanted to surprise him, in fact, gauge his face when he saw her unexpectedly, see if he'd truly meant it when he said 'anytime.'

Plus, she wanted him off-guard, wanted to see how he really lived—no time to clean up or hide the dirty nasty under the bed.

Up the thirteen flights, she debated her tactic.

Sexy vixen coming for more?

Old friend to see the city?

Or, if a woman answered, maybe jealous ex. That could be fun.

She felt like playing a part, figured David might get into that. Plus, it kept the vulnerable truth of her hidden under the rug, until she was ready to let it out.

Deciding to wing it, she approached number 1342 and knocked, a few hard raps, not to be missed. The door swung open without her having to knock again. David, topless and in plaid pajama pants, drawstring tied neatly. As he registered that it was her, many miles from home and unannounced, he hung his hand along the top of the door, relaxing into it, as a smile spread across his narrow face.

Good. He was happy to see her, no reservations.

She reached out to undo the perfect little bow. He'd learn soon enough that life wasn't tied up that way. That he couldn't tie her up that way.

Fingertips dipping beneath his waistband, she pulled herself a step closer. "Hi, David."

"Who is it?" a woman called—the same high voice that had answered the phone.

Clutching tighter to David's waistband, Gwen cleared her throat and leaned in. "Who do you want me to be?"

"Samantha?" he yelled over his shoulder. "You're gonna have to go."

Slipping away from her grasp, he walked across the spacious living room. Arrogant bachelor pad, as she'd suspected. The furniture was all smooth clean lines in grays and whites, a bit of smoky blue thrown in for accent.

Samantha came out in a man's button down shirt, bronze hair all the way to her ass. No boobs. No fat. No extra little oomph of anything. She was tiny, short, and drowning in that shirt. Gwen was sure she could fill it out better.

David scratched the back of his head. "This is Gwen. A very, very good friend from home. I forgot she was coming for the weekend."

"David,"—sexy whine from the booty call—"you promised me sushi."

"I'll call you in an order and have it delivered to your place, okay?"

"We have reservations!"

"Under my name, for two."

Gwen crossed her arms with a smug grin. God, she loved to win. How had she let it go on so long that she hadn't been winning?

The woman huffed, spun for David's room, and reemerged with a large purse, Gucci or Burberry or something fancy. Gwen shook her head. What a waste. She could buy *thousands* of ramen noodles with the money it took to buy that purse. How much room in the dry foods section of the Aaldenberg General Store would that fill? A ton. That would have been a good tactic last winter. Order a whole store of ramen noodles, up to the ceiling. *Financial problems? What are you talking about, this place is stuffed!*

Samantha slammed the door as she left. Its echo left a heavy silence which David and Gwen let simmer as their eyes got reacquainted with each other.

"She left with your shirt," Gwen realized.

"I have an unworn pile for that very purpose." He smirked. "That's a secret I'm only telling you. Because you're my very, *very* good friend from back home."

"Gross." Gwen wrinkled her nose, the scent of second thoughts wafting to her on his cologne, which he hadn't worn back at the bar, or at the hotel. "You're filthy."

He moved toward her. "I'll put your name on the tags of each one if it'll make you feel better."

She put a hand out to stop him. "Were you two just in bed together?"

"No," he delivered this casually, levelly, truthfully? "We were only getting comfortable. You came at the perfect time."

"You said I could come anytime."

"And weeks went by."

She crossed her arms.

"You want me to chase you? Long for you? Trust me, I did enough of that in high school to last us both the rest of our lives. I'm not a kid anymore."

"So romantic." Though, it was what she liked about him— he wasn't that kid anymore.

"I can be romantic. I can be monogamous. I can be almost anything you want me to be. But you get what you give, Gwen. You act temporary, you get temporary."

"How'd I act temporary?"

He snorted. "It was you using me in that hotel room. I'm not an idiot."

"So you're getting back at me now?"

"Not at all." He placed his hands on her arms. "I was happy to be used. Two percent of me hoped it meant more to you, but it didn't. I get that. Fine."

She frowned. "I'm not using you now."

"I hope you're not. So far, though, as distant as you've been? Hard to tell."

They studied each other. Gwen felt hollowed out, even though she'd left her guilt at home. It didn't matter here. Gage didn't matter here. Her past didn't matter here. David's words, though, caught up to her and slapped her across the face: *you get what you give.*

He might be a player, but he wasn't playing around. He would tell her how it was, call her on every step. It was transparency or nothing with him, when it was difficult enough to be transparent with herself, let alone another human, let alone a one-night stand. Maybe that's how he'd turned into what he turned into. Women who were after sex and money were more transparent then the ones trying to snake a husband. Maybe that was the draw. He knew what they wanted; he knew what to give them.

Decision time, then. Ball was in her court. Time for her to make things clear by giving what she wanted to get.

Slipping her heels off, she dropped her bag on the floor. "Did you miss me?"

"I did."

"Did you miss me more than you'll miss her?"

"I kicked her out, didn't I?"

"Had you slept with her yet?"

"Last weekend." Good. So he would be transparent too.

"How many girls have you slept with, since me?"

"Only her."

"You're not an every night kind of guy?"

"I work during the week."

She set a palm on his bare chest, her fingers catching in the whorls of his hair.

"Interrogation over?" he asked.

If they were aiming for transparency, if he thought she'd used him and led him on… "It was my first time, with you."

Eyebrows high. She nodded. He let out a breath of disbelief.

Chin up, she asked quickly, "Does that ruin it?"

He shook his head, gently touching her jaw. She placed her other palm over his heart, to feel if it was beating as fast as hers.

"Does that ruin it for you?" he asked.

Leaning her face into his palm, she replied, "I mean, the cheating part… the guilt. I don't regret it, though. I'd do it again."

"I'm glad you told me."

She tried out a smile and hoped it wasn't sad. "You get what you give." She pressed her fingertips hard into his muscle. Was his heart beating? "I want honesty," she said. "All of it, all the time." No more secrets, no more quiet plans, no more hiding money or lack thereof, no more decisions made before she knew about them.

Honesty. Living bare. Out in the open with the breeze and mist on your face, even when it was uncomfortable.

Especially when it was uncomfortable. So it could be dealt with and flushed, instead of being brushed to the side until it towered so high it tumbled over to crush and suffocate you.

Yes, she wanted bare and alive. So that's what she would give him.

* * *

Wanda and Harvey sat at an oceanfront table, waiting for Mae and Richard.

Wanda kissed Richard once, way back in junior high, but she hadn't mentioned that to Mae or Harvey because she figured everyone had kissed everyone else in town, at one time or another.

It also wasn't why she'd picked him.

Harvey's leg was beating a frantic rhythm under the table as he stared off at the boats moored in the bay. The sun worked its way to setting, and the Davidson boy played an electric violin on the boardwalk. The smell of seafood and boiled butter wafted from the restaurant.

At least the setting was lovely, this night where she would see how her husband and his ex-girlfriend might interact. She hoped they wouldn't give anything away, but she had to test them before her relationship with Mae went any further, even if she'd rather live in denial. Denial might put her to bed for a few weeks here and there, but it wasn't the aching dagger that truth could be.

Problem was, she'd come to adore Mae, and having a friend. A real one. Not the locals who stopped to chat with her in the store or on the street, but someone to unload on when she needed to unpack the suitcase of issues she was carrying.

Tonight would be a true test, and it would determine which direction their relationships would go—if Wanda was more important to each of them than they were to each other.

If she wasn't, well, her bed and her soap operas and her racy romances were waiting for her. She would live there until she wasted away.

"How're you feeling, Harvey?" Wanda asked, sipping her cocktail.

"What kind of question is that?"

She slid a hand on his knee to still it. "You seem a bit anxious."

"I'm fine." Sweeping up his Sazerac, Harvey took a big swig.

Sure. Fine.

Scanning the street and restaurant one more time, Wanda caught sight of Mae heading up the large wooden deck. She wore a loose black tank under a white cardigan, with a geometric black and white patterned skirt. Wanda was self-conscious of her knees, but to each their own. Mae's blonde hair was layered and fluffed, bangs brushed to the side, and a hollow metal heart lay on a fat chain around her neck. Red lipstick on a beaming smile—so the walk over must have gone well—and flat strappy sandals.

Wanda checked herself over with her hands. Her hair was

shorter than Mae's—shoulder length—but also layered to show off her loose curls, and her bangs were also brushed to the side. She wore a white oxford shirt under a green cardigan, sleeves rolled, and dark jeans with espadrilles. Small, understated, classy diamond earrings, and a thin bangle bracelet on her wrist. Wanda's make-up was dewy and glowing, last she'd checked, and her lipstick pink.

Good. Straightening, Wanda waved them down.

Mae brightened more when she spotted her, if that were possible, and Wanda stood to give her a hug. Harvey stood too. Wanda noted they were careful touching each other— like they were too comfortable and knew they shouldn't be, or conversely like they hadn't touched in twenty-five years. Richard stretched a hand out to shake Harvey's, and the four of them sat.

Mae spread her napkin on her lap. "Great choice, Wanda."

Wanda nodded. "Can't beat the waves and the sunset."

"The food," Harvey added, reaching for the rolls Wanda had insisted he leave alone until the other couple arrived.

"The company," Richard added, smiling about the table.

Wanda grinned at him and squeezed his hand quickly. If she did this, she figured, it would allow Harvey and Mae to touch each other at some point too, if that's what they wanted. She motioned a waiter over.

"Could we get these two drinks?"

"And me another Sazerac," Harvey added.

Wanda raised an eyebrow at him. She didn't want him so sloshed all his secrets came pouring out, all the ways she failed him and all he wanted in a wife that she couldn't be. She only wanted the one, if even.

Lacing her fingers through his to hopefully keep him focused and grounded, she smiled across the table. If they could get through tonight, the three of them, then they could get through the rest of it.

If they couldn't, well, at least Wanda would know that bed was the place she was meant to be.

* * *

Gage slumped down next to Betta and checked his watch. "Let's order Chinese."

"It's only four," Betta pointed out. It was also Saturday, so she'd eaten a late breakfast and a later lunch. She'd brought her laptop to Shelby's and had been camped out since noon— working and reading, reading and working.

"Let's order Chinese for a snack, and stay here all night reading. If we get hungry later, we can order pizza."

Shelby looked up from where she sat at her chair, the seasonal help she'd hired working the register for her. "Chinese outside so you don't get my couch greasy."

"Sure," Gage agreed. "Do you have a blanket we could use?" He turned to Betta. "Van want to join us? Is Kate home this weekend?"

"The whole family isn't sitting on my curb eating Chinese," Shelby said. "That would be bad for business."

This business was stirring around them. It was odd for

Betta to get used to the tourists inside the store. She was well acquainted with their buzz on the streets and adept at slipping through them unnoticed, but after the quiet hours she'd spent at the bookstore over the winter, so many it felt like home, the noise was unsettling. The motion disorienting.

Shelby leaned over and touched Gage's knee. "You, though, are good for business."

He shifted uncomfortably, closer to Betta, and Betta raised an eyebrow.

"It's been long enough," Shelby said. "I think it's time you find someone to do."

"I'm pretty busy between work and here and exploring town, actually."

"Some*one*, Gage, not something." Betta echoed with Shelby, then pulled her lips into her mouth to bite off her smile.

"Too obvious?" Shelby asked Betta.

Betta grinned. "I've heard it before."

Gage shifted again, his shoulder pressing into hers.

"It's okay. She takes no for an answer." Betta had seen a few people come out of the back room in the last year, while Gage had seen only one. That one was apparently enough. Gage crossed all his appendages, and Shelby chuckled.

A young girl in a bikini and cutoffs walked up. "Excuse me, ma'am. Could you help me find something?"

"Of course, hon."

As they were swallowed by the hive, Betta snickered. "Don't want someone to do then?"

"She's not my type."

Shelby was loose and flowing, bohemian to the core. Gwen was polished, smooth and shiny. "Yeah, I can see that. All buttoned up and battened down that you are."

"I can loosen up." Gage frowned. "You don't think I can loosen up?"

"Oh, certainly." She played serious. "I'm sure you can."

He pinched her side, and she let out a burst of laughter. Gage crossed his arms. "Wait and see what kind of crazy I order." Picking up his phone, he dialed for take-out.

Betta grinned out the window at the tourists on the sidewalk, while the movement and mutters of those inside milled behind her, filling the space.

As Gage hung up, Shelby threw a blanket over the two of them and tucked them into the couch together—a little deeper on Gage's side, so much that Betta winced. That was a lot of boob in a face.

Throwing the blanket off, Betta balled it up in her arms. "Let's go sit outside and discuss your imminent deflowering."

Gage coughed and sputtered while Betta laughed. Now she could see why her brother made jokes like that. It was kind of hilarious. Hopping up quickly, away from Shelby's chest, Gage glued himself to Betta's side as she made her way through the crowded store. "I'm not going to sleep with Shelby," he whispered.

"Just gauging your looseness," she said. "Not really my business."

Together, they spread out the scratchy plaid. Settling against the stone wall of the bookstore, Betta rested her head on the edge of the window pane and pulled her knees up to her chest.

Gage lay back on one elbow, legs stretched across the sidewalk. No one seemed to mind; they smiled and nodded and stepped over him, likely due to his warm greeting and pretty smile.

"Loose," he muttered, motioning to his relaxed position.

"You are wearing a *tie*."

Sitting up, he loosened it, whipping it over his head to slip it over Betta's. Then, furthermore, he unbuttoned his dress shirt and shrugged it off.

Betta took in his remaining white t-shirt, still partially tucked in where the untucking of the Oxford hadn't pulled it out, pressed navy pants, and shiny, shiny shoes with pointed, raised eyebrows. "You still look like a city rat."

With determination set in his jaw, he slid off his belt, kicked off his shoes, ripped off his socks, and rolled his pant legs up a few times.

Betta reached over to ruffle his hair. "A few days of scruff and no one will take you for a tourist."

He stroked his smooth cheeks with one hand, then resettled where he'd been, pieces of his outfit scattered around them. Gwen's friend, Sara, nearly tripped over his shoe, which sat precariously on the curb.

Sara gathered all his things and set them nearer the building, then took in the situation. As she lifted an eyebrow, Betta slid Gage's tie off her neck and tried to remember he was not half undressed, but still completely clothed.

"Where's Gwen?" Sara asked, her eyes flitting back and forth between them.

"Working, probably," Gage muttered, frowning toward the store.

"I was just there. Ez said she's been gone the last few weekends."

They both looked to Betta. She sighed, not wanting to rub it in, but also not wanting to lie. "She's been job hunting in Boston."

Sara crossed her arms. "She staying with David?"

"Who?" Gage asked.

"My high school boyfriend, who broke up with me every time she smiled at him. She promised to never-" Sara bit down on her words. "I don't know why it bothers me so much. It's been years."

"Gwen would never screw you like that," Betta assured.

Gage sat up, no longer anything loose about him, even in the more relaxed get-up. "High school boyfriend?" he asked.

"I know, I know." Sara put a hand up. "You're right—it's stupid I should care."

"I'm going to get some spiked coffee." Gage stood. "Without the coffee." He looked down to Betta. "You want anything?"

Betta blinked at him and shook her head. When he was gone, back inside the tourist hive, Sara stared at Betta like Betta herself had done something wrong.

Maybe she had. Maybe she shouldn't be spending time with Gage.

"She loves you," Betta offered. "I wouldn't worry about it."

"Breaking promises means something, no matter when you

break them. I think that's what's bothering me."

Betta didn't know why she felt like Sara was trying to make a point for Betta's sake. Gwen never asked Betta to stay away from Gage, and at this point, she'd have to give up Shelby's if she wanted to avoid him, which wasn't fair. It wasn't fair they couldn't both frequent the book store in town, when they were both in love with books like they were.

Sara shook her head, but what did she want Betta to say? Betta was not going to offer her sister up on a skewer, and she'd already defended her twice. She also was not going to spit out that it wasn't what it looked like, her and Gage. No matter that she'd only had one other man's tie around her neck, the one time James attempted to wear one.

This was a totally different situation and a totally different story. Sara should not put that on her.

Good riddance.

* * *

Esmerelda had thought, that by the time summer hit, everyone would be over her body and her pictures. She hoped they'd be over her altogether.

Just in case, she took to covering up, sunbathing even in a muumuu.

She and Christine staked out the same spot every afternoon, hoping that in time no one would bother taking it.

They'd thought about signs or peeing on the perimeter, but settled for crossing their fingers.

"Hi ladies." Ez's eyes popped open at Celia's voice. "Can I join you?" Of course it wasn't really a question. Celia laid out her towel next to Ez, smiled brightly at Christine, and sat down.

"Uhhh…" What Ez meant by that was, *last you acknowledged me, it was to trip me and look like you were going to rip your earrings out of my ears.*

"Listen, I know we left things kind of bad,"—Celia popped open her sunscreen and handed it to Ez—"Do my back?" She turned around. "But I'm here because I've seen that awful grandma dress you've been wearing and felt it my duty to talk you out of it. No need to be ashamed, Ez."

"I'm not ashamed." What she was, was cursing herself for applying the sunscreen as if it were a given, because of course she would, because this was Celia and Celia commanded it.

Ez snapped the bottle shut and tossed it on Celia's towel.

"You are, clearly. Don't you agree, Christine?"

"Modest might be the more appropriate word."

"Fine." Celia twisted her long dark hair into a bun. "But I can't have you going all frumpy when I created you as a star."

Esmerelda frowned.

"You might hate me for it, but those pictures are still whispered about. Because they're hot." She shook the fabric hanging about Ez. "Take that off and own yourself, Ez. First lesson if you actually want to be on stage someday."

Ez narrowed her eyes. Did Celia have spies everywhere?

Possibly.

"Duh. I know who you've taken up with."

Ez tucked her muumuu under her thighs, so there was less of it for Celia to touch, and asked, "Why are you here?"

Celia stretched out on her towel. "Sometimes I like to help people, Ez. And on this beach, this summer, you need the most help."

"We don't buy that for a minute," Christine said.

"Calm down, ladies, and go with it. Worst case scenario, I draw all the boys to your yard. And whether you believe it or not, I'm happy to share."

Esmerelda and Christine shot a glance at each other. Christine raised an eyebrow. "I mean, she is right about the muumuu. And I could go for a summer fling."

"There's got to be something in it for her," Ez muttered, ripping said muumuu off herself. Her boobs were literally two sizes bigger than they'd been for Gavin, and that was the last thing she needed all the drooling hormones on the beach to notice. She wasn't even used to them yet herself.

Celia shrugged. "Or maybe I'll surprise you."

* * *

Betta stood on the creaky stairs, smile so big she was embarrassed, yet she couldn't shut it down.

Gage stood before her in full work attire, briefcase at his side, and she was about to show him around her house.

She hopped down the bottom few steps. "Where's

Shelby?"

"Well, when I stopped by to grab her, there was moaning coming from the back room."

"Oh, boy."

"Guess she hired him so he could slip in once in awhile, instead of so she could slip out."

Betta gasped, as such a joke was thoroughly unexpected coming from him, then burst into laughter.

"Trying to be looser," he explained with a smirk.

She nodded with approval, then shook her head. "Still the tie, though."

With a defeated sigh, he opened his briefcase and dropped his tie into it, then the shirt.

When he went for his shoes, she put a hand out. "Nails and who knows what," she warned. "Keep those on."

He set his case against the stairs and rubbed his hands together. "Let's see this place, huh?"

Betta led him down the hall to the kitchen, through the galley workspace, back to the small foyer, and on to the living room. It wasn't half as grand as her parents' Victorian, but it would be hers.

Someday.

Hopefully.

It was interesting having something to work for other than a legacy. Something you wanted, that you poured your heart into. Making money for a purpose—buying a house, for example—was a new concept. Before, she'd only worked for the sake of doing something, because it's what they did. Tradition.

Gage ran his hands over everything—the sanded down fireplace surround, the bricks inside it, even the wide floor planks in the living room, interspersed with thin strips. He touched the beams of the ceiling he could reach and the copper casement for the master bath counter, windowsills, doors, hallway walls, you name it.

In the bedroom, he stood in front of the bookshelves for at least five minutes, legs spread and arms crossed. When she started snickering, he moved, but only to run a fingertip along the edge, pout visible. "I was counting how many books this thing could hold. You messed me up."

"You're going to get a splinter," she told him. The house was torn up where it needed to be torn up, and framed in where it was being rebuilt, things poking out everywhere. Pieces were beginning to come to life, but mostly nothing was finished and nothing was clean.

He winked at her as they headed out of the master. "I'll be all right."

"I don't know. Soft city boy hands."

"Hey!" He looked at them. "Okay, they are pretty soft. Let's see yours."

She offered them up.

He took them in his, rubbing his thumbs along her palm and up the pads of her index fingers. Dropping them with a smirk, he said, "Clearly you haven't been doing the hard labor around here."

With a huff, she shoved into him a little, to beat him to the stairs, except he caught her waist and tossed her out of the way.

Hand on the stairway rail, he asked, "So, what are you going to do, then?"

"What do you mean?"

"This or the store?" He sat down on the bottom step, like they were staying awhile. Betta leaned against the post and wrapped her hands around the top of it.

Of course she wanted the store. She'd wanted it since she was eight and understood it to be something she could have. But same as she couldn't tell Brennan the deal she'd made with her sister over that bottle of wine, she couldn't tell Gage she wanted to be a property developer.

"Okay, then." He slid along the step and rested his back against the wall, facing her. "What do you want, in general?"

The words got caught in her throat: Mas Properties, tradition, the shelves of Aaldenberg Hardware and that desk, finally hers. The view from reception at Brennan's office, the camaraderie of his people, *not* the loneliness of the store. She used to love that for the time it gave her to read, but lately doing had been better than reading.

All this ping-ponged through her mind while Gage stared at her, face smooth, no ripple.

"Big or small, now or later," he finally said. "Go."

"I want to do something. Be somebody. Make a difference in this town. Feel a part of it. Be proud of myself."

He squinted at her. "I think you're doing that."

Betta swallowed. "With Mas Properties, but not with the store."

"The store's a staple."

"Yeah."

"Part of the town."

"I know."

"Either way, you win."

"It feels like either way, I lose," she whispered.

Their eyes locked. "That's where I was at, with your sister and my job."

"James, too," she said. "With me and California."

"You miss him?"

"Sure. You miss my sister?"

Deep frown, and one quick shake of his head. "Nope. Some of the things she did—said—made it easy to get over her."

Betta raised an eyebrow. Some of the things she did? Betta had sworn she wouldn't get into it with him though—too sticky to find a balance there, between her sister and this new friend she'd found. "That quick, huh?"

"What, you're not over James?"

"No, I am. Moved on anyway." Onto better things she wouldn't have had if she'd left with him. Proof she made the right decision, not that it had been much of a decision to make.

Her current decision was harder, which path she'd take, which career she'd choose. She only hoped when it was all said and done, she'd feel as sure of herself as she did when she'd watched James walk away.

As sure as Brennan. Sure of her life.

JULY

Ez and Christine let it go on for awhile because any teenage boy who looked their way, Celia did her little wave at, which meant most of them came over.

They milked it for the benefits, because they'd decided one late sleepover night that it was about time they got some benefits from Celia, instead of Celia reaping them all for herself. Plus, they were kind of curious what she was after.

It was a sweltering afternoon when it finally came to light. "That's your brother, right?"

Ez squinted her eyes, shielding them with her hand to look in the direction Celia was facing. "Uh huh." Then she turned to settle on her stomach.

"Christine, you should go get us some sodas," Celia suggested.

"No thanks."

"Please." But Celia's please was never a request.

"Go get your own soda. And get me a candy bar while you're at it."

Celia huffed, but her eyes were still on Van. He was

playing volleyball with some high school friends who were home for the summer.

"Does he lift weights?" Celia asked. "He must have when he played football, right? I mean, I can see the definition from here. Look at his *thighs*."

"Ha!" Christine cried, sitting up and shooting a look at Ez. "Celia wants to lick your brother's thighs!"

"Mm, maybe his biceps. His legs are bound to be hairy, right?"

"That's disgusting." Ez wrinkled her nose.

Indeed, Celia stared in Van's direction like he was a fresh pizza dripping with cheese. Well, Ez had to give her that he was oiled up.

"He has a girlfriend," she informed, dropping back flat. "Also, I can't just serve you my brother on a silver platter."

"Well, that's how you thought it worked with Gavin, isn't it?"

Esmerelda's heartbeat thumped in her ears, the noise of the crowded beach and the waves fading away. She waited for the threat. The manipulation. The angle.

Celia smirked, breaking the moment. "Relax, Ez. Water under the bridge. We're even, right?"

That's how Ez saw it, but... "What do you want then?"

"God, I don't always have to want something."

Christine snorted, and Celia rolled her eyes. "Your brother's too old for me. Just enjoying the eye candy." She rolled onto her belly so quick Ez shrank back, thinking she was coming for the earrings. "You definitely have good genes though. If you worked them a little harder..." Celia kicked her feet up and down, the sand spray sprinkling over Esmerelda's calves. "Really? No one wants to get me a soda?"

"No," they said at once, united.

"Fine." Celia made a big deal about getting up, like the thought of walking over to the soda machines was excruciating in and of itself. "What do you want? I'll show you how I've changed my ways—*I* will serve *you*." She even curtsied.

"Cola," Ez said.

Christine smirked. "Diet cola."

Celia worked her hip sway as she made her way across the sand to the boardwalk, and when she was out of earshot, Christine said, "You can kick her out whenever you want."

"It seems harmless though, right?"

"Seems harmless, yes."

"Right. So we stick with our original plan." Which was use Celia for the summer and drop her after, if she didn't drop them first. It was she who'd taught them about using people, after all.

* * *

Dana and Sara did not seem pleased to see her when Gwen walked into the bar. She sat next to a paunchy, liver-spotted man who'd gone to high school with her parents and gave them a huge smile anyway, because she was in a huge smile kind of mood.

257

The pleasures of the flesh. She got it now. And the hot cocoa shop had been as good as she remembered. It hadn't even felt weird being there with David instead of Gage— she'd thought she might buckle at the knees from guilt, but David pointed out that she and Gage hadn't even been together a full year, and how many months of that were long distance? So their relationship was more like a month long, compared to the years she and David had known each other. He'd wrapped his arm around her in the booth, the scent of cinnamon in the air, and she let herself enjoy it, her favorite place in the city.

"Didn't think I'd see you in here for awhile." Sara muttered, settling her hips against the opposite side of the bar in front of Gwen.

"Maybe never," Dana added.

"Considering."

"Considering what?" Gwen asked.

"Considering where you were last weekend, the weekend before that, and probably the weekend before that."

Dana raised an eyebrow. "Sleeping with David now?"

Gwen went cold. "I'm looking for jobs. He's being helpful." Helpful insomuch as teaching her all the things— about the city, and fine wine, and good food, and yes, about her body, and she took home one of those *shirts* every Sunday when she left. Soon she'd be through them all. Soon they'd all be hers.

Sara narrowed her eyes. "He wouldn't be entertaining you at his apartment, if he wasn't getting some."

"You guys know I'm not like that." Also, it was none of

their business, and now they'd ruined her mood. That was irritating. They were irritating.

"We know what he's turned into," Sara pressed.

"A man whore," Dana added.

"God, you guys are like Tweedle-Dum and Tweedle-Dee." In the city, their generation was all about sex; Sara and Dana knew nothing. Sex was inconsequential. It was so overdone it was boring. That's what David's friends said anyway, before they took girls home for hours of sex.

Not so boring, was it? Gwen had whispered to David one night, after. *You're not boring,* he'd replied.

Sara shoved off the bar. "I don't know why I care."

She shouldn't. She should leave Gwen alone. She shouldn't make assumptions. "Just because you gave him what he wanted every time he snapped his fingers, doesn't mean he's going to expect the same from me."

Sara balled her fist around a towel. "Fuck you, Gwen."

Yeah, that's how Gwen felt, too. David and Sara were so far in the past, and Gwen was not bowing to his every need. Screw her for implying it.

"Guess it serves you right," Dana muttered.

"Guess what serves me right?"

"James…" Dana made a nasty face—one of snotty, pompous righteousness, if Gwen read it right. "And *Gage*."

"What are you talking about?"

"Betta." Sara's nostrils flared, and if Gwen had a drink, she might toss it at her to wipe the damn sneer off her face.

"Betta what? What does Gage have to do with it?"

"They were pretty cozy when I saw them last." Sara started

wiping down the bar. "Almost as if they were on a date in front of the bookstore. Gage's tie around her neck, and his work clothes strewn across the pavement. When Betta told us you were in Boston and I pegged you for fucking David, he didn't even flinch. Like he didn't even care."

"No doubt they're together now," Dana surmised. "The minute you broke up."

Gwen rolled her eyes. "Please. James was one thing. Gage would never do that, and he'd never go for Betta."

Why? Because she and her sister were opposite—complementary maybe, but opposite. Gwen was the center of attention, while Betta was calm and quiet background noise. Boring, maybe, but that's how Betta liked it. She didn't want to be in the middle of the chaos, and Gwen always had.

Until the chaos was real, anyway.

Whatever. Had they seriously just gone after her sister? "Betta's a saint. What'd she ever do to you?"

Nothing, so they had no reply.

"Be pissy with me, fine. But don't take it out on my sister—don't be bitches just to be bitches."

Dana cast her gaze down and mumbled something that might have been an apology. Sara, however, still had a sneer on her face, nostrils flared in disgust.

In case it was directed at Betta, Gwen threw it out there to needle at her, to put her back in her place, "Maybe I will sleep with David."

Sara bristled. The towel stilled.

"You always said he was good," Gwen tried to play off flippant, but she was testy.

Tight-lipped, Sara didn't respond. Instead, she quickly made her way along the bar with her rag.

Gwen bit the inside of her lip until it bled, then decided to go drink somewhere else, since they didn't seem to be serving her.

Whatever, she didn't want what they were serving anyway. How *dare* they go after her sister.

* * *

Betta worked the fourth of July for Ez, who was supposed to work for Gwen, who was in the city again. Van left at eight-thirty to meet up with Kate for the fireworks, because really, he kept saying, he was only doing them a favor, and her dad left shortly after Van, due to Wanda calling him incessantly— she'd made last minute plans for them with their new friends.

So it was Betta, closing the store down like she owned it. Walking up the center aisle, she trailed her finger along the shelves, which Van had straightened before he left.

No one in the store, everything neat—exactly how she liked it. Not quite as satisfying as it used to be, though. Filling in during season was a bit like coming home to an old hobby. Not like she thought it would feel, all those months she longed for it.

Reaching the front door, she startled as Gage appeared, bottle of wine in hand. He shoved his way through, and she locked up after him.

"Beverage?" he asked. "It's been a rough day."

Betta shrugged. "Sure."

On their way to the office, Gage pulled a few paper cups from the dispenser by the water cooler. Swinging through the doorway, he set them on the desk and retrieved a bottle opener from his pocket.

He sat in Gwen's chair and swung his feet onto her desk. Betta hopped up next to his bare toes and took the glass he filled for her. Bare toes because he finally bought himself flip flops, and as he hadn't worked that day, he wore board shorts and a very clean, pressed white tee.

She reached a finger out to touch it. "Do you iron everything?"

He bunched the front of it into his fist, which lifted the fabric up off his stomach. His shorts were slung low and his belly button bare. Betta looked up quickly.

"Better?" he asked, releasing it to slight wrinkles.

"Your face!" she cried, running her knuckles along one of his unshaven cheeks. "Here I was starting to think you couldn't grow facial hair."

With a grin, he nodded. "I'm going to take that as a yes." He tapped her tiny paper cup with his. "Cheers."

They drank. "What's with the wine?" she asked.

"I snuck into work to grab a few files this afternoon. Fern was there—our secretary?—both hands in the petty cash drawer. I double checked with Frank that it was okay for her to close up, and he asked me to keep her there until he arrived. Then he fired her. Over twenty bucks. I feel awful."

"*You* feel awful?"

His foot began to shake. "She has three kids, and between those three kids, they've got two deadbeat dads. All she needed was twenty bucks to get dinner for them. I tried to talk Frank out of it, but it didn't work. So now I'm not only the city rat with his fancy pants apartment, but also the new guy crushing locals every chance he gets."

"You aren't crushing the locals," she assured, a hand to his ankle to calm it. "Fern will be fine. She moonlights at The Cat's Tail, and has a sugar daddy who's kept her in those funky heels for the last six years. Don't let her fool you. She ain't hurting."

Gage was torn between disgust and laughter. The disgust won. "She moonlights at The Cat's Tail?"

Betta nodded. "Wanna go check her out?"

"No! Never!"

"Are you sure?" She hopped off the desk to dance—not that kind of dancing, of course, but she threw in enough hip action to give him the general idea, hopefully inspiring an image of Fern doing the same thing, only with her clothes off.

He was not the sort of guy who'd go for a forty-year-old stripper, so she was laughing, until she realized that he wasn't. He wasn't leaning in to pinch her either. Rather, his face was drawn and confused.

"What?" She stopped and checked herself over for spills or holes or something not right, but everything was in place. "What?" she asked again, hand fluttering over her scar.

He shook his head, one shake.

She slid back across the linoleum, but before she had a chance to hop up on the desk, he stood and caught her there.

"Betta."

"Yeah?" Her breath was audible, from the dancing. Not because his lips were coming for hers.

Okay, maybe because his lips were on hers.

Her gut lurched forward, into him, and she kissed him back, skipping right over the moment where it's what you do—kiss someone back—simply because they're kissing you. She skipped over it, because in some deep part of her it made so much sense to be kissing him. It was easy, and heady, and *oh*. Like, of course, *now I see*.

Heated, while at the same time slow and steady. The heat of his palms against her back, the heat of her fingers in his hair, the heat of his hips pressed against hers.

She was as much to blame; she was pressed forward, too, connecting them in so many spots. Her hips, his hips—Gage's hips, her sister's fiancé's hips. And she didn't mean hips, she meant-

Wait.

Weren't they friends?

Wasn't he her sister's?

Yanking back, she put a hand to her throat. Scrambling across the room, she tore through the store to get away. She couldn't think straight with his lips on hers.

That must have been the problem.

* * *

It was Sunday morning, the morning after the fourth, and Wanda carried a breakfast tray into their bedroom. She used to bring Harvey breakfast in bed, before the kids. In fact, some of those lazy Sundays probably brought them their kids.

Speaking of, Wanda was close to being in the mood to lock the door behind her, except she'd noticed Harvey staring at Mae during the fireworks the night before, when everyone else was looking up.

While Wanda's hand was on his thigh, he'd been staring at another woman.

Harvey sat up with a smile. "It's been awhile," he noted.

Letting some sunlight in, she crawled back into bed and grabbed a piece of toast to nibble on, while Harvey dove into the omelet.

"I'm looking forward to Betta's housewarming party," she said.

"Your housewarming party, you mean?"

It was Wanda's idea, but every girl and every house should have a party, should they not? "She's too busy to plan it herself." So Wanda was planning it. Mae would cater it, Betta would make the guest list, and Wanda would do everything else. "Then Van almost has enough saved for a ring, so there'll be an engagement party-"

"We cannot repeat the last one, Wanda."

"The last one was mostly favors."

"Okay, but can we do it here? And you cook?"

"I think I've been doing quite well, Harvey." Partially because she had no credit cards and the checking account would stop working when empty, but she wasn't bitter.

"You have, I'm not saying that."

"I'm not buying things anymore, Harvey. Haven't you noticed?"

"Yes, I have."

"I'm buying experiences. Mae"—Wanda made sure to watch Harvey closely every time she said Mae's name, but he'd perfected a straight face—"says it's experiences that last a lifetime, and I think she's right."

"Can I give you a budget? Because Mae's catering is expensive, Wanda, and everyone agrees your meals are a treat."

She stared at him, at this open opportunity he'd laid out for her. Her or Mae, who did he prefer? "Mae's is the best food in town, everyone says. *Food Magazine* even says."

"Because she's got a place. If *Food Magazine* came to eat here, they'd forget about her in a second."

She shifted onto her hip, a little closer to him. "You really think?"

"One hundred percent. I would do anything for your chicken pot pie. And Mae should give you a cut of her business to get your gnocchi soup on her menu."

Glancing down at the comforter, she plucked a piece of fuzz from the fabric. "I'm sorry I stopped cooking for you, Harvey."

It was quiet a moment, and the guilt climbed up her, binding her shoulders, whispering at her to just lie down, just give in, just give up.

Harvey's soft voice called her back. "I'm more sorry you were sick."

Wanda ran her hands down her arms, peeling the guilt off, and shook depression's bony, gnarled knuckles from her neck. "You know why I got out of bed?" she asked.

"Because Gwen got engaged and there was a party to plan?"

She shook her head. "Because Mae was cooking for you." Because she'd been woken a bit when Betta needed comfort herself, and then Gwen's engagement, at least, was something to do, something to look forward to, and then third time's a charm, Wanda supposed, with the news that came on the lobster mac and cheese.

If only it always made that much sense, that she could trace it… understand it.

Harvey slid a hand to her cheek. "She cooked for all of us, because we helped her out when her husband died. Mowed her lawn, brought her casserole. She was paying us back."

"I only brought her food then because you were doing so much I felt like a bitch not doing something myself."

He dropped his hand and chuckled, but it was true. She wasn't going to let her husband help the widow out and not be involved herself. Not when said widow was his ex-girlfriend.

Oh, this town.

Wanda sighed. "Why did you help her so much?"

"I kept thinking of what it would be like for you if something happened to me, with four kids and the store." He gazed out the window at the peak of Mae's house. It hadn't been weird living close to them when her husband was alive.

"That's sweet, Harvey." If it were true. "Does that also

explain why you were watching her last night?"

He took a drink of orange juice—delay tactic?—then licked his lips and set the glass down before he replied. "I don't know what you're talking about, Wanda."

"During the fireworks. You weren't watching them, you were watching her."

"I checked on her a few times because she was crying. Didn't you see?"

Wanda blinked. No, she hadn't. She'd been watching him watch her. Pinching the piece of fuzz tight between the pads of her fingers, Wanda took a deep, cleansing breath and let it out, steady, steady. "She's my friend, Harvey. I know you guys were together, but that is ancient history. I want us to be able to hang out with her and Richard, but if you want to be with her, then you need to tell me now."

Harvey took his time removing the tray from his lap. He set it on the nightstand and turned to her. "Her dad died on the fourth—remember?"

She stared at him. So maybe Mae had been crying. Maybe Wanda should be glad Harvey hadn't reached for her hands like he was doing with Wanda's right now, easing the lint from between her fingers and kissing her tightened knuckles.

Maybe she should feel bad that she hadn't been a very good friend to Mae, prodding her until she finally agreed to go to the fireworks with them.

What she did feel bad about was that Harvey hadn't exactly answered her question, which meant until she had the strength and fortitude to actually ask *did you sleep with Mae, are you sleeping with Mae, do you want to sleep with Mae,* she would likely never know.

* * *

Van was helping Betta with a few final things in the house and in general helping her move in, not that she had much. A box or two from her room and a few of Pops' pieces she'd stored in the basement. The rest of the furniture had been slowly procured over the past month.

The house was an accomplishment all her own. She should be proud instead of horrified. She should not be in a state of certain crisis.

She'd been in a state of certain crisis since Gage had kissed her, and every time he called or texted, it made things worse. She couldn't face him, couldn't answer, couldn't reply. She couldn't give him answers, afraid she'd say all the wrong things, and so she rejected his every attempt to contact her.

Everything felt wrong. Every word, every sentence, every sentiment swirling in her brain. It was all working its way to a hurricane, hot and cold and passionate and wrong.

Most mortifying was the realization he'd begun to feel like home, and that he'd become the kind of man she burned to get back to.

It was ludicrous.

She couldn't. She wouldn't. What would her parents say? What would *Gwen* say? Her sister was graceful enough about James, but he came to Betta years after he was Gwen's, not months. Plus, it would look like Betta took advantage of him. Wounded and broken, but hey, want another Aaldenberg sister? Same stuffed, dimpled lips. Same body shape, but with darker hair, and don't mind the scar on her face—look, though, she has that cute, button nose to make up for it.

The devil on her shoulder: *They broke up three months ago and barely saw each other since December. That's seven months of nothing between them. And before that, long distance? Please. Old news. He should be yours. Take him and don't look back.*

The angel: *No one will ever see this as okay. No one. Not again. Not Gage. Most definitely no, not ever. This is a small town you live in. You can only get away with things like that in the city, where it's anonymous. You think no one will ever know?*

"Bets!" Van's call startled Betta out of her stupor. She was in the family room, setting out pillows on the couch. Brennan offered her some interior design money in the end, because he wanted to shoot it for her portfolio, an idea of what kind of aesthetic she could bring to future clients.

Another lie, as the store was almost hers. Like Gage could almost be hers.

She held her breath to choke out the desire—every time it rose, it nearly gave her a panic attack—and swung past the stairs, down the hall to the kitchen. "Yeah?"

He crouched atop the island, wiring a last-minute wrought iron chandelier she'd found at the flea market the next town over. It was Brennan's idea, when he'd seen how poorly the original came out. He gave her a work credit card—flea markets for permanent fixtures were part of the remodel, not the renter's expense.

Van hopped down. "Your phone's doing something."

Betta glanced at it and swallowed. Gage's last text had been: *I miss my friend. If nothing else, can't I have her back?*

No, he couldn't. Kisses lost friends; that's what they were meant to do.

Betta stared at her phone, buzzing along the counter. The closer she was to it, she knew, the harder to stay away.

"Lovers' quarrel?" Van teased. "Who you been spending all your time with?"

She blinked at him, willing him not to notice the tear or two that snuck into her eye. How could it have happened twice? How come she couldn't find a man who wasn't her sister's first?

"It's Brennan, isn't it?" He waggled his eyebrows, but all Betta could do was wrinkle her nose to get the tingle out. The smile died on Van's face. "You okay?"

Her phone started buzzing again. Van reached for it, spurring her into action, but he read the name before she could pounce. Snatching it, she pressed it to her chest.

Van let out a low whistle, and Betta looked up to the ceiling. The tears could only drain back inside her that way.

"Gage?" he whispered. "Really?"

"Please don't. I already feel like an animal."

He raised an eyebrow. "An animal, like, you guys have…?"

"No!" She shook her head violently. "He kissed me. Once."

Van scanned her with the kind of look that said he was taking stock of her state of mind and doing the math. "He's blowing up your phone, and you're moping because you won't let yourself answer it?"

With the heels of her palms to her eyes, one still clutching her cell phone, she pressed hard and nodded harder.

"Back to this animal comment-"

"Maybe it's pure physical instinct, like, animal urges."

"If it was pure physical instinct," he said, in his quietest tone, "it wouldn't make you cry."

"What if it's about Gwen?" she whispered. "Have I always hidden behind her? The store... James... now Gage... Where's the line between us?"

"There is none."

"What do you mean?" she asked in alarm. "You think we're the same person?"

He raised an eyebrow. "No. I mean you are two totally different people on two totally different paths and there is no line because there doesn't need to be. I swear, Bets, I know your thing is moody and introspective, but sometimes you make problems for yourself that just aren't there."

"The problem is here, Van!" She held her phone up between them. "The problem *kissed* me, and now I have to do something, say something, *choose* something. The problem is fucking here!"

"Shh." He took the phone from her and set it aside. "Okay, okay. We'll figure it out."

"We will?"

Setting a hand on her shoulder, he ducked his head to meet her eye. "Who do you want to call first when something awesome happens—like this house project—who were you most excited to tell?"

"Gage."

"What do you want to do after a long day?"

"We've been reading, almost every night, at Shelby's. Or working, side by side, or drinking coffee and talking. He needed a friend—I didn't mean for this to happen. You don't have to quiz me, okay? He's... he's..." She couldn't get it out, what he was, how much he meant to her.

Van let go of her shoulder. "Shitty luck, sis."

Her shoulders slumped. "I can't fall for him, of all people."

"Can't or won't or shouldn't, doesn't matter if you did."

Her phone was a black hole on the fresh butcher block counter. "So I could choose to won't?"

"Huh?"

"You said can't or won't or shouldn't. You said won't. Like I won't, I refuse, I can choose not to."

"You can. But that would suck just as bad."

She nodded.

"Maybe worse."

She continued nodding.

"Well, how 'bout this. If you go ahead with it, I'll propose to Kate. That should give you some time before anybody notices the Gage thing."

"You're proposing to Kate?"

He winked.

She threw her arms around his waist. "Yay, Van, I'm so happy for you guys."

He returned the hug, and when they dropped out of the embrace, he nodded to her phone. "You gonna take care of that, or we gonna finish up?"

273

"We should finish up."

"Wrong answer."

"What?"

"I thought we just decided," he said. "So go. I'll finish up."

Betta looked around. There wasn't much left.

"Seriously, I'm not giving you the choice."

"Okay." She grabbed her phone and tote and headed for the door, pretty sure she'd never won a war of wills with her brother.

"Hey, Bets?"

She turned, hand on the doorknob. He stood at the end of the hall, imposing form backlit by her kitchen.

"It was nice working with you again."

"It really was." They worked well together, always had. "Too bad this is my last reno, huh?"

"Yeah. Too bad."

Then she was gone. Racing up the hill. Tripping over herself. Imagining how she'd feel if the situation was reversed, if she were Gage. How it would feel to cut open your chest and offer someone your deepest self, knowing it wasn't an ideal situation but not being able to stop yourself any longer, only to be shoved away and run from, then ignored.

She could think of nothing more awful. She had to make it up to him.

* * *

Betta's knock was loud and frantic, only partially because she was afraid who might see her, panting in the hall outside her sister's ex-fiancé's apartment.

The door swung open immediately, as if he'd been waiting for her. His expression was a mixture of surprise, then pain and hope. "You've been avoiding me," he said.

"May I come in?" she asked, checking the hallway, both directions.

He moved aside, and she hurried past him. As he closed the door, she studied his facial hair, almost bushy now. He must have left it since that night, let himself go worrying over her.

She meant to kiss him, to make up for it all, but words came out instead. "You're my sister's ex-fiancé, which means unavoidable, miserable consequences."

He closed his eyes. "I get it. I don't know what I was expecting. Can we please go back to how it was? Whatever it takes so I don't lose you."

"You haven't lost me."

"I haven't?" He opened his eyes.

She took a step back. "I wish I could come to you with no reservations, but with James before you, I can't. I can't do this in public. I feel awful asking that of you, to keep us secret, but this town... my family... I'll be..." She swallowed her horror because there was no way around it, if she kissed him again. "I'll be *that* girl. *That* sister."

"So, what I'm hearing isn't bad, though, right?" A smile started, cautious and careful, waiting for confirmation before it bloomed.

"I missed your-" She was going to say his soul, but the words echoed in her head in James' voice. That was what he said; now she understood. She understood and it ached; that James felt that in her and the simple fact of it. "We're on the same page."

Gage stepped toward her. "I'll make sure I'm worth you ruining your reputation."

She smiled. "Stop being so melodramatic."

"I'm not. I will. I'll be everything, Betta, if you let me."

"I don't need you to be everything, Gage. I just need you to be you." Because she couldn't stand it anymore, she rushed to the window and dropped the blinds. His was a first floor apartment, and Van was the only one who could know. At least until they were sure of each other.

She did not plan to sleep with him, not tonight, not for awhile—he'd been her sister's—but she moved through his place and did the same with the rest of the windows, the rest of the blinds. No one could know she was here.

As she emerged from his bedroom, he met her in the hall, one hand on the wall. Dress pants rolled, t-shirt wrinkled, hair *askew*.

Closing the bedroom door behind her so he'd know, she took the distance between them in a hurry. Betta felt the difference immediately, in both his lips and hands. No reservations this time, and though he might have been the right amount of sure before, he was now the perfect amount of confident. So sure and confident that she felt her surety and confidence reaching up to him from deep in her gut.

In the hall, they searched out a deepening mess of tangled

emotions while slow hands skimmed across the surface.

AUGUST

Betta woke up to the white beams of her new bedroom ceiling.

Rolling over, she found Gage rifling through the books on her shelves, still in the khakis he wore yesterday. They were crumpled, only one of the pant legs still partially rolled. He must have slept in them. When she'd fallen asleep, he still had his white tee on, but not any longer.

Last night was the first she'd let him stay. They were already in bed, him nodding off, and Betta couldn't stand the thought of shoving him out into the night, even if that's how secrets were kept.

The sky was barely lit, the second best time to sneak out—before the sun rose and the neighbors sat in their windows with coffee, before her parents or sister walked by on their way to work.

But wanting a few more minutes to run eyes over the bare expanse of his torso, she started with, "Good morning."

Spinning, he lit up the room with his grin. "Betta. Do you know what today is?"

She pretended to think about it. "My housewarming party?"

"Our one month anniversary." He crawled onto the bed and kissed her forehead, her cheek, her neck, and shoulder. Closing her eyes, she leaned into it, breathed into it. He sat back. "Tell me the truth—you're throwing a party for our one month anniversary, aren't you?"

Betta giggled. "Shh," she told them both. Because she didn't giggle. But then, her boyfriends didn't normally act like children with cotton candy in one hand and a pony in the other. "No, my mother is not throwing us a one month anniversary party."

"Then I'll give you your present now."

"You got me a present?" She propped herself up on her elbows. He'd bought Gwen a locket for their one month anniversary. If he got her a locket, or even jewelry, she was going to cry. Talk about feeling second-rate. Plus, she might wear a lot of eyeliner, but she'd never worn jewelry.

Hopping off the bed, he stood against her bookcase wall and held out his arms.

"You're my present?" She sat up, cross-legged and half under the blankets. "That's subtle."

He grinned wider. "No. Not me." Spreading his arms even further, he also pointed down.

She scooted over to the side of the bed to find a vintage rug running the entire length of her bookshelf wall. Clasping a hand over her mouth, she shook her head. "I can't accept that." It had to cost hundreds of dollars. It wasn't a standard size, so maybe even more than that.

How had he found it?

Sliding off the bed onto her knees, she ran her fingers across it, beautiful as she'd imagined and as perfect as the pictures.

"I was a little worried about the pattern; I know they're all different. It reminded me of the ones in your binder, but I made the lady promise that if you wanted to exchange it, you could."

She looked up at him. "It's amazing."

Crossing his arms, he looked smug. She would've laughed, except, "I didn't get you anything."

"That's not true. You got me a party."

Then she did laugh. Standing, she wrapped her arms around him and pressed herself against his skin. His fingers wandered up the back of her shirt, down her sides, then to her waist. This meant he was going to pull back and look at her, but she curved into him, holding tightly, not wanting any point of contact disturbed.

He kissed her heavily-lined eyes and leaned his forehead against hers. Brushing the hair from her face, he ran his thumb along her scar as if he cherished it—as if he appreciated all the ways she went against the grain. It got her every time.

Granted, it was also something that set her apart from her sister.

If someone who'd never been with Gwen would love her that much. Her eyes flitted to the ceiling. No. She was here and she wasn't Gwen, and he knew she wasn't Gwen, and they were happy.

"What do you want?" he whispered.

"Now or later, big or small?" she asked.

"Exactly."

"You," she replied.

He lifted her up and walked her backward to the bed, one hand holding tight to her bottom and the other searching out her curves. She should take him for their one month anniversary, that would be a second present to remember, but *Gwen*.

Always Gwen in her relationships.

Gage swore they'd never had intercourse, but the fact he'd used the word intercourse, as if all other bets were off and that was the only word that would do, well, all she could see was her sister naked in front of him, doing God knows what. Or God might not want to know what.

He waited for her to make the next move like he had every other night, to stop them or continue them, but she hadn't brushed her teeth, and if he stayed, someone would see him leave.

Running her hands along him one more time, she pressed her lips against his bare shoulder. "You should go. Before the town wakes up."

He dropped his head against her, lips to her neck, and she worked to calm the insistent tingles that threatened a certain sort of urgency she would not be able to resist.

Slipping from his grasp, she sat on the bed while he pulled on his shirt.

Quietly, she walked him out. He squeezed her hand as he stepped through the back door, and she shut it behind him, pressing her forehead to the wood. "Happy anniversary," she whispered.

Because it was kind of a big deal, the two of them, and she was touched he remembered. She played it off, but she'd known full well when she woke up that it was their one month anniversary. There'd been no Gwen-and-James benchmarks in recent history with which to compare relationships, but with Gage, she couldn't get them out of her head.

She could see clearly each gift he'd given Gwen and when, and she thought it might just kill her.

* * *

Esmerelda invited Celia to Betta's housewarming party because Christine couldn't go and everyone else would be old or older.

They sat on Betta's couch with a clear view of the front yard, and Ez whispered the low-down on the guests as they appeared on the front walk. By the time Betta was greeting them at the door, Celia was shouting a hello based on whether or not they sounded like someone she should know, or someone she would like. Celia could do this with a straight face, but Ez was snickering, giggling at best.

Betta, Gwen, and Wanda were there when they arrived, and Celia knew them all enough. "If I had that scar on my face," she whispered when they first sat down, "I'd wear less clothes than you wore in those Valentine's photos."

At least Betta's smiles, Esmerelda thought, weren't fake sticky sweet and spinning a trap.

You know my dad, from the store. "Hi, Mr. Aaldenberg! Navy is a fabulous color on you!"

Plus my mom's new best friend Mae, from the sandwich shop? Anyway, don't even get me started on that because it's super weird. First because my mom doesn't have friends, and second because I swear they had some longstanding rivalry all the way back to high school. "Hello, Mae."

That's Richard, the guy Mom set Mae up with. Cue head nod and fake smile meant to fool adults.

Shelby and Gage—that's Gwen's ex-fiancé, so that might be interesting. And she's the lady who owns the bookstore. Celia swung her face in Esmerelda's direction, "I hear she's a total cougar!" Ez shrugged, and Celia leaned closer. "Books or entertainment, if you know what I mean."

"Ew." Ez wrinkled her nose. "She doesn't work at The Cat's Tail."

"Oh, no. My cousin says she's picky and not for profit. Supposedly, he was hot enough to shag her. It's a thing they try sometimes. A dare—oh! Hi Shelby! Hey, Gage."

Ez bit down on her snicker.

You know Brennan Masowicz from Mas Properties? Betta works for him. Those must be people from the office.

"He's sexier in person than in his ads."

His billboard shots always had him in a plaid collared shirt under a crew neck sweater, hair smoothed back and face clean-shaven. That Brennan didn't know casual. But in person, his hair was less slick, a few strands falling over his forehead, and he wore jeans with a long sleeved t-shirt.

"It's August," Ez whispered as his group stepped inside. "He must be gross and sweaty under that." Betta gave each of the group a quick hug, and they filed past her into the house, leaving Brennan last. She took the bottle of champagne he offered, and he held her a touch longer than the others had.

"He never wears short sleeves," Celia whispered directly into Ez's ear. "He has burns on his upper arm."

"How do you know all this?" Ez asked, meaning the intel on both Shelby and Brennan.

"I make it a point to know things, Ez. Hi, Brennan! Love your work! Huge fan!"

He and Betta glanced at them, him with a creased brow and Betta shaking her head. The girls leaned again, trying to catch a glimpse of Brennan's backside as he followed Betta down the hall to the kitchen.

"Truth is, my mom's a total gossip," Celia admitted. "If you listened to one of her phone conversations, your eyes would bug out of your head."

"Sounds like fun."

Celia shrugged. "You should come over sometime."

Ez stifled the snort she wanted to throw back at that, considering what happened last time, and urged Celia up to join the party.

Everyone fell for her, and quickly, like they couldn't see—like they didn't remember—the girl in high school who pulled the wool over everyone's eyes over and over again.

Charisma. That's what it was. Undeniable charisma. So Ez studied her, because she figured such a thing could only help on stage.

She studied how Celia built her plate, how she ate her appetizers—dainty and with a smile. She studied how Celia cocked her hip when talking to Van and Gage and Brennan. How she stood taller and more serious with Gwen and Betta and Kate and Shelby. How she clasped her hands in front of her when she talked to Mae and Wanda, Harvey and Richard, keeping her face open and her eyes wide—innocent.

Celia pulled out her phone, chattering with Wanda and Mae, Harvey and Richard. "Man, they are *so good*. She should seriously use them as head shots, if she really gets into this theater thing."

Were they talking about her? Headshots? What pictures...

Ez tried to shove through Van and Betta. Celia stood across the kitchen, and Ez had to get there, had to stop her, but her brother and sister were all 'relax, Ez, what's up, Ez, hey, Ez' and she was too late. Her mom's face was white.

It could only mean one thing.

Ez snatched the phone from Celia and sure as shit, those damn pictures...

"What the hell is this, Esmerelda?"

"Mom, I-"

"You have *no clothes* on in these."

"Oh, she has clothes on, Mrs. Aaldy." Celia took her phone back from Esmerelda's stunned grip. "Bra and undies, at least. Oh, just undies here, you're right."

"You know better than to take photos like these." Her mom gripped Ez's arm. "Tell me you know better than to take photos like these."

Tears sprang to Esmerelda's eyes and she felt bare, everyone watching her. Brennan and Gage, Shelby and Kate. All her siblings, her mom, and her mom's best friend. Staring at her. Nude. They didn't need to see the photos themselves after what her mother had just announced.

Brennan ushered the Mas Properties crew out of the kitchen to show them the rest of the house, and Shelby hooked an arm through Gage and Kate to follow them for the tour. Richard said he needed a smoke, and asked Harvey if he'd like a cigar.

A bomb hit in Ez's gut. This was what Celia wanted; not to make up for anything, but to deliver one last deadly blow.

She should've known.

She would never learn.

"You put these online?" her mom yelled. Okay, maybe she wouldn't have yelled if Ez had said something, but her mouth was empty. Blank. Useless.

She tried. She opened her mouth and tried, but what could she say? She'd done them for her boyfriend? They were supposed to be private? She felt too stupid to admit that in front of her entire family, all of them smarter than her, clearly, after she'd let this happen.

"She didn't." Betta stepped forward, a hand to Ez's back. The warmth of her sister drew the cold terror out, and Ez leaned back into it. "She was mortified. And it's all been taken care of already. I took her phone away and grounded her."

Celia offered Van her cell, the picture refreshed and bright on screen, and Ez wanted to slap her. Snatching the phone from Celia, Van scrolled through. What he must be thinking,

287

his little sister, the type of girl who sent naughty pictures to the football star.

Esmerelda wanted to sink into the floor. She wanted to disappear. She wanted Mae to stop looking at her like that, and Gwen, who couldn't even conceive of doing something wrong.

Ez pressed her fists against her eyes, and Van said, "Deleted. Gone."

She peeked at him, and he squeezed her shoulder.

Her mom stared at her, shook her head, opened her mouth, closed it, opened it again.

"Can I walk Celia out?" Ez asked, hands folded in prayer at her chest. "Can we talk about this later, and not ruin Betta's party?"

"Betta already took care of it," Gwen said. "I promise." So they were all standing behind her. She'd never been more grateful for her siblings.

After glancing over the four of them, multiple times, her mom finally nodded. Wasting no time, Ez grabbed Celia by the arm and dragged her out the front door. She about threw her down the steps, staying at the top to be taller and more formidable, to have the power of the house and her family behind her.

Celia snickered, a shit-eating grin on her face. Pleased. Proud. Planned.

"You're the worst," Esmerelda muttered. She would not fold. Not anymore. Never anymore.

Celia lost the smile and narrowed her eyes. "If you only knew the holy hell I got when Gavin's parents showed up on my front steps with naked pictures of me on his phone."

Good. "Not my fault you were stupid enough to take nudes for a guy who doesn't even like you."

"Because of you!" Celia cried, pointing her finger at Ez.

"Because of everything you did to me!" Esmerelda cried. "Just leave me *alone* already!"

Celia sneered so hard her nostrils flared. "Give me back my damn earrings, and I will."

Ez scoffed, at herself more than anything. Ripping them out of her ears, the backs tumbling to the ground, she threw them at her. Celia could go fetch if she was going to be such a bitch.

Celia got on her hands and knees and grabbed the most obvious, then felt around for the other.

Ez would never steal anything again. She'd never screw with anyone, she'd never be a bitch, she'd never… she didn't know what she would never, but she would be better.

Betta's room had been whispering to her—a new room, with new things. But she wouldn't. She would be good. She would put her head down and do her plays and be a good friend to Christine, and then someday she'd earn her karma back, and she'd move to New York City and become a star.

Celia stood, earrings in her fist.

She would not flinch in Celia's glare. She would not back down. She would not look away. She would stand there until she could no longer see her, until she knew she was gone.

The farther down the road Celia got, the more Esmerelda's cheeks ran with tears, the more her nose dripped, the more her chest heaved. When she could see her no longer, Ez crumpled to the steps and held onto them.

She had lost. She could never hope to win. But at least she was free.

* * *

Wanda tried to burst outside after Esmerelda, but Gwen and Betta stopped her.

With hurried words, her other daughters spoke on top of each other, a team, a volley.

"She already got in trouble."

"She learned her lesson."

"There's nothing more to say."

"It's okay, Mom, really."

"Don't make her feel worse than she already does."

"That Celia girl is wicked."

"Don't punish her."

"It's over."

Wanda hadn't been there, and this loomed over everything she wanted to say about it. How could she yell or scold or lecture, when she'd been vacant at a time like that? Those months, lying in bed, aching to be needed, to have a purpose, to give a damn, and the whole time her purpose hadn't left her. She had been needed, and she hoped that if she'd known, she would've given a damn.

Then maybe not. That was how depression sucked on a soul after all, and if Wanda wasn't careful it would angle in on this failure and take her again for its own.

By the time Ez made her way inside, Wanda met her tears with open arms. She pushed the older girls out of the way and clutched Esmerelda to her. Ez hadn't wanted her lunches made or her hand held, but there was so much left to do that Wanda had forgotten about. The important stuff. The dangers of social media and high school and bullies and *men*, and the joys too. Wanda was the light to guide her through it all, wherever she was headed. She wasn't done yet. She was still a mom.

A lighthouse. She had to hold onto that.

* * *

It was awkward for Gwen, Gage being at the housewarming. Betta asked her ahead of time if it was okay, and how could Gwen say no? She couldn't avoid seeing him, now that he lived in town.

One more reason to move to the city. Now that Betta's house was done, she could go. The store no longer needed her. She found a job and a tiny efficiency in case things didn't work out with David. If they did, she hoped to spend most nights stretched out in his bed anyway. Her lease didn't start until the first, but she could crash with David for a week. Better there than here.

She'd done a good job avoiding Gage so far, but he was talking to Betta, and Gwen wanted to leave. They were in the kitchen, Gage propped against the stove and Betta against the island, comfortable. Of course they were comfortable. They were friends. They'd been friends before she broke up with him, and they'd been friends since.

She wanted that for him, people in town, even if it was her sister and brother. Her brother—Gwen rolled her eyes—who she had to *peel* off her, insisting she did not need to be walked home. It was only dusk and the walk was maybe two blocks.

The only problem was etiquette required her to say goodbye to the host.

So here she was, listening to *shoulds* again. With a tsk of disgust, she forced herself closer.

"Tonight," she caught Betta saying.

"Tonight?" Gage echoed.

At Gwen's approach, they retracted their feet from the center of the walkway, causing them to stand straighter, at attention almost.

"Gage." Gwen nodded.

Like a deer in headlights, he stared at her. "Hi, Gwen."

"That's a lovely rug up in your room, Bets. It's perfect for the house. I know I told you a million times, but you couldn't have done a better job."

Betta looked to her feet, the sweeping curve of her eyeliner more obvious, and her hair falling over her scar. She covered her scar when she was uncomfortable, self-conscious—embarrassed.

"You should be proud," Gwen told her. "Really."

"Thank you."

"What's tonight?" Gwen asked.

They looked at her. Then at each other. Then back at her, faces blank.

"You were saying something about tonight."

"Oh! It went really well," Gage said. "I think it went really well, don't you think it went really well? Couldn't have gone better. Quite a celebration." His Adam's apple bounced.

Gwen narrowed her eyes. He was shit for lying. Looking to Betta, she tried again, "Something happening later?"

"No. Why?"

"What were you talking about?"

Betta raised an eyebrow. "Little cranky from all your travel lately?"

Gwen crossed her arms. Crappy of her to bring that up in front of Gage, but at least he didn't know what she was really doing there—or who she was really doing. With a sigh, Gwen put a hand to her head. "I'm sorry. I'm tired. Heading out."

She wasn't the first to leave. She'd waited until the guests started trickling out. It was only Wanda and Mae cleaning up the kitchen, Harvey and Richard out back smoking cigars, and Van, Kate, and Brennan in the front hall, talking about development in town.

With a hug to Betta and an almost-hug-but-then-they-decided-against-it to Gage, she headed outside and started down the darkening street.

That was when she realized Shelby left before her. Shelby, who'd been at Gage's side all night. It would have made sense for them to leave together. Plus, Gage had been lying about something. And their feet—tangled, for sure. An accident or on purpose?

Gwen gulped and lost sensation along the surface of her skin. Or gained sensation maybe—she was both prickly and numb at once. Spinning on the corner, the one with a burnt out streetlamp, she watched the house as Brennan left, then Van and Kate.

Gage should be next.

She waited.

The prickly numbness spread to her gut.

Maybe he was smoking a cigar with her dad. Yes. She hurried, almost weightless, around the back street into the alley until she could catch a glimpse of them, of Harvey and Richard—no Gage.

Betta was likely Gage's best friend at the moment. Best friends helped pick up after a party. That meant he wasn't sleeping with Shelby, which Gwen should be grateful for. Only, right now she wasn't feeling so grateful.

A few more steps and she could see into the kitchen... her mom and Mae. Where were they? A light flipped off in the narrow galley up front. Gwen hurried to catch them, Betta and Gage. As if she thought they'd make out on the small, narrow table while her parents were there.

She was being silly. Stupid. Delusional. Sara putting thoughts in her head.

Betta's laugh rang out—her flirty laugh. The windows were open and the light from the kitchen slanted into the narrow space. Gwen crept closer.

Simply turning out lights together. Okay. Phew. Gwen put a hand to her chest, calm now. He was only helping her clean up after the party.

Betta almost slipped out of sight when Gage reached a hand for her waist. She hung back, resting into him.

Gwen clutched tight to the windowpane, knuckles white. She looked like a freak.

Gage felt his way along Betta's stomach, and Betta took another step back into the darkness with him. Gwen heard nothing but the scream in her skull, only it must not have been only in her skull, because they were staring at her now.

All three of them stared at each other with horror. And she, some weirdo, nose pressed against a window.

Flying to the front steps, she launched herself up them and flung open the door. Heaving with outrage, she landed at the edge of Betta's stupid galley, whatever the hell that was, one hand clutching the doorframe to hold her up.

She swept her hand across the nearest plant, sending it to the floor. The pot broke, dirt and ceramic scattering. She felt spittle on her chin, but she would not wipe it off, she would not clean herself up. She did not care if she looked like a monster.

Betta shook her head. Gage put his hands up.

Tonight.

She stifled another scream. "You know he's only using you to get back at me, right?"

"I'm not." Gage turned to Betta as if Gwen wasn't there. As if she wasn't the fiancée. As if Betta was all that mattered. "I swear, I'm not. I promise, I would *never*." He glanced back at Gwen. "I would never do something like that to someone."

Betta glanced from Gage to Gwen, her face ashy white,

but she needed to know, if she was going to get into bed with the scoundrel. Not that she wasn't turning out to be quite the tart herself, but she was her sister. Gwen took a step forward. "I cheated on him. He tell you that?"

By the look on Betta's face, the slight uptick to her eyebrows and how she shot a glance at him, he most certainly hadn't.

"I cheated on him, and now he's using you to get back at me." Gwen put a hand to her forehead. "And you, Betta! I ruined a relationship,"—she threw an arm out in Gage's direction—"and saved the goddamn store, for *you*. You have no idea what kind of hell I've been through, and this is what I get?" She let out a short laugh of disbelief. "I protect you and save you, and this is what I get. Good. Sleep with each other. I hope it's miserable."

Taking a few more steps, she shoved at Gage with one hand, the bastard, using her sister, her little sister. Then, without acknowledging Betta, not even a glance, she couldn't bear to look at her, the anger would crack and she'd explode in sobs if she did, Gwen spun and raced home.

Everything she'd done. For nothing.

* * *

Wanda and Mae hadn't missed a thing while doing dishes, and while Wanda violently dried and slammed plates into the open red cupboard, Mae washed silently.

Depression or not, Wanda had raised her kids right. Yet there were scandalous pictures of Ez online and Betta was with Gage? Not to mention, *Gwen had cheated on him?*

Where would they have even gotten such ideas?

Harvey.

Was this proof, staring her in the face?

Wanda ripped a coffee cup out of Mae's wet hand. "Have you ever cheated on someone, Mae?"

"Oh no, Wanda."

"Oh no? Or no?" She slammed the cup down in its place.

"Of course I haven't." Her gaze was slippery though, Wanda thought.

She gathered the silverware, dried them, and ripped open the drawer to put them away. She didn't want to know. If she knew for sure, she couldn't be friends with her anymore, and she would never forgive Harvey. Better not to know.

Starting this thing with Mae had been about keeping the tramp occupied and away from her husband, but it was for Wanda's sake she kept it up. Mae was good for her. They were good for each other. She didn't want to lose that, but she was pissed and mouthy.

Setting her hip against the counter, Wanda folded her arms, dish towel hanging. "Have you ever been a mistress?"

The room shifted, Wanda could sense it. Harvey cleared his throat. He stood on the other side of the screen, Richard behind him.

She glared at him while she waited for Mae's confession.

If Mae slept with her husband but chose now to deny it, she cared more about Wanda than the affair. It would be a clean slate going forward, and Wanda would trust that their friendship was strong enough to prevent it from happening further.

Then again, Gwen and Betta were sisters.

Wanda clutched her stomach and looked to Mae. *Answer me*, she willed. *Answer me right.*

Mae held tight to the lip of the sink, but smoothly she replied, "No, Wanda. I've never slept with another woman's husband." It was low and quiet, and Harvey didn't flinch. He opened the door and stepped inside, then held it for Richard.

"What'd we miss?" he asked.

Richard looked around. "Everyone gone?"

"Yes," Wanda spat. "Everyone is gone." And she went back to doing the dishes.

* * *

Betta paced the dark workspace galley while her mom and Mae finished up in the kitchen. Gage followed her awhile, whispering denials and sweet nothings she covered her ears to, as they sounded too much like what she imagined he whispered to Gwen all those months ago when Betta watched their reunion. The day she hurried to James and compared them—Gage and Gwen versus James and Betta, James and Gwen versus James and Betta. Now, Gage and Gwen versus Gage and Betta.

The commonality that *Betta* was always last.

It was convoluted and wrong, and she snapped at him that she wasn't having this conversation until they were gone.

So he went to move things along.

Tonight. She'd meant it, too. She was going to sleep with him tonight—it could be happening in moments actually, as soon as her parents left. Why not, she'd thought, as she watched him with Shelby across the kitchen. Why wait? She had to get over her sister and Gage somehow, and she figured there was no better way than to jump ahead of where they'd been.

How stupid of her to think such a thing were possible, and how much she ached for a Gage without a Gwen-stained past. No matter how much she felt for him—and it was a lot, it came on fast and overwhelming—she deserved better than a compromise.

His voice drifted to her from the kitchen, somehow managing a tone like nothing had happened. *Betta's not feeling well, I'll walk you out. Oh, no, I'm not staying, I'll just lock up for her. No, no, it's okay, it's been a long day.*

They must have heard. She hoped they wouldn't turn around and peek through the windows to watch the aftermath unfold. Apparently, that was a thing now.

Betta hid in the shadows of the galley, behind the light slanting in from the kitchen, as her parents' voices moved down the hall to the front foyer, until their chatter became a remnant on the breeze coming in the windows, until it wasn't even that.

Gage stood in the front hall, staring at the door.

"I'm revenge?" she whispered.

"*No.*" He stared at his feet. They were alone in the house—he alone there, and she alone here.

She'd never felt lonely with him before.

Moving closer, she leaned against the doorframe. "I'm revenge."

He shook his head. "How can you believe that?"

"I'm trying not to, but my sister doesn't lie."

His head snapped to her. "She cheated on me. She lies."

Clearly bitter, which a potion for revenge did make. "Something you failed to tell me, which makes it even more suspicious."

"I couldn't voice it. Couldn't say it. Couldn't make it real." He moved toward her, leaving a foot between them. "It's not about her, Betta. She might have brought me here, but I have no doubt anymore that you are who I was meant to be with."

"It's been a month, Gage. No time at all. You can't know anything."

"I know you make me laugh, Betta. Relax me, loosen me up. If all we did the rest of our lives was read together and talk about books, that would be enough for me. If I only saw you at Shelby's, on our couch, I could live off that." He reached for her hand. She let him take it. Holding it loosely, he continued, "I know that we, together, are something special. Our relationship works like nothing in my life has ever worked. We can't give that up."

"What about my sister?"

"What about her?"

Betta wrinkled her forehead. She wanted him to tell her

why she was special over Gwen, but that wasn't what she was supposed to be worrying about right now. Even if she didn't completely buy the revenge—let it be her own denial, she didn't really care, she couldn't let anything ruin what they had because he was right, their relationship worked more smoothly, more sweetly, more easily than anything she'd known—the point was Gwen's heart, broken and oozing on the windowsill.

"She didn't let me see inside her the way you do," he whispered. "She was always protecting something. The us of me and Gwen was barely formed. The us of you and me felt solid since our first afternoon at Shelby's."

Betta rested her temple against the wood and focused on his thumb pressing down on her knuckle. Not too hard, but as if to hold her there.

"I loved us, too," she whispered.

"Past tense?" He tilted her chin up, but gently. "Please don't trash us because of something we have no control over. Something that's over and done, and that I can't change."

She'd been trying to keep Gwen at bay for a month, out of their relationship, out of her mind, only for her to storm her way in tonight. Maybe it saved Betta some heartache, ruining it quick instead of giving her more time to love him.

Tears sprang to her eyes, harsh ones that wouldn't take no for an answer, and so, through their descent, she said it as quickly and concisely as she could. "Please know it doesn't lessen what you mean to me." She untangled her hand from his and curled it into her chest. "I believe you that I'm not revenge, but I can't do this. I'm sorry."

Was she hyperventilating? No, those were just tears. How could she do this to him? To herself?

She had to pick her sister. It didn't matter if he loved her or not. What mattered was this town and her family and her sister, and that could never be righted if she stayed with him. Plus, she wanted something better for herself than her sister's leftovers, no matter how perfect he was, no matter how perfect they'd been.

A new job. A new house. Both showed her what it felt like to be clean and free. Gage did not feel like either of these things anymore. He felt like betrayal and pain and misery.

Betta could do nothing but drip from her eye sockets and shake her head, back and forth. *No, don't take these tears the wrong way. No, I don't want you to go. No, I don't want you to stay. No, I don't want to have you. No, but I do, so desperately.*

Pain creased his brow, drawing his eyebrows together, and she couldn't stand it, so she threw herself at him and hugged him fiercely.

He rested his lips against her temple and pressed a thumb against her scar. Their foreheads bent to meet. Betta couldn't let go of him—she tried and tried again, and when she almost had it, when she thought she was there, it was no longer their foreheads bending to meet, but their lips and their hands and their hips.

Undoing his buttons, loosening him up, untucking his shirt, she couldn't stop. He slipped out of his sleeves and let his shirt drop to the floor, no folding tonight, and yanked his white tee over his head. Betta did the same with her top, and as she reached behind her to unclasp her bra, he took her face in his hands.

"You wanted me to go," he said.

She stared at him, but she wouldn't say it again because not one ounce of her did. She wanted him more than anything, even if she couldn't have him tomorrow, or again after this. Thank God they hadn't more time for her to know for sure if she loved him. She could tell herself otherwise for the rest of her life, shrug it off that it was only one month and he was her sister's, truly. At the same time, though, she couldn't usher him out the door. She had no strength left, no resolve. She was weak and sorry for it, but not going to fight what she wanted right now, this minute.

If she didn't take it, she could never come back. She wouldn't have another chance.

Unclasping her bra, she let it fall. His choice now, to stay or go. One night or none.

Slipping his hand in hers, he tugged her to the stairs, and they ran up the steps.

September

High school lunch on the first day of school.

Always brutal, the lines being drawn.

Esmerelda took a deep breath and crossed her fingers that they still had spots at the theater table. Not that she really cared. If she and Christine had to sit in the corner and eat with their hands, she'd survive.

It would be nice though, to have a table. To be insulated by a crowd. To have a place.

Not necessary, but nice.

Christine walked through the hot lunch line with Esmerelda, and Ez put exactly what she wanted on her tray. She followed Christine through the cafeteria, past Celia, who ignored her as if she'd never existed and last year had never happened, thank God.

Past Gavin's table, Ez couldn't help but look, and Gavin smiled. She smiled back.

Almost there.

"Ez?" From behind her.

She turned. Gavin shook his hair out of his eyes. He needed a haircut.

"So, um, Ben's having a party. Tradition, you know?"

She set her tray on her hip with a smirk. "You're cute."

He grinned, missing perhaps that the compliment was a tad condescending. "I miss you, Ez."

Well, that she liked. She liked being missed. "I'm sure Celia will pick someone nice for you."

"What?"

"You know, tell her you won't go because I won't take you back, and she'll find a way to get you there. Like last year."

"Or you and I could go as friends."

She laughed. "That worked out for you last time, huh?"

Full grin now, he replied, "It did, until I got stupid."

She shrugged. "Live and learn, I guess."

"Yeah, I guess."

"I'll see you around, Gavin."

"I hope so."

Ez turned back to where she'd been going, and Christine waved her down. She was there, at the table. One more spot for Esmerelda.

Take two: sophomore year.

* * *

Betta walked into the office and set her purse down. She

headed down the hall and stood in Brennan's open doorway. "I need to talk to you, sir."

"I'm too young for a sir. You know I hate that."

"I'm sorry." She made her way over to the chair in front of his big desk.

"When people use sir, they usually give me bad news." He shut the file he was studying and set it on his second most important to-do pile. "Word in town is Gwen's disappeared, so I'm afraid you're going to tell me you're leaving." He was no chump. It was one of the things she liked about him. "Is that what's been eating you all week?"

No. Missing Gage had been eating her all week. She crossed her legs and set her hands to her knees, taking a deep breath in. Not here. She opened her mouth, but the tears were too close, so she shut it.

"I feel like I'm getting broken up with, Betta."

She squinted at him, his words not helping her composure.

"Listen, I get it. This place is a family legacy too."

Betta shook her head and forced herself to get it together. "This is what I want, Brennan. I need to figure out a way to do both. What I have to do, and what I want to do."

"Your brother won't take the store?"

"He's an electrician."

"I know. He does good work. Ez?"

"Doubtful. She doesn't like to get her hands dirty."

"And Gwen is out."

She released a forlorn sort of smile. "I can't go full time here. Even part, I'm going to need to be back and forth for awhile, more than you'd probably like. I don't want to abuse your kindness, or your flexibility, but if you'll still have me, I'll work here when you most need a receptionist."

"Anyone can be a receptionist, Betta." He tapped his pencil against his desk, *click, click, click.* "If you don't have time for a full reno yourself, I'll find you a team or give you smaller projects. Hell, maybe you and I can work together. I haven't done one in ages, but I miss it. And to be honest, you inspired me with that little saltbox."

She melted back against the chair, struggling to get a hold of her tears again, but for a different reason—good ones like relief and gratitude and hope. Reno projects still on the table? "I can't tell you how much I appreciate this."

"As slow as the store is off-season, couldn't you work from there?"

Crossing her legs, she pumped a foot up and down until she could speak without a quiver of emotion in her voice. "I'm sure I could."

He shrugged and looked back to his work. "Some of our parents work from home a few days a week. Don't know why that would be much different."

* * *

Wanda thought it would be hard, having one less child in the house, but walking to work and seeing Betta drinking coffee on her front steps every morning was almost better.

A girl with a house like that had her shit together, no

matter who she was sleeping with, and Wanda had a part in that.

"Morning, honey," Wanda said, checking her watch. She had a few minutes, so she headed up the walk.

"Hey, Mom." Betta patted the space next to her. "Want some coffee?"

"Nah, I'll make some when I get to work."

"You've been working for Gwen a lot… I've been hoping to see her. She hasn't been answering my calls."

"You haven't spoken since your party?"

Betta shook her head.

"You and Gage are…?"

Shaking her head again, Betta gripped her coffee so tight her knuckles went white.

"Gwen won't come out of her room. I mean, I'm sure she has—food is gone—but only when no one's home." Wanda noted the guilt etched in the concern on her daughter's face. Easing the mug from her hands, she set it on the step next to her and massaged her fingers to loosen her grief. "I think maybe she needs her sister."

"I'm sure she doesn't want to see me."

"Sometimes what we want isn't what we need." Wanda squeezed her hand tight before letting go. "Speaking of, I've been meaning to thank you for last winter."

"Mom." Going slightly awkward, Betta averted her eyes. "Don't be silly."

"No, you don't be silly. You're a formidable girl, Betta. You can handle a lot."

Betta swallowed hard.

Leaning in, Wanda whispered, "This too shall pass."

She hoped Betta heard her—that she was talking about it all, and maybe even more than Wanda had overheard. Whether she was destroyed by Gage or in pain from letting him go, the stuff with Gwen, the pressure Wanda knew Harvey put on them regarding the store, the stress of a real job at Mas Properties on top of it all, maybe even living on her own in an empty house.

Wanda shivered. She hated empty houses.

But there was one thing she knew, one thing she'd experienced in all her years, multiple times, one thing she held onto, even in her darkest hours when it was hardest to believe. She leaned her shoulder against her daughter's and said it again, in case there was any doubt. "This, too, shall pass."

* * *

Gwen ignored the footsteps in the hall, and she ignored the knock on her bedroom door, same as she'd been ignoring everything all week.

She felt as if she brought karma on Betta, Gage using her, after what she'd done with David. At the same time, she was so mad at her sister for allowing it to happen, like it was nothing to stab your sister in the back.

If Betta and Gage stayed together, two happy townies, Gwen would just vomit. She wasn't sure she could bring herself to go to the wedding without causing a scene. That's how they'd made her feel, like she was unhinged, the type of girl who caused scenes.

She startled when her door opened, because it had been locked. Betta stood in the doorway, a skeleton key in her hand, and the sisters took stock of each other.

Gwen put a hand to her hair; she was possibly nesting rats.

Sweeping in with some sort of purpose, Betta opened the curtains, the blinds, even the windows, letting the cool crisp scent of September in. She threw open Gwen's closet, tugged out her suitcase, and plopped it open on the bed next to Gwen herself.

"I'm sorry," Betta muttered, but quietly and without looking at her. The syllables floated disjointedly on the fresh air, and by the time they made their way to Gwen, they had no meaning left.

Gwen crossed her arms and clutched her biceps. She had no meaning left, either. She had nothing left. She had so much of nothing, she couldn't even see herself anymore.

Betta glanced at her like she was real though, as she grabbed clothes from her drawers and packed them neatly in her suitcase. Her favorite dresses from the closet and her fanciest shoes. Jewelry. Make-up. Lingerie.

Gwen put her hand on Betta's wrist as the lingerie went in the case. Their eyes caught.

"You're moving to the city," Betta said. "You're doing it now. You're not wasting any more time."

"I'm sorry for what I said. I was mean."

Betta shrugged. "Sometimes we're mean to each other. We're sisters."

Gwen gulped back a sob. "I want you to be happy, if he's what will make you happy."

Betta covered Gwen's hand with her own, sandwiching her there. "Men are not going to make us happy, Gwen. We're going to make ourselves happy, and then the men in our lives are going to come along for the ride."

"Is Gage...?" Gwen closed her eyes. She couldn't ask but she had to know. "Is Gage coming along for your ride?"

"No. I chose you."

Gwen opened her eyes. "You can have us both."

"No, I really can't." Betta straightened, their hands coming apart, and she sighed. "There has to be someone out there for me, Gwen. Someone who's only mine. Not ours."

"I've always wanted that for you." She said it before realizing how wrong it sounded, like she wanted Betta to keep her hands off her boyfriends. "That's not what I mean. I mean-"

"It's okay." Betta shut and latched her suitcase.

"You're taking the store, then?"

"Not necessarily." Standing, Betta put her hands on her hips and looked around. "But figuring that out is my problem, not yours. My turn, okay?"

Gwen nodded.

"What else do you need?"

"A shower."

"Yeah, I think I could braid that leg hair."

They smiled at each other. Gwen swung said hairy legs off

the bed and stood up.

"Go make yourself pretty for the city. I'll drive you to the train."

"That's a long drive."

"I took the day off to talk some sense into my sister. I have plenty of time." She put a finger up. "You still have that apartment? They didn't give it to someone else because you didn't show up on September 1st?"

Gwen nodded. She paid through September. All she had to do was pick up the keys. If there were any problems, David would save the day. His bed was still hers. Or it better be. She'd only missed one weekend, and she could use a little medicine: bright lights, good food, hot cocoa, maybe a serving of bliss.

She stood to hug her sister, easier now that she wasn't keeping Gage, and went to rinse the disdain and sorrow off. Time to start over.

No, she corrected herself. Actually, it was time to just plain *start*.

A Year Later

The barn was a fairytale, tiny lights heavily draped along the high beams to make the space glow. One chandelier over the head table and white swaths of cloth draped from the beams over the others. Sprigs of wildflowers and fresh herbs, small twinkling candles, pictures of the families and the couple over the years.

A wedding, two years after a funeral. Betta traced Pops' face on a stray picture, one of the many strewn across the table. How far they'd come in those two years. And then not really very far at all, as everyone was still fawning over Van. He and Kate were greeting people off to her right, a two-person reception line for a casual wedding and casual celebration. All Betta could hear was a lot of smoke being blown up his rear end, because he'd paid for the wedding all by himself. No longer a football star, yet he could pick his nose and the town would still applaud.

Trailing her hand the rest of the way down the table, studying the pictures and not where she was going, she almost walked into Gage before she realized anyone was standing there.

Too close. Terribly close. So close she could smell him— heat as if the iron were still on his clothes, and the minty scent of his aftershave, the spice of his hair product. She swallowed and shifted her weight to her heels so she could breathe.

She knew he'd be there, knew Van kept in touch with him after he moved down the coast, but the onslaught of memories flooding her were unnerving just the same. Amazing how strong one month could feel an entire year later.

He looked impeccable, of course. The only one in full suit and tie for a wedding in a barn, and her heart folded in on itself a little. Navy suit with a baby-blue collared shirt and black tie, chunky man watch, and shiny black shoes, so high-end looking, all of him, even the smile and clean-shaven face, his styled hair—the city was bright in him like he never left, like she never taught him to loosen up.

Maybe that month hadn't stuck with him the way it had with her.

"Hey," he said.

"Hi." She nodded, as if she agreed. Internally, she rolled her eyes at herself.

"How are you?"

"I'm great, you?"

"Good! Good."

Betta frowned, wishing it weren't so awkward. Wishing they could talk about things like they used to, like there was nothing between them. Only, she didn't want to lose all the things that were between them, even if it was over.

"I hear you've hired a manager at the store."

"Yeah. I'm still in weekly, here and there, but Brennan's got a big project coming up, a hotel we're taking down to studs. All hands on deck, you know?"

"That's great, Betta. I'm happy for you."

"Van said your new boss wants to retire. You're buying the firm?"

He nodded.

She smiled. "Small town city rat."

"Small town, my way," he corrected. Hand up between them, he showed her a place setting card. "We're not sitting together, so I was hoping you'd save me a dance."

"I'd like that." Betta looked to the stage, where the band was setting up. Esmerelda was to sing for the couple's official entry. "I need to check on Ez, though. Catch up later?"

"Of course."

As she moved away, though, he caught her hand. She closed her eyes but didn't look back, waiting for the squeeze, the dart of his thumb, the release.

*

Ez was going to throw up. It didn't matter how many times she sang on stage, her palms went sweaty and her throat dry.

Christine offered her a bottle of water—thank God for best friends who knew what you needed at your worst times. She downed most of it. Enough to lubricate her vocal chords, but not enough she'd want to pee her pants by the time she was done.

It was only the first dance, she told herself. No big deal if she screwed up.

Except it was always a big deal if she screwed up, which was why she made it a point not to, and why she was now known as the girl who didn't screw up.

Betta came around the corner. "Ready?"

She nodded. "Van ready?"

"Yup. I just checked on them."

Right. Go time.

Ez took the steps to the platform and one of the band members handed her the mic. Rehearsal went well the night before. The band had been impressed. Now, she had to impress everyone else who hadn't a tie to the high school, who hadn't seen her at a production this year.

Her final debut, at her brother's wedding. Taking a deep breath, she scanned the crowd. About all of town was there, plenty who only knew her as Gwen and Van's little sister. Betta's too, now that she had her hands in everything—zoning meetings and restorative projects and other things supporting the town that Ez couldn't wrap her mind around, even when she heard the whole long discussion start to finish, when Betta and Brennan discussed it at the store on his all-afternoon lunch breaks. Every day this summer it seemed like, she wished they'd just shut up sometimes.

But she couldn't shut up now. She had to do this. After she opened her mouth and made them take notice, after everyone saw she was the artist in the family, she'd finally be her own person, with her own thing.

No longer just the little sister.

*

Wanda and Harvey swayed on the dance floor while Ez stepped off the platform and got mauled by everyone who hadn't heard her sing before.

"We only have one kid left after tonight," Wanda said, tilting her head at Harvey. Kate was an only child and her mother too lonely to let them move in with Wanda and Harvey. She'd already signed her house over to them, which wasn't something the Aaldenbergs were quite ready to do.

"Shall we spoil her while we can?"

"Do we have the money for that?"

"We could invite Richard and Mae over more often, instead of always going out, and shave enough for those acting programs she keeps going on about."

Wanda rested her chin on Harvey's shoulder with a snort. Ez left pamphlets everywhere, Boston-acting-this and Boston-acting-that. Good thing she got free voice lessons from the choir teacher or they'd need to fork out for that, too. "I guess she could stay at Gwen's."

He put his lips to her ear and whispered, "We'd have the house to ourselves again."

Betta and Gwen leaving so close together was hard, but the girls' weekends in the city curbed that blow. And now Van, but he picked up Saturdays at the store so he could save for some fresh furniture and maybe a little remodeling—a new deck was first on his list. Wanda could work Saturdays if she wanted, if she missed him, or at least bring him leftovers to take home, especially since Kate wasn't very domestic. All brains that one, future pediatrician.

Plus, with Mae and Richard in their backyard, there was hardly a night the four of them didn't share dinner, a drink, dessert, or a cigar.

It wasn't as bad as Wanda had thought it would be, having less chaos around her. Fewer people. Less need. Retirement wasn't as empty as she'd expected. In fact, it was kind of nice, choosing what she filled herself with, rather than not having a choice in the matter.

She simply had to keep choosing, one step in front of the other, one choice after the next. Not let the options overwhelm her. Choose anyway when they did. So far, so good. Only one week in bed this last winter.

It had been a better year.

*

Gwen stood to the side, watching Esmerelda soak it up: *congratulations, your voice is amazing, I can't believe we've never heard you before, why don't you sing at church?*

"She's somethin' else," Gage said, sidling up next to her.

She smiled. "Yeah, she is."

They stood near the cake table. Gwen had perfect sight of her parents on the dance floor, laughing and leaning into each other. That's what she wanted when she was their age: to know that no matter what they went through, it was worth it. To know that if one of them strayed, even emotionally, it was possible to come back together again.

"I hear you're managing a store?"

It had broke her and David, due to the opposite hours—him busy during the week, her mostly on weekends—but she loved it. "Ridiculous, right?"

"Well, high end boutique is a far cry from what you had here. Fits you well."

"And you've moved again?"

"Yeah. After everything that happened, well, I get why you wanted out. No one ever forgets what you've done or said. No escape, no avoiding it."

"That's for damn sure. Not in a small town."

"I'm being more careful this time. Getting everyone's family trees before I start dating."

Gwen glanced over. He was smiling. "Sometimes you have to be careful," she agreed.

Not as careful as Brennan was being, though, so if there was one thing she did this weekend, it would be to prod him and her sister along. Gwen saw how he looked at Betta. She knew how much time they spent together, and she noticed how quickly he sat next to her at their assigned table, how his body oriented toward her whenever she was around. Even across the room. And hers to him. The number of times they brushed hands or shoulders or elbows, Gwen should have kept count.

Not that she wanted to ruin whatever working relationship they had—it was probably what was holding them up—but for the sake of striking nieces and nephews... his curious grey-green eyes with Betta's lips and nose? Both of them with such beautiful, dark hair?

Kismet, for sure.

Shelby sashayed over to them. Her dress was slinky and black, nothing like her normal hippy garb, and her hair was twisted off her neck.

"Come eat cake and dance with me," she told Gage, with a hello smile in Gwen's direction. "I'm bored."

Gwen raised an eyebrow at them—*were they a thing?*—but Gage smirked and shook his head—*silly you'd think so*. Still, he went, led by Shelby's hand to a table where she fed him a few bites, wiped frosting from his lips with her thumb, then pulled him out to the dance floor to rub up against him like a cat.

Betta, laughing, headed for the cake table. Gwen intercepted her, linking her elbow and holding tight. Betta was an anchor, and Gwen soaked that up as much as possible. It reminded her who she was and what she'd done and what she was meant to be, in the softest, most understanding of ways.

"Take a piece back to Brennan too, and scoot your chair closer to him, and ask him to dance, and then take him out back and kiss him silly, the way James did with you."

Betta blanched. Then stammered. Then blushed from cheeks to chest. "I can't do that," she whispered. "He's my boss."

"Exactly why he won't do it, and why you have to."

"I can't."

"You can."

"I won't."

"You will."

"Gwen."

"Betta, trust me."

"It will ruin everything."

"It will ruin nothing."

Side by side, arms linked, they stared at Brennan, strumming his fingers along the table. He searched the room, glancing from dance floor to bathroom to picture table to cake. Once he caught sight of them—of Betta—he relaxed into a smile, fingers settling.

"Mmmhmm," Gwen murmured.

Betta blinked a few times, turned to the cake plates as Gwen released her, chose two different flavors—nice touch, an excuse to share—and wove her way back to him.

When she was halfway there, Gage came in from Betta's left and touched her elbow.

Betta stopped.

He said something, glanced behind him toward the dance floor.

"No," Gwen whispered. She couldn't pick him. It wasn't right. He was tied to another town anyway, and Betta couldn't leave this one.

Betta looked between Brennan and Gage, between the cake in her hands and the dance floor.

How serious had they been, Gwen wondered, that Betta was faltering? *Don't take the sure thing,* she wanted to yell. Sure things were sometimes the most difficult in the end, with the least payoff. Life could be better than that. She wanted Betta's life to be better than that.

Betta said something to Gage, drawing him to the table with Brennan, setting the cake plates down and reintroducing them maybe.

Sit, Gwen willed. *Choose Brennan.*

With a shudder, Betta's words from the year before echoed in Gwen's ears: *I chose you.*

Gwen closed her eyes on the scene—the barn in all its loveliness, the white of the chairs and tables brightening the space, her beautiful dark-haired sister wrapped in a delicate indigo dress, standing between two men—and the truth of the situation flooded her.

If Gage was who Betta should be with, it was time Gwen let that go.

Betta had chosen her, and she would do the same.

ACKNOWLEDGMENTS

Thank you, again and always, to Mairead Ahmed and Kat Abbott for being the best critique partners a girl could ask for. Thank you for telling me when I could do better – for your confidence that I actually can, and for your honesty in pointing it out. As much of a critique as it is, it also feels like a compliment and a challenge. Please continue to check me and keep me working harder.

Thanks to Lauren Mueller, my perfect reader, for the never-ending enthusiasm—every writer needs a girl like you. Thank you also to Kat and Sarah for pushing me to rewrite this whole damn thing, and for reminding me what a better writer I am today than when I first drafted this.

Thanks to those who've helped me learn and grow as a writer, and those who greeted me with open arms as I entered the writing community. Your kind words, honest critiques, and bits of advice have been much appreciated.

Thank you to my family and friends for your overwhelming support. And thank you to Kat, Moy, Lauren, Emma, and Neva for talking books with me, always an inspiration and reminder of how much I love words and the stories they create.

Of course, and always, thank you to Joel for all the things, but especially for allowing me to change and morph and discover this somewhat consuming passion you didn't originally sign up for.

Finally, thanks to passions meeting up with talents, whether natural or hard-earned. And related, thank you to Gina Ardito and Chris Slabber, for lending a little of your passion/talent/magic to this book.

ABOUT THE AUTHOR

J. Mercer grew up in Wisconsin where she walked home from school with her head in a book, filled notebooks with stories in junior high, then went to college for accounting and psychology only to open a dog daycare. She wishes she were an expert linguist, is pretty much a professional with regards to competitive dance hair (bunhawk, anyone?), and enjoys exploring with her husband—though as much as she loves to travel, she's also an accomplished hermit. Perfect days include cancelled plans, rain, and endless hours to do with what she pleases. Find her on Facebook or Instagram @jmercerbooks or online at www.jmercerbooks.com.